LETHBRIDGE-STEWART

TIMES SQUARED

Rick Cross

CANDY JAR BOOKS · CARDIFF
2021

Range Editor: Andy Frankham-Allen
Editor: Shaun Russell
Editorial: Lauren Thomas & Keren Williams
Licensed by Hannah Haisman
Cover by Martin Baines

Printed and bound in the UK by
Severn, Bristol Road, Gloucester, GL2 5EU

ISBN: 978-1-913637-59-0

Published by
Candy Jar Books
Mackintosh House
136 Newport Road, Cardiff, CF24 1DJ
www.candyjarbooks.co.uk

This novel is dedicated to Heather Cross and Declan Smith. My light. My life. Love you, monkeys.

PROLOGUE

THE HULKING, hirsute creature lumbered up the mountainside, and Professor Edward Travers followed.

Clambering over icy rocks, he hardly noticed the wind stinging his eyes or the jagged granite abrading the skin of his palms. He even ignored the burning stitch in his chest, which he supposed must stem equally from his excitement at this unexpected discovery and from the energy he was expending in pursuit of it.

No small thing for a man of middle age and appalling diet, Margaret would no doubt add. *Let alone one barely accustomed to the thin air and harsh terrain of the high Himalayas.*

The thought of his wife's wryly disapproving voice caused his cheeks, sweaty and wind-bitten, to grow hot with dismay. *You don't even have your camera to hand, Edward, let alone your rifle. Just what do you plan to do if you do catch up with the bally animal?*

The bally animal in question was now loping over a scrubby, snow-streaked hummock just thirty or forty yards ahead, clearly desperate to be away from him.

If he was being honest with himself – and twenty-four thousand feet above sea level, honesty was as crucial to survival as a sure footing – that niggling voice wasn't wrong. It also hadn't escaped his attention that his inner voice sounded more and more like Margaret's lately. When it wasn't aping that of Professor Walters, of course; his smug, hectoring rival in the Royal Geographical Society.

1

He supposed it was an indication of how much he missed her. And he *did* miss her. And hoped to see her soon, back home in the relative warmth of England's more civilised clime.

All of which now brought him up short, even as his quarry disappeared down the other side of the snowy hillock. *Damn.* His rifle had been shattered early on, and his camera, a brand-new Voigtländer with the Skopar lens, a gift from his wife, was probably still lying somewhere in the tent he and Mackay had pitched weeks ago, before his dear old friend had been attacked and the whole ruddy affair set in motion.

No camera. No rifle. No one at his back. So just what *was* he thinking, haring off all alone after a six-foot-tall, clawed and muscle-bound *animalia paradoxa?*

Words replayed in his mind. *It's a splendid thing to have a dream, even if it does turn out to be a legend.* That had been his strange new friend, of course; the unkempt little man who became their saviour in the end. Aided by the cocky young Scot and the waif-like English girl, the stranger had unravelled the curse of Det-Sen Monastery and caused its unnatural attackers to be destroyed, leaving the monks to rebuild the fabled Buddhist priory and start again. Travers and the strange trio had climbed into the highlands for a last check on their 'equipment', which looked to the stunned professor very much like one of those Gilbert MacKenzie Trench Police Boxes, only to have their goodbyes interrupted by the very thing he'd originally come here to find: a true Yeti! And not one of the bulky monstrosities that had laid siege to the monastery, but a taller, more graceful thing. Lithe as a panther, with silky fur like a great housecat and ringed eyes like those of a lemur.

At last, Travers had found evidence that his life's work had not been mere folly. *This* was the lost creature of lore. A living, breathing Yeti!

And a fast one at that. It had squealed in surprise and fled up the mountainside, cat-quick. Travers had barely managed a farewell wave to his friends before bolting after the thing. *No*, by heaven! He refused to let it escape him again!

Despite his misgivings, despite the stitch in his side, he would not stop. *Could not* stop. He set forth again and topped the hill the Yeti had climbed a moment earlier. The landscape here, so close to the lifeless heights dubbed 'the death zone' by that mad Swiss climber Edouard Wyss-Dunant, was almost devoid of greenery. Without crampons and safety gear, his quarry would very shortly be beyond his reach.

'No!' Travers moaned, scanning the slope for sign of the beast. It must not elude him now, after all he'd seen and endured in the last few weeks. Where in *blazes*—

There! A shadowy cleft in the rock face, twenty yards off. A cave mouth. Travers drew in a reedy breath. There was simply nowhere else the animal could have gone. He steeled himself and jogged towards the black slash in the grey expanse.

But the logic-driven part of him still spoke up, this time in his own brisk voice. *The question now is simple: Will it submit meekly, or turn and fight like a cornered wild animal?* If it were indeed a mild-mannered plant-eater, he had little to fear. But if it was a carnivore, accustomed to running down goats and other prey...

The robotic Yeti certainly hadn't lacked for claws, but he'd seen no sign of sharp incisors among the brutes, or teeth of any kind. If they'd actually been modelled after the real creature, perhaps he was in luck. Those fearsome claws might be meant primarily for digging up roots and grubs, rather than, say, disembowelling its prey.

He swallowed. *Analyse the facts, man. Bipedal ambulation, indicating evolutionary advancement. Still able to run on all fours, however. Probably enabling short bursts of speed necessary to run down a meal on the move. Eyes facing front, thus good depth perception for tracking quarry. Skull structure suggests pronounced temporalis muscles, for pushing teeth into meat and locking the jaw, permitting the animal to hold on whilst its prey struggles its last.*

What further evidence of carnivorousness would you require? Its teeth sunk in your throat?

He pondered a moment longer, then took off his parka and wrapped it tightly around his left forearm. He approached the cave mouth with this crude protection thrust out in front of him. Should the thing swipe at him with its claws, or snap at him with whatever sort of teeth it might possess, he would block with his padded arm, hopefully protected from a serious wound by the extra layers of the coat.

And, so resolved, he stepped into darkness.

The temperature seemed to drop twenty degrees at once, and he felt panic try to boil up his throat. He slipped further forward, and shortly realised he could make out shapes in the blackness: rock outcroppings and a distant red glow. Fire light.

Then he heard the Yeti's distant grunt, and a voice answering it.

A human voice.

Travers crouched, listening. He could make out no words, only murmurs. The voice was male, but young or old he couldn't tell. It almost sounded as if it were… By Jove, *yes*! As if it were *addressing* the newly arrived animal!

'*Ah, Kabadom, tashi delek.*'

That much Travers grasped. *Tashi delek. Welcome, my friend.* And *Kabadom…* Might that be the Yeti's name? Had this stranger *named* the beast? Fascinating!

Despite his nervousness, Travers was grinning in delight, once more overcome with child-in-a-sweet-shop excitement. His eyes continued to adjust. The narrow passage sloped downward perhaps thirty yards to the large chamber occupied by the Yeti and the stranger. There were side passages cut into the rock about a third of the way down, permitting access to other areas of the hideaway.

At the tunnel's far end, he saw flickering, orange light. He supposed, from the crackle of wood, that it was a small fire on the cave floor. He also heard a low, vibrating thrum. *Something*

4

mechanical, he thought. *With a bellows or an air bladder.*

He itched to move forward. But partially visible through the cleft was the Yeti. *His* Yeti. It stood motionless, back to him, head cocked to one side, listening to the speaker as the cave around them crackled and thrummed. *By the stars, it was* listening! Surely there could be nothing else like it on Earth.

The unseen cave dweller began to speak more rapidly, his voice raised but his words still unclear. He sounded angry. Travers wondered who he was. Not one of the Det-Sen monks, it stood to reason. After the chaos wrought at the monastery, none of the monks would have so agreeably welcomed the Yeti.

That strange thrumming rose in volume, and the angry speaker fell silent. Travers shook his head in wonder and fear and—

Something shifted behind him. Outside the cave entrance.

He turned his head. In the rapidly falling sunlight still creeping into this deep expanse, he could see shadows shifting on the rocks behind him. *Big* shadows.

Something was coming.

Heart banging in his chest, he duck-walked further into the passage, wincing at every scrape and crunch of the gravel beneath his feet, but the brute did not turn. He slipped into a side passage, crouching low, breath burning painfully in his throat.

A moment later, something big tramped past his new vantage point. He risked craning his head upward, and saw the brief flash of two great, lambent eyes.

Another Yeti, of the kind that had wreaked terror on the monastery below. It swept on past. Another followed. And another. And another. A column of Yeti filed in, their bulk filling the narrow corridor. Claws scratched the stone and clittered menacingly. Robots or not, their fur was real enough, and the stench clogged Travers' sinuses, turning his saliva into a sour paste at the back of his mouth.

5

He clamped a hand over his mouth, sinking lower with each passing Yeti. All it would take was for one of the brutes to glance down. He choked back a moan.

A cry of surprise from the unseen stranger. Travers looked up again. The last of the Yeti had passed. Twelve of them? More? He wasn't sure. But now that thrumming note was once more—

No. Not a thrum. A *voice*. So deep it was almost beyond hearing.

…must come, I have work for you yet. Yeti to London, you to New York… new source…

Babbling from the stranger, words too thick with imploring obeisance to be anything other than fearful pleas to a terrible master. *Oh my word*, Travers thought in horror. *It's him*. It. *We ended our campaign too soon, Doc—*

The stranger cried out again. Several Yeti snarled threateningly, clearly warning against the stranger's protests. The humming sound rose, becoming a rushing torrent of wind and noise. Travers felt hot air push at his face, then a stranger sensation: a pull on his clothes, a tug at the skin of his face. His hair blew back, then forward.

Another shout from the stranger, diminishing in volume as if he were being rapidly carried away, and cold white light abruptly filled the world, blinding Travers. Forgetting the need for quiet, he shouted in surprise. It made no difference.

Because the light began to pull at *him*.

He fought to see, fought to understand. He could see nothing of the large cavern now. Just a swirling brightness that seemed to reach out for him. *So bright.* The tumult of wind and alien noise increased relentlessly. He shielded his eyes as chips of granite and shale pelted him, flying from the mouth of the cave towards the glow. He felt tiny gashes open on his cheek, on the back of one hand. Something sharp tore his trousers and gouged his shin.

If I don't get out, he thought wonderingly, *I'll be stoned to death.*

He began to shuffle back the way he had come, hands still protecting his face. One thought now ran through his mind. His friends. He had to warn his friends.

The Great Intelligence lived!

He made it halfway back up the stone throat towards the entrance, staggering through the hail of debris. Then the relentless wind and light stopped him in his tracks, dragging him backwards. Travers scrabbled desperately at the walls, felt a fingernail peel back, and shouted one last time. It might have been his wife's name; it might have been nothing but a last, wordless, defiant shout.

Then he was pitching backwards into the maelstrom, eyes rolling wildly as he plunged into blinding white nothingness.

CHAPTER ONE
The Mystery in the Tunnels

THERE WAS a throbbing hiss, a grinding mechanical roar. In answer, Alistair Lethbridge-Stewart simply lowered his head, clenched his jaw, and braced for what was to come.

From the air around him, a voice. 'Hello again, uhh, ladies and gentlemen,' drawled the American pilot in his syrupy southern accent, addressing the passengers via the in-flight radio. 'We're on final approach to John F Kennedy International Airport, just about, uhh, fifteen minutes from our scheduled landing time.' A pause. 'I'm, uhh, told the current temperature on the ground is a bracing fifty degrees Fahrenheit, which for our European friends would be, uhh, ten degrees Celsius. Cool and clear out there, a little after three o'clock local time, but they're, uhh, tellin' us there's a chance of rain tonight, so if you're headed out for a night on the town, I'd bring your umbrella.'

He clicked off. Lethbridge-Stewart sighed.

He wasn't sure whether it was the cancerous *basso* tone, the deep-fried *y'all*s or the lingering *uhh*s, but he fervently hoped that was the last time the pilot would find it necessary to speak to them.

Another click. Lethbridge-Stewart closed his eyes wearily.

'Finally, on behalf of the crew of Flight 503, I'd like to welcome all of you to the United States. Y'all have a great weekend, and, uhh, thanks for takin' a ride with us here at Trans-World.'

'Darling?' said a voice to Lethbridge-Stewart's right. He looked up, shifting his long frame in the tight confines of the chair, and found his seatmate watching him bemusedly over a flutter of magazine pages. Sally Wright, his fiancée, let slip a wry smile. 'You've flown simply hundreds of times, Alistair,' she said, gently mocking. 'I know we're nearly there, but shall I ring the stewardess for a last drink? Something to calm your nerves?'

'I'd rather not meet your American friend with alcohol on my breath,' he replied, only to see her teasing grin widen further. 'I've no problem with air travel, Sally. When, that is, there's a qualified military pilot at the controls, as opposed to commercial aviation's version of a near-sighted city bus conductor. And as for the civilian accommodations...'

He waved a hand at the confines of Flight 503, Trans-World Airlines' state-of-the-art, wide-bodied 707. Sally followed his gestures, took in the cramped rows of narrow plaid seats, the lolling heads of a hundred passengers visible above pillows or head-rests. A few read or talked quietly to their neighbours; others dozed fitfully, or tried in vain to do so. Two rows up, an elderly gent periodically uttered a rattling cough. It sounded bronchial, contagious. He followed each bout by spitting thickly into one of the plastic cups the complementary drinks came in, an action punctuated each time by the horrified chirp of his seatmate. *'Really,* Ralph!' A baby somewhere aft had wailed incessantly for much of the flight. Lethbridge-Stewart supposed its parent had either given up the struggle to soothe it, or had gone deaf from the racket.

And finally, as if to cap off the argument for him, the *No Smoking* signs posted at intervals along the length of the cabin suddenly lit up, eliciting groans from travellers in the rear third of the plane. Most – Sally included – began taking last frantic puffs before stubbing out their cigarettes, adding a final set of smoke-signals to the blue fug lingering overhead, further straining the airliner's overtaxed filtration system.

Not that the burned tobacco smell quite masks the creeping, cabin-wide eau de body, Lethbridge-Stewart thought bleakly. He did not bother to say it aloud. He was marrying one of those habitual smokers after all. Besides, truth be told, he could have murdered a cigar. A good Cohiba and all would have been right with his world.

Sally's smile never wavered. 'Still beats catching the night bus to Bermondsey.' She laughed, her own energy and

9

enthusiasm unfazed by the long flight.

'It's *indistinguishable* from the night bus to Bermondsey, give or take some thirty thousand feet at cruising altitude,' he shot back, a smile lifting one side of his mouth. She saw it, flushed happily, and gave him a chaste peck on the lips. He had to fight the compulsion to glance around, worried that some previously unnoticed ranking officer had taken a seat nearby, and might now be frowning at the inappropriate display of affection. Even more worried that Sally was so completely *un*worried.

For God's sake, man, he scolded himself. *Let it go.*

He cleared his throat and glanced at the magazine she'd been reading. 'Your *Look* is a bit out of date, my dear.'

She threw him a mock glower, chuckled, and regarded the cover. *Look* was her favourite American monthly; this issue, dated 10th June, was four months old. She shrugged. 'I don't know why I don't let the subscription lapse,' she said. 'I'm always ages behind. If it weren't for the occasional train trip or some madcap holiday with my handsome fiancé, I'd never get caught up.'

Lethbridge-Stewart ignored the flirtatious tone; he was reading the top headline on the magazine's cover. '*The Wedding Racket*,' he quoted curiously, raising an eyebrow. She frowned and turned it around again to read the headline for herself. He saw her bite her lip, and knew what it meant.

Dash it all, he thought. *Can't we go eight hours without tripping over this topic?*

It seemed they couldn't; lately she'd pushed him less and less gently to confirm a date. As her persistence grew, so too did his reluctance. From the moment he'd impulsively asked Sally to marry him the whole business had gnawed at Lethbridge-Stewart in a manner he found disheartening. And, if he was being truly honest with himself, *vulgar*. It was like something out of *The Archers*; a guilt-riddled cliché he wanted no part of.

For months he'd kept reassuring himself that he hadn't made a mistake. That he would eventually, sensibly, overcome these worries in his own practical, studied way. His disquiet had continued though, and after that business last month with the Grandfathers – and the *other* bit of news she'd sprung on him in the wake of it, her reassignment to Dolerite Base, with him – the nagging concern had become so pervasive that when his bride-to-be breezily suggested they take a New York holiday, he agreed on the spot, booking it before either of them could come to their senses. It was rash, he knew. As rash as that initial proposal of marriage had been.

But they both *were* overdue for some real time off. And for Lethbridge-Stewart, it seemed the perfect opportunity to resolve his inner conflict, one way or the other.

They would have five days together, he'd reasoned as he booked their travel, asking the agent to spare no expense finding suitably romantic accommodations in downtown Manhattan. Five full days in New York City, the fabled Big Apple itself. Free to enjoy themselves without the overshadowing rigours of the job. Away from the exacting, omnipresent code of military propriety. And temporarily unburdened by the increasingly strange turns life had taken over the last eight months or so.

Sally was still looking at the magazine cover, and still biting her lip. Colour had risen in her cheeks, and her eyes shone. Lethbridge-Stewart imagined at least some of his thoughts had played out clearly enough on his face, and regretted it.

'Sally,' he started to say. 'We—'

'Darling,' she began at the same moment. 'It's—'

'Miss anything good?'

They both broke off and looked up to see Owain Vine approaching from the toilet at the rear of the plane, stepping aside to allow another passenger in a New York Mets baseball cap pass by. Eighteen, good-looking in an unaffected way, his long ash-blond hair hanging over the collar of his battered jeans jacket, Owain was wrinkling his nose and waving a paperback book in the air. He jerked a thumb over his shoulder at the smoking section. 'Blimey, that pong can't be healthy, can it?' he asked, cheerfully enough. 'Pity it doesn't cover up the BO.'

Lethbridge-Stewart smiled at the echo of his own earlier thoughts. 'We're about to land,' he told the young man. 'Better strap in.'

Owain slid into the empty seat to his uncle's left, balancing the paperback on one thigh. 'I don't think I'll ever truly enjoy flying,' he said as he buckled his seat belt. 'I love to travel, but give me a nice, slow freighter any day. Open air. The sound of birds. Plenty of time to play my guitar or just... be. Sure, there's the diesel stench to contend with, but the wind whisks it away pretty effectively—'

Lethbridge-Stewart chuckled. 'Sorry, we don't have two weeks to get where we're going.'

Owain snorted. 'Oh, now you're coming down on the side of the capitalist pigs of the aviation cartel, eh? Weren't you telling me earlier you'd send the whole lot for scrap and happily go back to riding your rucksack on a military cargo plane?'

'There's something soothing about the drone of a Hawker Siddeley,' Lethbridge-Stewart protested. 'And nobody asks you to check your bags.'

'Fair enough. Just keep in mind, you fly military and sooner or later someone's going to start shooting at you.'

Isn't that always the case? Lethbridge-Stewart thought wryly. He watched as Owain checked the shoulder bag he'd slung under the seat in front of him, carefully tucking his book – *Man's Eternal Quest* by Paramahansa Yogananda – into it and settling back for the last few minutes of their trip.

Lethbridge-Stewart realised he *was* glad they'd come, very glad, in spite of all the issues he and Sally needed to iron out. It meant a chance to spend some time with Owain, and the lad never failed to brighten his outlook.

'Looking forward to exploring New York?' Lethbridge-Stewart asked.

Owain nodded. 'Too right. Do you know the kind of venues this city has to offer? The Café au Go Go? Max's Kansas City? Fillmore East? I'm buzzing.'

'I take it those aren't local places to eat,' Lethbridge-Stewart quipped.

'Square.' Owain laughed. 'They're only the hippest music clubs on the planet. Procol Harum. Jefferson Airplane. Cream. Dylan. Even Bowie and The Stones play those joints when they come over to the States. And Them!'

'Them who?'

'Them, man! Van Morrison? G-L-O-R-I-A?'

Lethbridge-Stewart sniffed. 'That doesn't spell "them".'

'You're so unhip it's a wonder your bum stays on.' Owain laughed affectionately, earning the prerequisite raised eyebrow. 'It's New York City, Uncle Alistair! If London is the eye of the world, New York is the centre of all time and space.'

After all we've seen, I wouldn't be so sure about that, Lethbridge-Stewart thought. He nudged the boy. 'You *will* try to find time to have at least a couple of meals with Sally and me between rock concerts, won't you?'

'Oh, please do,' Sally chimed in, and Lethbridge-Stewart was relieved to see she had herself back under control. 'Tonight certainly. We're due to have dinner with Adrienne, remember. She has us a booking at Sardi's!'

As Owain promised Sally he'd stick close this evening, Lethbridge-Stewart found himself recalling the other purpose for their New York getaway. The telephone call Sally had received a fortnight ago.

The final minutes of the flight were uneventful, and they disembarked right on schedule to find Lieutenant Adrienne Kramer waiting patiently for them in the bustling concourse. She was a pretty, petite black woman with sharply observant eyes and short hair cropped close, accentuating the striking bone structure of her face. She was dressed in civilian clothes: black boots and trousers, a black windbreaker over a hunter green turtleneck.

But if she was trying to appear nondescript, her parade-rest stance and general air of keen observation, of *readiness*, surely botched the disguise. She looked tough, no-nonsense, every inch the soldier, and when she recognised the trio she'd come there to meet, she even appeared to struggle for a moment against the compulsion to come to attention and salute. Lethbridge-Stewart stifled a chuckle, suddenly sure that if he had been in uniform, she would have done.

Sally chirped in delight and hurried to embrace her friend, both of them laughing in delight. The soldier-in-disguise was gone; Kramer was just a twentysomething woman happily meeting an old friend at the airport.

Lethbridge-Stewart and Owain approached them as other passengers hurried past, the Trans-World waiting area rapidly filling with the din of various reunions and homecomings. The lad was smiling uncertainly, one eyebrow raised. *Did he pick up that affectation from me?* Lethbridge-Stewart wondered, startled but not displeased by the idea. He clapped Owain amiably on the shoulder.

Sally beckoned. 'Alistair, Owain, come meet my dear friend, Adrienne Kramer.'

Lethbridge-Stewart shook Kramer's hand as Sally made introductions. 'I appreciate you refraining from saluting, Lieutenant.' In deference to her, he said it 'loo-tenant', the way the Americans did. 'We're making every effort to keep this a true holiday. The less pomp and circumstance the better.'

Owain smiled broadly as he greeted Kramer in turn. 'Don't mind my uncle,' he told her. 'He's never truly happy unless there's action afoot. If you check his luggage, I'm pretty sure he even packed his swagger stick.'

Kramer smiled, but Lethbridge-Stewart saw that it ended well below her eyes. 'I understand the desire to check duty at the door, sir,' she said. 'There's no better place on Earth for a few days of R&R than New York City. But the truth is, I'd hoped to talk a bit of shop with you first, if that's all right.'

He sighed. *So much for the notion of civilians on holiday.* He gestured at the deplaning passengers heading for the baggage claim area. 'Business before pleasure. Shall we?'

Owain followed them through the crowd, Uncle Alistair walking up front beside Kramer with Sally close behind them.

Owain drank in the chaotic scene all around them. They weren't even out on the street yet and already he was agog at the riot of colour and noise: the people, the shops full of trinkets and tourist memorabilia, the fashions and hairstyles, the rich melange of accents and languages. Even the overhead Tannoy was a polyglot wonder, directing the crush of humanity and identifying current arrivals and departures in English, French and Spanish. Owain liked to think of himself as having travelled, even at a relatively young age, but New York was a whole new level of experience. He grinned, excited to get out of there and into the city proper. The record stores and art galleries. The parks. The cuisine and culture and every marvellous thing that awaited them. Not a very Eastern way of thinking, perhaps, but hadn't it been said that one must first walk in the world to truly appreciate the value of living free from the world's influence?

Shaking his head in wonder, he murmured a quote from Gautama Buddha himself. 'As you walk and eat and travel, be where you are. Otherwise, you will miss most of your life.'

Sally had donned her wide-brimmed yellow travelling hat. She hooked her arm through his. 'What was that?'

He shrugged, cheeks colouring slightly. 'Just taking it all in,' he said.

'Wait until we head downtown,' she told him. 'You haven't seen anything yet!'

Ahead of them, Lethbridge-Stewart and Kramer were deep in conversation. 'In fact,' she was saying, 'I was doing double-duty, meeting you here. I was scheduled to check in with a friend of mine, a detective who does a little off-the-books research for me now and then. We meet here when we need to chat away from prying eyes.'

'Sounds a bit clandestine,' Lethbridge-Stewart said. 'Sally led me to believe you handle liaison activities between the US Army and the UN here in New York. Surely you aren't expecting trouble?'

She shook her head. 'No. I don't know. I don't think so.' She sighed. 'Truth be told, Brigadier, I'm really not sure what to think. It's these damned coma patients.'

Lethbridge-Stewart frowned. 'Coma...?'

'Seventeen now. First turned up almost a month ago. No one made a connection between them until there were a dozen in Manhattan General Hospital, among them a high-profile foreign dignitary at the UN, which is why it hit my desk. It's easy to overlook such things; the city is a big place. You don't start to see patterns until...' She paused. 'I'm getting ahead of myself. Anyway, these don't appear to be ordinary comas. Total paralysis, but they can breathe on their own. No reaction to external stimulus. Health seems stable, no deterioration, but no improvement either. And far as anyone can tell, there's no pattern, except that quite a few are city workers; Metropolitan Transportation Authority.'

'The city's subway system?'

'That's a big part of it, yes. A few others have connections to the subway as well. Homeless, mostly, but also a kid we learned like to play in the abandoned tunnels.' Kramer shuddered. 'Honestly, if you'd told me five years ago that anyone in their right mind would let their kid go near some of these festering old hellholes...' She shook her head. 'I'm from Washington, I should know better, right? Anyway, it's all just a theory. I have a C-I, a confidential informant, who first called my attention to it. I brought in Paulie – that's Paul Dawson, former NYPD. Took a bullet on the job two years ago, now a private detective. Paulie agrees, it's not normal.'

They came to a long, descending escalator beneath signs pointing them towards the baggage carousels. They queued and descended.

Lethbridge-Stewart decided to forego asking why Kramer thought *he* was the right man for this discussion, and stuck to the subject in hand. 'There *is* some linking factor among the coma patients? Something worrisome?'

Kramer glanced around, briefly studying the faces of the nearest travellers and airport staff. The slightly paranoid behaviour piqued Lethbridge-Stewart's interest even further. 'Rat bites,' she said simply.

'Rat bites,' he repeated.

She nodded. 'Hard to say definitively without proper assessment of every patient, and I couldn't get access to them all. But in numerous cases, at least one bite mark was found. Among the majority of those, the wound or wounds indicated the bite of *rattus norvegicus*.'

Lethbridge-Stewart raised a questioning brow.

'The common-or-garden brown rat, as I believe you Brits would say. Also known as the Norway rat. Here, they're just "New York sewer rats" under the best of circumstances, and much more colourfully identified the rest of the time. Like the rare incident when they slip into a Hell's Kitchen tenement and take a bite out of somebody's baby in its crib.'

'Good lord,' Sally said, revolted.

Kramer nodded. 'Believe me, it happens. They're *everywhere.*'

They reached the ground level thoroughfare and began

16

wending their way through the crowd to retrieve the newcomers' bags.

'Omitting for a moment the comas,' Lethbridge-Stewart said. 'Surely even a couple dozen rat bites aren't that unusual in a city of this size?'

'Not before they began cracking down here in the 1920s and '30s. Extermination efforts really drove the brown rat population back. The city now tracks fewer than fifty rat bites per year, a two hundred percent drop since this time a century ago. But the rate they're happening lately…'

'I take your point.'

'And that's discounting the comas, as you said,' Kramer added. 'If there's a causal factor, no one's found it yet. If it's a new type of disease for which rats are the vector, it's not one that makes a lot of sense to the attending doctors. If it was just seventeen cases of rat-vectored rabies, believe me, I'd have recommended the UN to put pressure on city officials to clean up their act, bought new seals for the doors and windows in my crummy little third-floor walk-up, and that would be the end of it as far as I'm concerned. *But…*'

'But?' Lethbridge-Stewart prodded helpfully.

'But it's *not* rabies, and something tells me it's going to take more than political pressure and new door seals to resolve whatever's really going on.' Kramer checked her watch again. 'And it doesn't settle my nerves knowing Paulie hasn't shown up.'

'Your CI?'

'Right. I'd intended to meet with him, here in the airport café, before picking you up. He didn't show.'

CHAPTER TWO
The Dead Ender

MILES AWAY, deep under Manhattan, as the passing trains roared and rattled around him and the furtive, somehow menacing rustle of rats (*or bats?*) grew harder and harder to ignore in the dripping, echoing passageways, Detective Paulie Dawson crept down a pitch-black tunnel somewhere below Hell's Kitchen, trying to catch up with the shadowy figure he'd started following more than an hour earlier.

You should've checked in with her by now, he thought. *You missed the meeting at the airport, and you should've checked in. She's gonna read you the riot act.*

He had one gloved hand clapped over his lower face, trying to lessen the seeping garbage stench of the dark tunnel as much as he could, so his murmured response would have been unintelligible to anyone else within earshot. 'Yeah, but it's gonna be worth it when I bring in her Mr Mystery.'

The warm glow that idea lit in his belly was short-lived. There was a distant bellow of mechanical brakes and he jumped in spite of himself, drawing in a deep breath. The sour reek of the lungful of air made him wince. He spat into the darkness and it occurred to him – not for the first time – that when he got his gimp *tuchas* outta here, Adrienne was *definitely* gonna owe him a drink. Or two. Or six. With or without Mr Mystery in tow.

Drinks with Adrienne. He smiled. The glow in his belly was back.

Or you could get off your duff and straight-up ask her to dinner, his needling inner voice shot back. *You only been wanting to for like ten months. Be a man, Paulie, why don'tcha?*

'She's married, dumbkin,' he muttered. 'How many times I gotta say?'

Dawson sighed. He'd been having this argument with himself for quite some time now, but just lately he'd begun having it out loud. No strange thing in New York, right? But he'd lived alone almost five years now, since his ma had gone home to Jesus, and he knew *that* was gonna make him funny if he kept it up much longer. Plenty of funny guys in this city, sad sacks the lot of them, and he didn't relish the idea of ending up *being* one of them.

He'd tried dating once or twice, mostly when his sister Louise tried to fix him up with one of her giggling Bingo girlfriends, but it never seemed to work out, not even when he wore his best jacket and a tie and brought flowers and held doors and pulled out their chairs for them. He supposed his income was part of it. The private dick racket didn't exactly keep him flush, even in this city, and his police pension didn't help much, even counting what extra he'd got for taking a bullet on the job.

The other problem, he had to admit, was the fact that for at least the last year he'd been carrying a pretty fierce torch for Ade Kramer.

It was sad to the point of being ludicrous, he supposed. Or ludicrous to the point of being sad. He was thirty-eight, paunchy and already greying, a pencil stub of a guy who still said *youse* when he was tired or distracted. Adrienne was twenty-four, athletic, a smart, educated army officer with a light southern growl. Oh, and she was a Negro, of course. He knew people from his old Flatbush stomping grounds – his mother among them, God rest her soul – who would fall down in shock if they heard that Paulie Dawson from the neighbourhood had a crush on a coloured girl. But Dawson didn't give a damn. Never had. Bigots were dullards, and nothing annoyed Dawson so much as a dullard. He strived every day to improve himself. He'd read Proust and Faulkner, James Joyce and Ray Bradbury. He loved Steinbeck's *Grapes of Wrath* and John Howard Griffin's *Black Like Me*.

And since he'd met her in the summer of '67 he'd loved Adrienne Kramer too. Secretly... but he loved her.

He'd been part of a protection detail she'd briefed on security and etiquette during a critical series of UN talks on US-Russian relations in Indochina, and six months later she'd seen him coming out of a Chinese takeout joint on 8th Avenue and said, 'Well, hello to you, Officer Dawson.'

They'd kept in touch ever since. When he was still on the job, it had been about trading information, sharing contacts. She worked hard, and she valued connections, and he did what he could to be of help to her. It meant the world to him that she'd stayed in touch after he left the force and hung out his investigative shingle. She'd thrown him a research job now and again or pointed others his way when they had certain needs. Often of the broken-marriage variety.

Then *she'd* got married. It nearly broke his heart when she told him about the engagement, and he'd begged off when she asked him to dinner to meet her fella. He'd known for some time she had a fella, of course – an architect, she'd said – and knew that even after they tied the knot George Kramer was still living in Washington, only taking a train into the city to see her one or two weekends each month. He had no idea how any man could stand that, stand to do anything but hand in his notice, take the first bus or train north to be by her side, and sweep floors or dig ditches or do whatever it took to stay there.

But George did seem to treat her well. And she sure was sweet on him.

Damn it all.

Even without that insurmountable obstacle in his path, Dawson glumly had to admit to himself that Adrienne was just entering the prime of her life, while he was heading down the far side of his own. Hobbling down it, more like, thanks to the dumbkin with the thirty-eight who'd tried to rob the all-night Midtown Diner on that hot Saturday night in August, just a month or so after he and Adrienne had met. The kid hadn't been a *bad* sort. Paulie knew him from the old neighbourhood, had even played stickball with his dad in junior high, but he'd panicked when Dawson and his partner walked into the diner, when he saw their uniforms and their holstered weapons, and his own gun had gone off.

And an accidental bullet does the same thing to your left kneecap as one fired on purpose, ya hump, Dawson thought ruefully.

All things being equal, the saddest part of the whole thing had come next. Paulie's partner, Corey Donaldson, had drawn his piece and shot the dumbkin dead. Paul had insisted on going to the funeral, walking with a cane, still wearing the *fakakta* leg brace he'd be stuck in for months to come, and the dumbkin's dad had roared in anguished fury and blacked Paulie's eye for him.

'S'your problem, ya know, Paul,' his sister had said to him later, bringing him a cheap piece of flank steak to put on his eye. 'You're a nice guy. Nice guys finish last.'

He sighed, hunting in his coat for his torch. 'Maybe so,' he murmured. 'But not today.'

He'd spotted the skell he was tailing in Midtown, coming out of a Radio Shack carrying a paper bag full of what Dawson assumed must be electronics supplies. The guy's face jumped right out at him: Adrienne had briefed him a while back on the mutt Paul had thereafter dubbed *Mr Mystery*. She wouldn't go into detail about why she wanted him or what it was all about, but he'd been a cop long enough to know when the time was right she'd tell him everything. In the meantime, the sketch she'd showed him had been pretty dead to rights. She'd got it from some confidential informant of hers, somebody Dawson didn't know.

Come to think of it, she'd never really gone into detail about *that* character either, had she?

'Definitely owe me more than one drink for this one, Ade,' he muttered.

He found the wayward flashlight, switched it on low, and began to shuffle deeper into the tunnel, favouring his bum left leg. He kept the pale yellow beam pointed at the ground. He didn't want the skell to get wise – *if you ain't lost him already, Paulie, thanks to your gimp tuchas* – but he also wasn't exactly keen on the idea of accidentally putting a foot wrong and stepping on the subway's third rail, the one the juice flowed through.

He'd followed Mr Mystery from the Radio Shack to the nearest subway entrance, keeping well back, following all the rules he'd learned on the job and honed since then, keeping tabs on wayward husbands and tax-dodging white-collar crooks. He'd expected Mr Mystery to hop onto a train, but as one slid into the station he'd edged nearer and nearer to the far subway tunnel. He'd waited 'til the doors opened and the crackling loudhailer blared the stop information, and as the on-off crush peaked, Dawson had watched in surprise as the spry cat simply stepped down off the platform, disappearing into the tunnel from which the train had come. If anyone else saw him, they gave no sign. Dawson went to the edge of the tunnel and peeked around the corner.

Just in time to see the stranger disappear up a side tunnel.

Cursing, he thought for a moment, looked around 'til he saw what he needed, and ran to a nearby bank of pay phones. He found a dime and called Ray Reigadas, his old poker buddy in the MTA office. Ray assured him that while the subway line Paul was following was live, the one feeding that offshoot tunnel was most assuredly out of service. That was the old L line, Ray told him, part of a section begun in the mid-1950s but never completed due to problems in the bedrock, and it had been shut down as a dead ender.

A dead ender.

That was all Dawson needed to hear. He'd blown Ray a kiss, hung up on the man's laughter, and waited until the platform grew busy enough once more for him to mimic Mr Mystery's amazing disappearing act.

And now here he was, chasing the weird old guy in the cloak and hood up this smelly, echoing old tunnel, which grew more and more disused and dilapidated the further along he went. Even so, Dawson continued to eye the third rail nervously. He'd been relieved that Ray had pronounced it out of service, but Dawson hadn't spent fourteen years at Midtown Precinct South with his head up his hinder, and he'd only grown more cautious in the years since. He was also a New Yorker born and bred, and if there was one thing you learned from the time you were outta short pants (other than you backtalk your mother and you're gonna earn a smack) it was, don't never, *ever*, touch the third rail.

To kids like him, it was a mythical threat, a legendary way to shuffle off your mortal coil. To cops like him, there was no fiction about it. Twice in his police career he'd had to peel fried homeless guys off the tracks after they'd set a foot wrong. Both times it had been months before he could bring himself to eat barbecued pork again.

And where the hell is Mr Mystery going, anyway? New Jersey the hard way?

There hadn't been a side corridor or access point anywhere for the last mile. Just this endless, curving, pitch-black tunnel to nowhere, stinking like burned animal fur, like—

In the distance, something shifted. Something... large.

Dawson paused. Considered. There was nowhere the skell could run to now, except right into the waiting arms of his pursuer. Smiling, he raised the flashlight and pointed it down the tunnel.

Nothing. Nothing he could make out, anyway. The tunnel floor was growing ever more littered, not just with the usual windblown subway detritus of candy bar wrappers, old newspapers and the like, but back here in this abandoned tunnel there were smashed cardboard boxes and odd, unexpected mounds of junk. Just ahead, dented and bashed but still recognisable, was a rusty old child's tricycle. Beyond it was a pile of splintered wood that might have been an antique sideboard or just an old pallet of crates. Here were discarded tires, and piles of rubbish. The door of an icebox. A surprisingly clean and new-looking woman's purse.

Another shuffling noise ahead, and what sounded like a deep sigh.

Dawson decided he was done playing hide-and-seek with Mr Mystery.

'I know you're there, and you know I'm here,' he said suddenly, raising his voice so it echoed around the cavernous passage. 'You wanna stop fooling around back there, pal, and come on out?'

Only silence from the dark tunnel.

Dawson grunted. 'That was some disappearing trick on the platform, but now I'm tired and I want you to come on out so's I can ask you some questions. Then we can both go our way. What do you say to that?'

He started forward again, still holding out the flashlight but increasingly aware of how thin and pallid its beam had become. Maybe *he* should've stopped by Radio Shack—

There was a grunting noise. He stopped again, frowning, and put his free hand to his lower face, trying to block the worst of the stench. *Criminy*, the stink of it! It was like the monkey house at the Bronx Zoo, and seemed to get worse as

23

he walked further into the echoing dark.

'Come out where I can see you now, fella,' he snapped sharply. 'Don't make me tell you a third time!' Yeah, he was a nice guy. Sure he was. But Mr Mystery didn't need to know that just yet. He cranked up his New York Cop voice still further. 'Listen, ya mope, I've had it up to here with the stink in these tunnels, and I'm losing my pa—!'

Something rose out of the darkness, a great, fur-covered creature that had been crouching amid the debris piles further up the line, and Dawson's voice stopped dead in his throat.

Luminous yellow-white eyes peered unblinkingly at him. Another deep grunt. This one sounded angry. Or hungry.

The thing had to be eight feet tall.

Patience, Dawson had been trying to say. It was one of the many characteristics he, the nice guy, was supposed to possess. He wished he'd had a chance to show it to Adrienne. *I really woulda liked to take her to dinner*, he thought glumly.

The shambling thing raised massive claws. It rumbled at him like a bull alligator, and before he could even begin to weigh his fight-or-flight options, it dropped to all fours and rushed at him, not like an alligator now but like a bear. A grizzly or – considering its mostly white pelt – a polar bear.

And it was *fast*.

Paul Dawson, who already knew he would not be able to get the gun out of his coat in time, heard his sister's voice in his head, very clearly.

Nice guys finish last, Paulie.

Dawson thought she was wrong about that. He was finished right now. Finished before he understood *any* of this. That disappointed him terribly.

But not for long.

CHAPTER THREE
Picking Up the Pieces

THE TAXI moved through the streets as if hounded by unseen hell-beasts, weaving in and out of the rush-hour traffic. The driver muttered impatiently at other drivers in a thick Slavic accent and occasionally worked his brake pedal like a bass drum, as if keeping the beat for one of the surly rock bands Owain enjoyed.

Kramer had respectfully offered Lethbridge-Stewart the front passenger seat. She sat in the back with Sally and Owain, pointing out landmarks and catching up on the latest about the wedding plans and Sally's new appointment to Edinburgh. Lethbridge-Stewart had to admit to himself that he was mildly pleased – at first – by Kramer's deference. Then the driver somehow managed to slalom across four lanes of traffic, whipping into a taxi-only lane and braking with a screech of tires as he joined the long line of exhaust-belching vehicles headed for the Queensboro Bridge. Only then, removing both white-knuckled hands from where he'd planted them firmly on the dashboard – to keep from being thrown headlong into it – did Lethbridge-Stewart understand that Kramer had done him no favour at all in offering up the front seat.

He gave the driver a caustic look. 'Steady on. We're on holiday, old chap; this isn't the World Rally.'

The big yellow taxi's driver merely grunted at him.

Ah, New York, Lethbridge-Stewart thought, bemused.

If the others were remotely bothered by the reckless speed and stop-start motion of the taxi they gave no sign. Sally was begging Kramer to drag her husband away from his Washington draft table and fly over for the wedding; Kramer, laughing, said she couldn't recall the last time they'd dressed to the nines and danced the night away. 'We'll have all the dancing you can stand, I promise!' Sally wheedled.

For his part, Owain was too busy gaping in delight at the approaching city to worry about their mad driver. His eyes moved ceaselessly, taking in the stone-and-metal forest of skyscrapers, the mix of vivid and drab colours popping out everywhere from the crowded buildings and billboards and giant, blinking neon signs. He'd told Lethbridge-Stewart during the flight that he really only knew New York from rock-band lyrics and from the Hollywood films that made it across the Atlantic.

Manhattan fairly pulsed with life. Lethbridge-Stewart saw that Owain couldn't stop grinning in anticipation of all its promised sights, sounds and experiences. Lethbridge-Stewart was more glad than ever that he'd invited the young man to join them.

Despite the taxi driver's apparent desire to break as many driving records as possible, it took them three-quarters of an hour to arrive at 59 West 44th Street in the heart of Manhattan. When they emerged into the bright, chilly afternoon sunlight, Sally gasped in delight and clapped a hand to the top of her hat to keep it in place as she leaned back, peering up at the towering, twelve-storey hotel.

'The Algonquin!' she exclaimed. 'Really, Alistair? You've booked us at the Algonquin?'

Lethbridge-Stewart permitted himself a pleased smile as he paid the driver, adding a modest tip. Glowering at him, the man went to the back to get their bags.

Sally hugged him tightly. He chuckled. 'You haven't even seen inside yet.'

'It's marvellous, darling,' she whispered, and gave him a peck on the cheek. 'This was Dorothy Parker's favourite spot in the city.'

'Who?' Owain inquired. He was helping the taxi driver extricate their belongings from the cramped boot, handing off items to a hotel valet, unmistakable in his dapper, eggplant-coloured uniform. Kramer stood nearby, checking her watch.

'Who!' Sally mocked in disbelief. She flapped a hand at Owain in reproach. 'Mrs Parker and her Vicious Circle! The Algonquin Round Table! Only the most glamorous, notorious band of writers, actors, journalists and *bon vivants* of their day. We're just a street over from Times Square. In the 1920s this was *the* place to be.'

'Rabble,' Lethbridge-Stewart said gruffly, his eyes twinkling. 'Harold Chorley would fit right in with that lot, I daresay.'

'Not a chance.' Sally laughed, and her eyes glowed with happiness, all their unspoken troubles on the plane apparently forgotten. She put a hand briefly to his cheek. 'Really, darling, it's *wonderful.*'

Yet despite his pleasure at having so thoroughly pleased her, Lethbridge-Stewart found himself struggling to meet her gaze. He glanced at the busy street, trying to lessen his own sudden discomfort by taking in their bustling surroundings. Taxis, delivery trucks and other vehicles zipped past them. Pedestrians moved in a steady stream in all directions; it was Friday afternoon, and the work week was over. The crowd-flow in front of the hotel parted wordlessly on the pavement near the kerb, skirting a small group of long-haired twentysomethings who had hunkered down there, panhandling, playing guitars and singing what sounded like protest songs. The valet glared at the vagabonds as he went past with most of their bags in his hands and looped over his shoulder. Owain followed with the rest.

There was a brief, burbling honk of a police siren, and they turned to see a broad, blue police patrol car pull up behind their taxi.

'Looks like those hippies are in for it,' Lethbridge-Stewart observed.

But the two uniformed police officers who got out of the squad car came directly over to him and his party, ignoring the muttering youths. The police car's driver, burly and moustachioed with a prominent five o'clock shadow coming in bluish and stubbly across the dark olive skin of his lower face, nodded in Kramer's direction.

'Excuse me, Ma'am. Are you Lieutenant Adrienne Kramer?'

'That's right,' she said. 'What can I do for you, Officer?'

'Your office said if we missed you at the airport, you'd be here, seeing folks to their hotel,' the big cop said. He looked unhappy. 'You're acquainted with a private detective by the name of Paul Dawson, right?'

Kramer and Lethbridge-Stewart exchanged a look. 'I am,' she said. 'What's happened to—'

'He was working for you?'

'He was making some inquiries, yes. What—'

'Ma'am, can we ask you to come with us? Our chief would like to ask you some questions.'

Owain had stopped outside the hotel's ostentatious revolving doors when he heard the siren whoop. Now he ambled back over, brows drawing together in consternation. Sally also drew close, looking confused, pensive.

Kramer folded her arms. 'I'd be happy to help in any way I can,' she said patiently. 'But first I'm going to need you to tell me what's going on.'

The cops glanced at each other, and the second one, slim and pale yet with a moustache almost identical to his partner's, nodded. They both looked back at Kramer, and the mix of sympathy and suspicion in their eyes said plenty.

'I'm sorry to have to tell youse, Ma'am,' the skinny cop said haltingly. 'Detective Dawson was found dead just a short time ago. Our team's still at the scene now.'

Kramer paled, but her composure never wavered. 'What happened?'

'Looks like he fell in front of a train,' the driver told her. 'He was down in Hell's Kitchen, apparently following a lead in the subway, and he...' He trailed off, waved a hand helplessly. 'He had your card in his pocket. Note on the back said the two of you were to meet this afternoon.'

Kramer nodded. 'Out at the airport. I was waiting on these folks to arrive from England. Paul was to check in with me there in regard to the case he's assisting me with.'

The cops gave Lethbridge-Stewart and the others what seemed like cursory glances, but Lethbridge-Stewart felt the keen eyes sizing him up, assessing him.

Kramer had put a hand to her forehead. 'Dammit, Paul,' she muttered.

The driver gestured lamely. 'Very sorry for your loss, if you and Paulie was close. He was a good guy. Good cop. It ain't right, this.'

'Lieutenant,' Lethbridge-Stewart said quietly.

Kramer looked at him, shaking her head. 'I knew something was wrong when he didn't check in at the airport,' she said in disbelief. 'When he didn't call me. But...' She looked back at the two cops. 'I want to go to the scene. Now, before a hundred people tramp through it.'

'Ma'am, I dunno,' the slim one started.

'You said investigators are still there, yes?'

'Well, yeah, but...'

Kramer looked at Lethbridge-Stewart. 'Will you join me?'

Sally took his hand. 'We both will, Adrienne. This is terrible. Of *course* we'll come.'

Her friend nodded her thanks, looked back at the cops. 'I'm a security staffer at the UN, and Mr Dawson was investigating matters related to national security at my behest. Do you need my identification? Do you need to contact my superiors? I can make that happen immediately if it will cut through the hassle and get me on-site faster.'

The cops traded another look. The slim one raised his hands, giving her a sympathetic look. 'No need, Lieutenant. Youse wanna ride with us?'

Lethbridge-Stewart gave their driver a quick glance. The man was sidling away, trying to make himself invisible, clearly wanting to be anywhere but here. *Illegal*, Lethbridge-Stewart surmised. *Expired work visa, if he ever had one in the first place.* 'Yes, I think we'd best let our driver go his way,' he said. He stepped over to Owain. 'Why don't you get us checked in, see that our bags are delivered to our rooms?'

'Happy to, Uncle,' Owain said. 'Do you think you'll be long?'

'No idea. But if you're hungry, go ahead and get something to eat, in the event we're detained. I'll see to some supper for Sally and myself when we get a chance.'

Owain nodded and turned away with the bags to follow the valet into the hotel. Lethbridge-Stewart returned to the others.

'Shall we?' he asked.

Owain watched as the bellboy deposited Aunt Sally's bags in her suite and Uncle Alistair's in the adjoining one. His own room – an extravagance his uncle had surprised him with, much to his delight – was another floor up, and he gawped as the young steward led him inside and pointed out the amenities. All three rooms were fairly identical, down to the idyllic pastoral artworks on the walls and the pattern on the quilt of the king-sized beds, but somehow this one, with its ornate wardrobe and sitting chairs, its gaudy lampshades and well-appointed lavatory, seemed the lushest of them all.

He tipped the bellboy a tidy sum, earning an enthusiastic tip of the youth's cap and a promise to assist with anything he might need during his stay, and closed the hotel room door behind him.

He sat down on the edge of the big bed. 'Glorious,' he murmured, allowing himself to collapse backward for a moment, revelling in the plush mattress and downy bedcovers. *This* was living. It might not jive with his spiritual quest, but he couldn't help but grin broadly.

It certainly *felt* right.

He got up and took a quick shower. The water pressure wasn't mind-blowing – not unexpected, given that he was on an upper floor – but it still felt utterly grand after the long day's travel. Towelling off, he dressed in fresh clothes: comfortable jeans, daps and his favourite t-shirt, the grey one with the Campaign for Nuclear Disarmament semaphore on it. He left his hair to air-dry, finger-combing it into some semblance of acceptability, and grabbed his wallet and room key. Then, thinking about the chill in the late-afternoon air, he threw on the battered denim jacket that had once belonged to his brother and headed out, intent on exploring a bit of the surrounding city before night fell.

He *was* worried about the unexpected mess Uncle Alistair and Aunt Sally (it felt a bit strange, referring to his adopted uncle's fiancée that way, but he'd used the term playfully a few times and it seemed to delight her) had found themselves in. But there was no sense sitting here fretting over it.

He descended via the lift and left a message at the front desk, giving the clerk Uncle Alistair's and Aunt Sally's room numbers and asking him to inform the late-arriving members of his party that he'd be back within a couple hours. The clerk in turn gave Owain a business card with the hotel's main phone number on it, in case he wanted to stop at a pay phone at any point and inquire about their check-in status. With that, Owain pushed out through the revolving doors, thinking with a kind of nervous glee, *New York's mine to explor—*

The thought vanished as he stepped onto the sidewalk and instantly found himself surrounded by clamouring, angry voices. He had emerged in the middle of an altercation which seemed on the verge of blossoming into a full-scale riot. Apparently unmindful of, or perhaps emboldened by, their earlier luck in avoiding a clash with police, the band of eight or ten hippies on the sidewalk outside the Algonquin, resplendent in coloured headbands and open-throated blouses, bell-bottomed jeans and sandals, had not taken the opportunity to move along unmolested. Instead, they'd apparently begun heckling hotel guests as well as the valets, and now were receiving in kind from representatives of both groups.

Owain heard shouts of 'Capitalist pigs!' and 'Bloated bourgeoisie!' Someone was beating a fast tattoo on a tambourine, adding a shrill, panicked note to the uproar. Most pedestrians on this side of the busy avenue attempted to put their heads down and pass by, ignoring the altercation completely, but the bottleneck only grew larger by the minute, and Owain could see that the sympathies of those just trying to get home at the end of a long work week were predominantly with the hotel personnel and their patrons. Two or three big men in their forties or fifties, wearing city worker fatigues and hard hats, led the on-looking crowd, and they were winding up to a dull roar themselves. 'Get a job, ya punks!' one of them shouted. Almost in unison, a passing taxi's driver-side window rolled down, and a wrinkled old codger with a crew cut leaned out, slamming a hand on the side of the cab in time with the beating tambourine. 'Cut your hair, you dirty hippies!' he roared, and was gone.

The crowd seethed and surged. Owain was bumped hard from behind, and he stumbled forward, colliding with a pretty girl wearing a beaded headband and flowing white smock. She had flowers painted on both cheeks, and she looked utterly terrified. Owain put a hand on her arm, steadying her,

31

and looked around in shock and confusion, seeking a way out of this mess. *This* was the New York he had so longed to visit?

A guy of nineteen or twenty with dirty blond hair hanging down his back – possibly the leader of the little group – poked a bony finger into the breastbone of a portly businessman, who clutched his leather briefcase to him like a shield. The youth snarled. 'How can you live with yourself, sleeping in this palace when kids in Vietnam are sleeping in mud, soaked in the blood of innocents?' The suited businessman used the briefcase to shove the boy away from him. A tall, muscular hotel valet intervened, stepping between the young protester and the hotel guest.

'The cops are on the way,' the valet said, clearly seething beneath his forced calm exterior, his hands balled into fists. 'I'd suggest you—'

Unbowed, the hippie spat at his feet.

Owain's comforting hand was abruptly slapped away from the frightened girl's arm, and he found himself nose to nose with one of the city workers. 'Draft dodger,' the man murmured. His hands were fisted too, and they were rising.

'I'm not—' Owain started, meaning to add *'even American'*, but the big valet had seen enough.

The man lashed out without further warning and knocked the spitter flying. Opposing sides slammed together, and the fracas escalated into a full-blown fist fight. In the distance, police sirens warbled. Owain and the city worker both glanced in that direction.

But before the man could accost him further, Owain felt someone grab him roughly from behind and drag him backwards. He caught a last glimpse of the girl cowering amid the fighters before losing sight of her in the altercation. There was a strong arm around his shoulders, and he was being hustled away as fast as his protector could go, muscling through the outer ring of onlookers. Owain glanced left, saw shoulder-length blond hair, a strong male jawline. Lips pressed tightly together, green eyes flashing.

'Who…?' he tried to shout over the din.

'Come on,' said the young man, his voice deep and clearly American, though almost without accent. 'We bug out or we're going to get our skulls cracked. If not by those city boys, it'll certainly be the cops.'

They were moving fast now, and the arm dropped away from Owain's shoulders, his rescuer trusting him to keep up. They hurried around the corner of the hotel, heading towards Times Square. The flood of rush-hour pedestrians made it difficult to move quickly, but it didn't take long until they were lost in the flow. Behind them, Owain could still hear the sirens and shouts – even an occasional scream – but it was all quickly swallowed up by New York's singular, multitudinous song.

'I wasn't with that lot outside the hotel,' Owain said at last, after they had walked another city block, as New Yorkers called their sectioned streets. His breathing had slowed nearly to normal, the oncoming evening air beginning to chill his hot skin.

'I know,' said the other youth, smiling. 'Reg, the guy yelling at that roly-poly fellow in the suit, tends to let things get out of control way too often. We're all pretty sick of his jive. Anyway, I saw you stumble into the middle of it and figured you didn't deserve to spend a night in the can with the rest of us.'

Owain looked at him, getting a really close look now. His saviour looked slightly more presentable than most of the hippies outside the hotel, clad in dark jeans, a plain white t-shirt and a black windbreaker. His hair, though longer than was considered respectable by the middle-classes on either side of the pond, was professionally cut and looked clean. He had shaved recently too. The young man glanced over, saw Owain looking at him, and grinned. 'I'm Simon. And I've got to hand it to you, buddy, I didn't have you pegged for one of the fat cats.'

Owain blinked, his cheeks flaming. 'I'm... Oh. No, I'm not.'

Simon gestured at the CND symbol on his shirt. 'That says you're not. Staying in that bourgeoisie mansion for the rich and feckless, though. Some people might jump to conclusions.' His grin stayed on as he spoke, and Owain saw that it was good-natured, not judgmental.

'I'm staying there with my uncle and his fiancée. It's my first visit to New York.'

'Somebody else paying for the digs, eh?' Simon said, and

laughed. 'Don't flip your wig, bro, I'm just giving you the business. You're English?'

Owain nodded.

'Far out. And do they give you English fellows names these days, or…?'

Smiling, the adrenaline beginning to drain from his system at last, Owain introduced himself. 'Guess I owe you my thanks, Simon,' he said sheepishly. He thought for a moment of the cowering girl back there in the crowd, wondered why Simon hadn't thought to pull her to safety as well, and dismissed it. *He* had been the stranger; it had been kind of Simon to get him out of harm's way. It wasn't Simon's fault he'd failed to recognise the girl's danger as well.

'It's copacetic, Owain, my man,' Simon said grandly, that big smile returning.

American culture might be all about the hair and the fashion, Owain thought, *but what sets these people apart the most is all those big, white teeth. And their readiness for a fight.*

Simon looked around, presumably getting his bearings. 'Tell you what,' he said, rubbing his hands together. 'You want to pay me back? I'm famished. What do you say to some grub?'

It was Owain's turn to smile. 'You're on.'

Simon clapped a companionable hand on his shoulder. 'My man!'

They continued down the avenue together, the bright lights and hubbub of Times Square rising in the distance to greet them.

As Owain and his new mate were exiting the scene outside the Algonquin, Lethbridge-Stewart, Kramer and Sally were being led across a noisy subway platform in Hell's Kitchen, following another interminable ride across the choked traffic grid that partitioned Manhattan's stunning tower blocks and skyscraper clusters. It had helped that this trip had the benefit of police lights and siren, speeding them a little more quickly to their destination, but by the time they arrived, Sally told Lethbridge-Stewart she could feel a headache coming on nonetheless.

For his part, Lethbridge-Stewart could also feel the jet lag catching up. He realised how desperately he'd been looking forward to lying back on a plush hotel bed, shoes off, eyes closed, perhaps with a nice cup of tea brewing somewhere in the suite. *It'll wait*, he thought.

But when they arrived at the subway station and realised the place was choked with rush-hour commuters furious at having their trips home delayed, he wondered how long it would be before he was fighting off a pounding head himself. Scores of tired, angry people blocked the station entrance. Most just milled about in confusion. Others jostled one another as they struggled to get back out to the street, hoping to hail a taxi or flag down a city bus.

Fortunately, for Sally's sake, Lethbridge-Stewart had a small tin of aspirins with him, tucked away for the flight. He shook two of the small white pills into Sally's palm and put the tin back into his trouser pocket.

A sharp whistle, and they looked around. Kramer had thanked the two cops who had driven them. The uniformed men were turning away to help with crowd control outside the station, stolidly resigned to the extension of their own workday. Kramer herself was waving Lethbridge-Stewart and Sally over. It looked like she'd found their on-site escort: a heavyset, stone-faced police sergeant named Hayes, who seemed adept at tuning out the clamour of questions from the civilians clustered all about them.

Or perhaps he's just deaf, Lethbridge-Stewart thought with wry amusement. *In this city, it wouldn't surprise me. The perfect antidote to the furore.*

The four of them made their laborious way down into the belly of the station, pushing against the mass exodus of huffy, protesting New Yorkers.

The cracked, faded tile walls, peeling hand rails and stained cement floor of the station were grim indeed, Lethbridge-Stewart mused, recalling some of the brightly lit, well-maintained Underground stations back home in London. He wondered at the poor condition of this facility. He knew, of course, that Manhattan's population had far outpaced that of Britain's largest city, exploding at the turn of the century and swelling ever since. Given that fact, he supposed the infrastructure here must take a beating as millions flowed into the city each day to work and flowed out again to the surrounding boroughs when the work day ended.

But privately he thought that Hell's Kitchen had been aptly named, or this subterranean thoroughfare beneath it had been anyway. The squalid corridor leading down into darkness was about as far from where he'd planned to spend his first few hours in New York as he could possibly imagine. Not even that cup of tea would suffice any longer. He wanted a good meal, a whisky and a cigar.

But they would keep, he knew, and be all the sweeter for it.

Ahh, New York.

On the platform itself, the cops had a little more success pushing back the complaining crowds, and as they crossed the dirty floor of the station, Lethbridge-Stewart spotted a water fountain and pointed it out to Sally. She crossed to it to take her pills and he glanced over at Kramer.

'My condolences again on the loss of your friend, Lieutenant,' he said uncomfortably.

Kramer looked as tired as he felt. She nodded her thanks, and added, almost as if she'd been reading his mind, 'Sorry to ask you to start your vacation in a place that smells so much like urine.'

'Yes, well. Needs must.'

Kramer turned to the uniformed officer who had escorted them inside. 'Can we go down now, Sergeant?'

Hayes nodded to her. He gave Lethbridge-Stewart a steely glare. 'I don't know about him,' he intoned.

Kramer glanced back and forth between the two men. 'Mr Stewart here is with military forensics. This is our case examiner, Miss Wright. They're integral to my investigation on behalf of the UN.'

Hayes looked them over again. He still seemed sceptical, but after a moment just nodded wearily and beckoned them all to follow him. They went to the far left edge of the train platform. Someone – probably the same tunnel workers now struggling to erect floodlights pointing into the gloom of the tunnel – had set up a folding metal staircase, enabling them to step down onto the tunnel floor easily.

'Power's been cut to the line?' Kramer asked Hayes as he

led them into the spacious cylindrical tube, pointing a bright torch beam at the floor to light their way.

More torches swung this way and that, carving the darkness roughly one hundred yards up the tunnel. A camera's flash went off repeatedly, the pulse underscored each time by the echoing, somehow grisly *crunch-pop!* of the strobe.

'Hadda cut power to at least a third of Hell's Kitchen down here,' Hayes explained. 'Got some pretty ticked off commuters cos of that, let me tell you.'

As if we didn't just wade through a mob of them, Lethbridge-Stewart thought dryly.

Hayes' voice had a deferential quality to it, but his stance and demeanour didn't echo it. Whether that was due to Kramer's youth, gender or the colour of her skin, Lethbridge-Stewart couldn't say for certain, but it irked him regardless.

'Yeah,' the heavyset sergeant said. 'The sooner we figure out this mess and amscray, the better. Looks pretty cut and dried, to be honest. Paulie D followed some skell onto the tracks, maybe homeless, maybe not – we got no shortage of 'em here, panhandling and scaring the respectable folks – and it looks like Paulie misjudged the next train. It happens. This city...'

He trailed off, leaving the last couple words to serve as an explanation of sorts, and perhaps doubling as a curse.

Sally stumbled on the loose debris and Lethbridge-Stewart caught her arm, steadying her. She held on to him tightly, and he didn't draw back. 'Thank you... *Mr* Stewart,' she said slowly, drawing out the words, suppressing her normally rich accent with its traces of her Northumberland roots. It made him look sharply at her, and when she winked he found it hard to suppress a smile.

They had almost reached the scene. Three uniformed cops stood by, one with thumbs hooked into his belt; the other two holding their torches steady now to help light the scene. All of them were watching a slim black man in a tan coat and beret finish up photographing the scene. The final member of the unit, a bald, bespectacled man in a suit jacket and blue rubber gloves, was crouched next to a huddled form under a dark plastic sheet.

Hayes cleared his throat. 'Mr Luck here's our forensic

investigator,' he said, jabbing a thumb at the crouching man. The camera's flash went off suddenly – *crunch-pop!* – turning the scene momentarily bright blue and white. Lethbridge-Stewart blinked to clear his vision and the man identified as Mr Luck straightened up and turned to face them.

'These are the folks from the United Nations,' Hayes told him. He nodded at Kramer. 'She's the one supposed to meet with Paulie this afternoon at the airport, around the time it happened.'

Luck nodded. He didn't offer to shake with anyone, merely tipped a gloved finger to one temple by way of introduction. 'You sure you're up for this?' he asked in a hoarse, cigarette-infused voice devoid of accent, New York or otherwise. They all nodded.

Sally now had her arms folded, clutching at her own sleeves to steel herself.

Luck turned, crouched again, and carefully pulled back the plastic sheet. It made a wet, sucking sound. Sally gasped, shuddering. Next to Lethbridge-Stewart, Kramer closed her eyes, turning her head to one side.

'Damn,' she said. 'Damn it, Paul.'

'City's been trying for years to introduce cost-effective safety systems in case someone wanders onto a track,' Hayes murmured. 'Spots like this, coming around a curve, bad lighting, it's no wonder things like this happen.'

Kramer steadied her resolve and turned back to her friend's mangled form. 'But we're so close to the platform here,' she said suddenly, looking around them at the tunnel. 'We're maybe a football field away. Coming in or going out, trains are moving much more slowly, aren't they?'

Luck shrugged. 'They speed up pretty quick, but even if they're going slow, those big wheels are gonna do some damage. That's a lot of weight to try to stop on a dime. A body gets pulled under...' He shook his head. 'We're collecting the rest further up the line.'

From the mouth of the tunnel behind them, the big floods came on, freezing the scene in an unblinking white glare, offering a stark view of the splashed gore on the tracks and the surrounding walls. Kramer put a hand to her mouth, and Sally shook her head in horror, turning away.

For his part, Lethbridge-Stewart took a careful step closer and crouched to get a better look, moving laterally alongside the partially dismembered corpse to get out of his own shadow. His stomach rolled over in revulsion, and he grimly crossed off the sumptuous meal from the list of things he was longing for in the wake of their long, long day.

But he couldn't avert his gaze. He was a soldier, trained to stay calm and self-possessed in the face of such horrors, his composure rigidly under his control. *Almost.* But inside…

Inside, he knew, you never grew accustomed to the sight of violent death. You never learned to handle the raw, awful smell of it, the way the stench clung to your sinuses. But it wasn't the sad, pitiable state of the body itself that transfixed him. There was no arguing the evidence here: Dawson had indeed been struck by a subway train, its travelling speed a moot point given the incredible amount of damage inflicted. He guessed they'd be quite some time yet, mopping up the glistening tracks leading into the distance.

Picking up the pieces.

But that wasn't it. He was looking at the victim's chest and abdomen, staring at three ragged gashes running upwards from the dead man's considerable belly, or what was left of it, nearly to his throat, which had been flayed open very nearly to the wet, white spine.

That hadn't been done by the train. Death by subway misadventure was a new one for Lethbridge-Stewart, no doubt, but he had seen men cut to pieces by anti-personnel fire in wartime. He knew the impact that flying metal had on flesh, large pieces or small: pellets, bullets, shrapnel or shards. And what he saw now was not *that.*

Paulie Dawson had been run over by the subway train, yes. But before that, it seemed fairly obvious he had been savagely mauled by something with claws.

Big *claws*, he thought. He turned grave eyes on Kramer. 'Lieutenant, I think we'd better talk further about your coma patients.' He pointed at the abdominal wounds. 'Those,' he said grimly, 'weren't made by rats.'

39

CHAPTER FOUR
Sleepers and Strangers

OUTSIDE THE subway entrance, the air was brisk. A welcome respite from the humid stink of the underground tunnel, even given the noxious rise in exhaust from the early-evening traffic which made a typical London rush hour look like a Sunday afternoon drive in the country.

Much of the waiting crowd out there had dispersed, finding other means of transport, but a few irate-looking pedestrians still milled about, watching the passing vehicles and glowering at the cops minding the station entry point. For their part, the boys in blue hardly seemed to notice, merely joshing one another about their weekend plans and dismissively waving off anyone who tried to get past them into the subway.

Policemen were policemen wherever you went, Lethbridge-Stewart mused.

He turned to his fiancée, saw she was still very pale, and put a solicitous hand on her arm, steering her away from the street and the knot of cars whizzing by.

'Are you all right, Sally?'

She took a deep breath. 'Better now. My head was beginning to feel like an impacted tooth, but it's easing a bit.' Sally looked past him, met Kramer's dark, hurt eyes. 'I'm terribly sorry, Adrienne.'

'I appreciate it, Sal.' Kramer shook her head, and the hurt changed to something else. Something flintier. 'Maybe bad luck, maybe something to do with this mess, I don't know, but I'm going to find out why he died.' A horn blared close by, shaking her out of her reverie. That flinty look, though... Lethbridge-Stewart saw it was apparently there to stay. She looked at the two of them, her jaw working reflexively. 'It's getting late, and you've been travelling all day. Why don't you go back to your hotel, get something to eat and get some rest?'

Lethbridge-Stewart was already shaking his head. 'I'd like to stick with you, Lieutenant, if you don't mind. We can take a look at your coma patients. Perhaps they'll shed some light on what happened to your friend.'

Kramer sighed. 'I was hoping *he* could shed some light on what's happened to *them*.' She studied Lethbridge-Stewart keenly a moment. 'What is it? Something about Dawson's wounds... You suspect something, don't you?'

Lethbridge-Stewart thought about it. 'Let's look at your patients first. I don't want to jump to conclusions, but something is niggling at the back of my mind, yes.' Beside him, Lethbridge-Stewart saw Sally rubbing her temples. He turned, taking her by the elbows. 'Darling, I really do think you should do as she suggests. You look done in.' Still pale, Sally was all set to protest, but he gently cut her off. 'Find Owain and have a bite to eat. And tell him not to wait on us. He should go on and investigate that New York music scene he's so keen about. I'll have a look at these victims and meet you back at the Algonquin before you know it.' He smiled. 'And tomorrow we'll start our holiday. Officially.'

He could tell she still wanted to demur, but it appeared her headache hadn't diminished as much as she'd let on, and instead of arguing with him Sally relented. It was a relief; the last thing they needed was further fodder for confrontation.

Perhaps Sally knew it too. She simply leaned forward and kissed him, before Lethbridge-Stewart went to the corner to hail her a taxi back to the Algonquin.

Across the street, a figure observed them. His diminutive frame was silhouetted against the lighted window of a small bodega, the glass pane behind him crowded with prayer candles etched with Virgin Mary portraits. All around him, scruffy kids bounded up to passers-by on the pavement, hawking postcards and tiny, painted-plastic replicas of the Statue of Liberty. They seemed adept at singling out the tourists for their most enthusiastic sales pitches, and flocked excitedly to them like pigeons mobbing old ladies with bread in their pockets.

But though the small man was not local by any stretch, the street kids ignored him as he ignored them, instinctively grasping that he was neither mark nor mook, not a sucker and certainly not stupid.

Pushing back the hood of his long cloak, he stared at the tall man on the opposite side of the street, watching silently as he flagged down a chequered cab. Its *In Service* sign stuttered alight. The tall man spoke briefly with his woman and put her in the cab with a quick peck on the cheek.

The observer's head abruptly cocked to one side, as if he were listening to instructions no one else could hear. He grunted, satisfied, and removed the hooded cloak. Beneath, he was dressed in an immaculate bespoke suit. He balled up the cloak and dropped it to the pavement below the window, where all those candled Virgins seemed to regard it piteously, and was instantly transformed from guttersnipe to gentleman, hobo to high-class man about town.

No one about seemed to notice.

And the man, now almost unrecognisable as the late Detective Dawson's intended quarry, moved to hail a taxi of his own.

The diner was small and bright, its surfaces all scrubbed clean, the whole place seemingly fashioned from smoky glass and Formica and stainless steel. It looked like something straight out of 1950s Americana to Owain, and smelled like bloody heaven on earth. A gum-chewing waitress in red-and-white-checked apron and smock brought them oversized menus that looked like Moses' stone tablets. There were a lot more than ten numbered lines on them.

They ordered coffee and mammoth plates of food: a rare burger, French fries and towering vanilla milkshake for Simon, an all-American breakfast for Owain, complete with extra wheat toast and heaps of potato hash on the side. *My god*, Owain thought, *the decadence of it!*

Simon kept up an almost nonstop line of chatter, telling Owain about New York City, about its music and night life, about the protest movements he was a part of and the ideals behind them; the notion of a world free of hoary old ideologies and awake to new possibilities for the first time in what might have been decades. Or centuries. He talked like a DJ, like a salesman, like a beat poet, and as they fell to their food like men home from the wars, Owain decided he liked Simon very much. There was the matter of the fracas Simon had just dragged him away from, too. It might not have wound up an actual *war*, per se, or anything more than a lot of overheated pushing and shoving, but it also might have been much, much worse. Owain wasn't sorry to have missed out on that. And he ate with as much gratitude for that fact as he did the simple pleasure of filling his empty stomach.

'So what do you think?' Simon asked, smiling at him past a mouthful of burger.

Owain swallowed, grinned back. 'About what?'

'The good ole U-S-of-A.' Simon waggled a fry. 'Gotta look a little better now than it did twenty minutes ago.'

'Exactly what I was just thinking,' Owain said, and Simon laughed appreciatively. It was impossible not to smile back; this easy-going American had a confidence and charisma Owain found every bit as appealing as it was daunting to him. He'd learned to relax a lot in his travels over the six months or so, but he was still a child of his simple Cornish upbringing, still bound up in his background and the ingrained tenets of his people despite all his studies, all the things he'd seen and experienced. He sometimes wondered if he'd ever be able to overcome his own history in that regard. If he'd ever truly escape Bledoe in his heart and mind, even if his feet carried him halfway around the world.

By comparison, the casualness and ease in almost everything Simon did and said – talking about the city, music, movies, ideology, tripping nonchalantly from topic to topic and treating each with the same insouciant humour, as if he were completely unchained by any sort of personal past, any personal *ghosts* – struck Owain as profoundly, unassailably cool.

'How do you do it?' Owain asked abruptly, startling himself. Red heat rushed up from his collar. He turned scarlet, his tongue tangling in his mouth.

'Do what?' Simon asked, swirling his straw in his shake and sipping at it.

Owain shrugged, fighting his embarrassment at having asked the question so baldly. He decided to press ahead. 'You seem to have it all figured out,' he said. 'I'm still shaking about what almost happened back there, but you don't seem the slightest bit... fazed.'

Simon raised his hands in a *search-me* gesture, slurped his shake once more and said, *'Be as simple as you can be.'*

Owain's eyes widened at the first few words, and they finished the quote in unison.

'You will be astonished to see how uncomplicated and happy your life can become.'

'That's the Yogi!' Owain said with a grin. 'How—?'

Simon laughed again. 'Not all of us Americans are Christians or rudderless pagans, you know. I've been digging on Eastern religion for years. Zen. Buddhism. Zoroastrianism. I've begun to lean away from the theists, but Guru Yogananda still has some righteous things to say about living clean, seeking truth and oneness.'

Owain nodded enthusiastically, all thoughts of awkwardness or embarrassment forgotten. 'The shedding of our craving for the impermanent things of this world, yeah, too right! I've got his book with me. No, seriously; *Autobiography of a Yogi.'*

An appreciative nod from Simon. 'Great read. What drew you to the Way?'

Once more, Owain felt his tongue tangle in his mouth, felt his eagerness slipping away. He cast his eyes downward, staring at his plate. How the hell could he tell this near-stranger anything remotely resembling the truth?

That back in March he discovered he was the reincarnated soul of his adoptive uncle's late brother. That centuries from now, via some arcane science or magic he could not begin to fathom, he himself was destined to be reincarnated as well, becoming the ascended, formless being they knew as the Great Intelligence. That it was his destiny, ultimately, to become unstuck in time, running mad over the long aeons and seeking to wreak vengeance across time and space on those he blamed for his condition. While, all the time, seeking to expand his own mind by bringing as many others as possible into his own.

Owain opened his mouth, trying to think of something witty to say, and glanced up just in time to see Simon staring back at him, eyes frank, almost... cold. It was, for just a second, nothing like his new mate's usual warm gaze at all.

Simon smiled broadly, digging into his burger again and talking through a mammoth bite of meat, pickle and catsup. 'C'mon, man, I can't read your mind. What was it?' He gestured at Owain's plate, chewing, his eyes twinkling. 'It sure wasn't the vegetarian lifestyle.'

Owain shrugged off the fleetingly weird feeling, lifting his shoulders noncommittally. He looked closely at Simon again. Nothing there now but the most casual, friendly curiosity.

And suddenly, without realising he was going to do it, Owain found himself talking about Lewis. Telling Simon all about his twin brother, and the hole his passing had left in Owain's life.

Manhattan General Hospital, positioned roughly at the midpoint between Times Square and the heart of the Hell's Kitchen neighbourhood, was clearly one of the city's older facilities for the professional treatment of illness and injury. Its ancient stone facings, high dark windows, and ornate merchant-metal fencing looked vaguely European to Lethbridge-Stewart, holdovers from the Old Country, and certainly antiquated. A hundred years antiquated or more.

Even so, as the blue-and-white cruiser pulled up, the old hospital appeared to be a fairly busy centre of activity, with a fair knot of people climbing the stone steps, pushing their way in and out of the heavy glass doors. Three crewcut young men in long white lab coats stood at the base of the steps, smoking and arguing, oblivious to the new arrivals. Several dishevelled old men and one woman, all of them clearly homeless, huddled on the other side of the steps, where the steep stone side cut the wind and heated steam from the subway vents at their feet rose up to keep them warm. Lethbridge-Stewart wondered if they stayed here all night, and shook his head in amazement. What a city this was.

As Kramer thanked the driver, Lethbridge-Stewart exited the cruiser, stepped past the trio of arguing doctors, and mounted the steps. Kramer hurried to catch up with him, and they entered the hospital together.

Shortly, after climbing a long interior staircase and passing through a number of windowless doors marked *No Admittance Without Authorisation*, they were ushered into the intensive-care ward by a small, intense man whose nametag identified him as Doctor Supravhal. It was all cold tile and tubing and clustered machinery in there, every footfall echoing below the vaulted ceilings and everywhere the pervasive smells of over-washed linens and disinfectant. The lights were dim. A nurse prowled restlessly, clipboard pressed to her ample bosom, but bobbed her head at the doctor when they entered, and left them to it. After a brief exchange, so did Supravhal; it was evident to Lethbridge-Stewart that Kramer, whatever her rank or status at the UN, was known here, and trusted. That said a lot about her, in his book.

Rows of beds were arranged against the left and right walls, each flanked by softly beeping machines tracking the vital signs of the beds' occupants. Seventeen in all, just as she'd said. Kramer led Lethbridge-Stewart towards the nearest of these, and bade him have a closer look.

'What do you see?' she asked.

He looked closely, studying the bed's occupant. Even in the dimmed light, what he saw was a singularly ordinary man of about thirty-five, appearing to sleep almost normally despite the IV in his arm, the oxygen line in his nose and the blocky, blinking apparatus crowding one side of his bed. He was swarthy, deeply tanned especially for the late season, perhaps a bit more muscular than the average city dweller but otherwise undistinguished.

Except for the strange, yellow-grey cast to his skin.

Lethbridge-Stewart glanced up at Kramer, who nodded and stepped closer herself. Carefully, she reached forward and drew one of the man's closed eyelids up.

'My word,' Lethbridge-Stewart breathed.

The pupil of the eye had shrunk to the smallest pinprick. Around it, the original colour of the iris was impossible to distinguish, the normal white of the sclera gone. Both had turned a virulent yellow-grey similar to the skin, the iris only distinguishable because the new colour there seemed to...

swarm, flecked with shifting prisms of darker grey and a deeper, more poisonous yellow. Beneath the glister of the cornea, the strange eye seemed almost to throb. To pulse.

Kramer was talking, he realised. '—no clue what caused it.'

Lethbridge-Stewart blinked, straightening up. 'Sorry,' he said, clearing his throat. 'What was that, Lieutenant?'

She gently closed the man's eye once more. 'I said, he's a construction worker, part of a crew working on connecting a new elevated track with the Hell's Kitchen train lines. Found by a watchman not too far from where we were, actually, with no clue what caused it.' She trailed off, her eyes distant. He knew she was thinking about her dead friend. A moment later, she was back. 'The rest are exactly the same. Skin. Eyes. Everything.'

Lethbridge-Stewart pointed at the man's waxy, discoloured skin. 'No one thought it might be prudent to seal them in protective enclosures of some kind?'

Kramer shook her head. 'They've run a hundred tests. It's not toxic or infectious, and no more radioactive than the backscatter you get from the X-ray machine at the airport. As far as anyone can tell, they're just… changed.'

Lethbridge-Stewart looked down the length of the room, mystified, at seventeen prone human beings, rendered unconscious by means he didn't yet understand, physically altered for some unimaginable purpose.

Behind them, the door opened. Both of them jumped.

Doctor Supravhal stood there, blinking owlishly at them, blowing on a steaming cup of coffee. A pair of nurses entered behind him, carrying trays of needles and fluid-collection tubes.

'Time to draw blood,' Supravhal said.

'Let's step out, get some air,' Kramer suggested. 'Now that you've seen them, we can talk more outside.'

Lethbridge-Stewart nodded agreement and mutely followed her out, tilting his head politely to the newcomers as he passed. He found it took a great deal of willpower not to turn and look back over his shoulder at the figures in the beds, all of them still to the point of lifelessness.

Owain knew he would be hard-pressed to replay that entire

dinner conversation in his head later. He remembered laughing so hard at one point he spilled his pop – fortunately, the glass was almost empty – and he remembered fighting to keep control of his emotions as he told Simon about Lewis's death and the start of his own journey of self-discovery. He told his new friend all about Bledoe, the little hamlet he'd left behind, and about his adopted Uncle Alistair, who'd proved such a vital touchstone as Owain had begun to make good on Lewis's dreams of seeing the world.

He omitted some of the more outlandish things he'd seen and experienced, of course. *Leave the craziness for another time*, he thought. *If there is another time.*

But he ended up talking at length about destiny, about the idea of speeding towards a future that might already be written. He asked Simon what he thought about fate, whether it was something over which ordinary people ever really had any control. He wasn't sure why. After all, he hardly knew this cheerful young American with his throaty smoker's laugh and his wide, infectious grin.

But this is what it's all about for our generation, in this country at least, Owain thought. *Opening yourself up, making friends wherever you go. Spreading a sense of community and brotherhood as antidote to the closed-minded, closed-heartedness of the older generations.*

Simon thought for a moment about what he'd asked. He slurped his shake and shrugged. '*Live quietly in the moment and see the beauty of all before you,*' he said, once more quoting Yogi Yogananda. 'The future will take care of itself.'

Owain smiled, shaking his head in admiring disbelief. He laughed and went back to his meal. Their generation or not, he doubted most blokes his age – those still relatively new to international travel anyway – were lucky enough to meet individuals as open-minded and in sync with the world as Simon seemed to be.

The blond man leaned back in the booth seat, chuckling, and winked at him. 'You ever drop acid? Amazing way to open the inner eye.'

Owain flushed again, but only slightly. 'I've dabbled in some... things, but no, I've never gone to that length.' He regarded Simon cautiously. 'Have you?'

Simon's broad grin faded, and he looked more serious than Owain had ever seen him. 'It's interesting. It's not for everyone, and I've known cats who've taken some *egregiously* bad trips, man. Walked on the wild side and barely made it back again. But you asked about the future. Sometimes, doing a tab, opening the inner eye, it feels a lot like opening a portal *to* the future.'

Owain raised a brow, remembering the Om-Tsor and his adventures on Fang Rock. 'Wow. Are you saying you've... seen things?'

That sober, downward gaze continued. 'I saw Martin Luther King's assassination.'

'What?'

Simon's piercing eyes rose to meet Owain's, nodding almost imperceptibly. 'Saw it like I was one room over from James Earl Ray, across the street from the Lorraine Motel in Memphis. I heard the shot. I saw it all.'

Owain shuddered, fascinated. 'Did you talk to anyone about it?'

Simon looked away again, shaking his head no. 'I didn't know what I was seeing. It's intense, like tunnel-vision. Everything goes cold, and there's this roaring that kinda overwhelms everything except what's dead-centre in front of me. It's so bright, like someone's turned a spotlight on the scene.' He trailed off, and blew air harshly between his lips. 'This recent one... I don't know, man. It's out there.'

Owain leaned forward. 'What? I mean, if you want to talk about it.'

The American sat quietly a moment, gathering his thoughts. 'It's a student protest,' he said, keeping his voice low. 'Looks like a college campus. Cow college, I don't know where, lots of white kids with good skin and money. The trees look bare and everyone's in jackets, but I don't see snow, so I think it's spring. Everyone's angry, shouting. Throwing things. I see a sign that says "US out of Cambodia".' He fell silent again. After a moment: 'In the distance, a burnt building is smouldering. I think it's the Reserve Officers' Training Corps building, "Rot-See" they call it, turning kids into soldiers.' He took another deep breath. 'This kid, this girl in a white bandana, comes running toward me, waving her arms. And then the gunfire starts.'

Simon fell silent. Watching him, Owain discovered he needed a sip from his own glass in order to speak clearly. 'And this hasn't happened yet?'

'No. Pretty sure it would make national news if it did.'

'Did you tell anyone?'

Simon shrugged. 'I tried. Visited some nearby campuses, ones that reminded me of the place I saw in the vision, but it could have been anywhere. I talked to organisers I knew about Cambodia protests they might be planning. Nothing.' His eyes said more: *No one took me seriously. Not a damned hippie kid from the sticks.*

They finished their meals silently, but by the time they were done, Simon had recovered his usual *laissez-faire*-bordering-on-Zen attitude, chattering away again about Creedence at Max's Kansas City and The Stones at the Fillmore, and dancing naked on the GWB, whatever that might be.

Owain, on the other hand, felt more disconcerted than ever. He found himself dwelling on the idea that had launched this avenue of discussion – a way to open the inner eye – and he pondered the teachings he had read on the subject, the guidance of Paramahansa Yogananda and other teachers. When it came to spiritual cleansing, to purifying the mind and spirit, the inner eye was key. Its most potent gift was the ability to grasp the aspects of your life which were hidden from you, those truths you were most reluctant to face. So what did it say about Simon that opening his inner eye had revealed a desire – or a helplessness – to effect change in the direst of circumstances?

And what would opening Owain's inner eye say about *him*?

Lethbridge-Stewart and Kramer exited the big front doors of the hospital to find the night was upon them, all the city's myriad lights shining now as the night assumed ownership of the city's vast stone and steel network and the millions of tiny lives housed therein. As the two soldiers started down the stone steps, both immediately and rapidly began to talk over one another. They both stopped, and he gestured for her to continue.

'I'm sorry to ruin your weekend, Brigadier, but if it's any consolation, I'm about to ruin lots of other people's weekends too.'

'Good,' he said.

Kramer broke off, staring at Lethbridge-Stewart in surprise. 'What?' she asked. She'd rounded on him when they hit the pavement, feet planted, fists clenched, clearly used to fighting to get what she wanted. The last thing she seemed to anticipate was agreement.

He smiled briskly, clasping his hands behind his back. 'I want you to see to it, by whatever means necessary, that all available forces here are put on high alert. You should argue to close the subways until we have an opportunity to investigate further, in order to protect the public from additional attacks.'

'Exactly my plan,' Kramer said, her sternly handsome face easing into the first hints of a broad smile.

'Once we know for certain there's an unnatural threat at work,' Lethbridge-Stewart continued, 'I'll alert General Hamilton in the hope that he can go through channels and help swing his US counterparts into motion to help your state and local law enforcement. He'll tell me the Fifth has no real pull here, of course, but...'

'And what'll you tell him?'

Lethbridge-Stewart thought a moment. Shook his head. 'Too early to say.' He nodded curtly to her. 'Facts, Lieutenant. We need more facts.'

Both of them were so deeply focused on their conversation that neither saw the shadowy figure approach, moving quietly along the building's edge, keeping out of the street lights. He stepped forward eagerly, reaching out, hands coming up—

Lethbridge-Stewart saw this last from the periphery of his vision and whirled at once, pushing Kramer to his left to put himself between her and the oncoming figure. He crouched slightly, left hand up in a warding gesture, right cocked back and fisted, ready to swing. 'Steady on!' he snapped. 'What's your business, sir?'

'Wait!' Kramer gasped, recovering fast and stepping between the two men. She looked flustered, but it was also evident she knew the man. 'This is my informant!'

Blinking, Lethbridge-Stewart straightened up, eyeing the figure warily. The man flinched back at Lethbridge-Stewart's shout, skittering back toward the relative safety of the high stone wall and its iron fencing. Now he stepped forward again, chuckling and briskly rubbing his hands together, his face still shadowed by the rise of the stone steps above them.

'My dear chap,' the newcomer said, his accent decidedly familiar, his voice at once jocular and brusque, like that of a curmudgeon with a particularly amusing secret. 'What a pleasure it is to meet you. For the, erm, first time, as it were.'

'You're English,' Lethbridge-Stewart said in surprise.

'As English as they come, old boy.' The man stepped into the light, and now Lethbridge-Stewart could see him plainly. A ruddy-faced man of fair middle age, soft in the middle, flushing redder still now at his own involuntary reaction to Lethbridge-Stewart's aggressive reaction. And there was *something...*

The man went on chuckling, observing him steadily. It took a moment before Lethbridge-Stewart recognised the eyes looking at him; they were much younger than Lethbridge-Stewart remembered. The same was true of the man's entire face. It didn't match the one that rose in Lethbridge-Stewart's mind. And yet it did. He knew this fellow. *Would* know him, perhaps. He wasn't sure of the vocabulary for this; there'd been the Fang Rock experience, of course, but otherwise...

'Good God, man,' Lethbridge-Stewart said at last. The husky chap standing before them chuckled again, delighted. Lethbridge-Stewart supposed now he knew why.

Kramer folded her arms against the chill of the evening, staring at the ground as she waited for the shock of adrenalin to subside. Seeing the mix of amusement and familiarity on her face, it occurred to Lethbridge-Stewart that she had no idea there was anything strange about the man. No idea at all.

'Brigadier,' she said at last, 'I'd like you to meet—'

'Professor Edward Travers,' he finished for her, still

hardly daring to believe his eyes.

Because the Travers he knew, the one who'd aided in the struggle against the Yeti in the London Underground and was even now begrudgingly settling in at his new home in Edinburgh, was well into his seventies. This Travers though... This hale fellow standing before him on a chilly Manhattan city street in late October 1969 was younger.

Decades younger.

Travers stepped forward and extended a hand in formal greeting. 'I suppose my appearance begs some explanation,' he said.

'That, Professor,' Lethbridge-Stewart replied, shaking Travers' hand firmly, 'may well be the understatement of the year.'

CHAPTER FIVE
Time Out of Mind

NIGHT WAS taking proper hold of the city. Realising he hadn't eaten since well before midday, Lethbridge-Stewart asked Kramer if they might find someplace to grab a bite and bring one another up to speed. She looked from the soldier to the professor and back again, recognising there was some twist here to which she was not yet privy, but apparently willing to wait for answers. For the moment, anyway.

It turned out she knew the area pretty well from her frequent visits to the coma ward. She led them a couple of streets west to a cosy tavern called *The Early Doors*. When they stepped into the place, all brass and burnished mahogany under a fug of blue smoke, Kramer headed directly to the long bar, nodding to several drinkers hunched over their glasses, and greeted the hawk-faced woman pulling drinks.

'Hey, Tanya.'

'Ade! Welcome back, honey. What'll it be?' Brisk, whiskey-voiced – roughened, no doubt, by shouting deadbeats out of the place after last call – she was the very picture of a classic pub keeper, lacking only the prerequisite Northern accent. Thin but faintly pretty, ciggy hanging from thin lips beneath long straight brown hair, a starched blue apron tied over plaid shirt and blue jeans, and a stained hand towel tucked into her back pocket.

Kramer ordered three pints of bitter, asked for menus, and guided the men to a booth at the back. It was enclosed in high wood framing that lent them some privacy. Seating herself, Kramer handed out menus and took a pull on her drink.

'Okay,' she said. 'What the hell is going on? How do you two know each other?'

Lethbridge-Stewart sipped, and nodded in satisfaction.

Between its barkeep and its bitter, he decided he approved very highly of *The Early Doors*. He looked at Travers, settling in next to Kramer, and drew in a breath.

'Professor Travers and I have worked together in the past,' he said. 'But...'

The professor was quaffing happily, nodding at them around his glass. 'There's a bit more to my story that I've never shared with you, Lieutenant Kramer. More than a bit, actually. Call it professional courtesy; I didn't want to make your life any more complicated than necessary.'

She stared at him, then at Lethbridge-Stewart. 'You worked together in the past, he said... But, Professor, you've been here years now. In the States. In New York.'

'Since early 1965,' Travers confirmed.

Lethbridge-Stewart blinked. 'Early 1965?' He was trying to do the sums in his head. 'But that's...' He trailed off. Blinked again.

'I'll tell you as much as I can,' Travers said. 'I've been waiting for Lethbridge-Stewart here. Or someone like him; possibly a rumpled fellow with a strange police box, and a *ghastly* recorder player. I knew one of them would arrive, sooner or later, to help me set things to rights.' Kramer and Lethbridge-Stewart looked at one another, both mystified, if for different reasons.

Travers cleared his throat and began. 'It was 1935—'

Kramer gawped. '1935!'

Travers went on without comment. '—and my dear friend John Mackay and I were in the Tibetan highlands, near Det-Sen Monastery, searching for a trace of the fabled abominable snowman. The Yeti.'

The phone rang just as Sally stepped out of the shower and wound a plush, cream-coloured towel around her. She swept her wet hair back and went to answer, certain it would be Alistair. Steam curled out the bathroom behind her as she rushed out.

Instead, she heard singing. A woman's voice, sounding far away and slightly indistinct. '...*you may lose them one day, someone takes them away, and*—'

'Hello?'

The singer broke off, and there was a short burst of embarrassed laughter. 'Sally!'

'Yes?' She smiled as she realised who was on the other end. 'Anne?'

Anne Travers was Head of Scientific Research at Dolerite Base, and ever-so-increasingly a friend of Sally's. Which was hardly surprising; other than the girls working under Jean Maddox there weren't any other women in which to confide while working at the Fifth. Despite what Alistair liked to believe, he wasn't solely the reason for Sally's transfer. Her friendship with Anne was part of it, too.

'I'm so glad I caught you!' Anne said. 'You weren't resting up, were you?'

Sally sat down on the edge of the bed, adjusting the towel. 'Not at all, we've... just arrived, actually.' She thought about Adrienne, the body in the subway, the coma patients she and Alistair had whisked off to investigate, and decided to forego burdening Anne with any of it. *Why muck up her evening as well?* Sally thought glumly. She glanced at the clock. Evening? Not where Anne was calling from, surely.

'My goodness,' she said, 'it must be after midnight in Edinburgh.'

She couldn't tell if the odd sound in Anne's voice was fatigue, the mediocre connection or something else entirely, but her next words made Sally frown in concern. 'I had hoped to talk with you before you left London this morning, but you know the job...'

'Never lets up,' Sally agreed, covering her concern with cheer, unwilling to add to whatever was troubling Anne. 'You never did give me that shopping list, you naughty thing. How are Alistair and I supposed to properly shop for your birthday? I *so* hate that we'll miss being there for it.'

An uncertain sound from Anne. Surprise? Had she forgotten her own birthday?

'That's not what I wanted to talk to you about,' Anne said. 'I—'

But there she stopped.

Sally stood up, began pacing. She had one hand clamped to the top of the towel, holding it in place as she walked back and forth across the bedroom suite. 'Anne? What is it?' A long pause. She couldn't tell for sure what Anne was doing. Pacing across her own room? Drinking? Crying? 'Anne?'

'Oh, Sally, I don't know why I called!' A quaver in her voice: real distress now. Sally lifted her free hand from the hem of the towel to her lips, truly alarmed. 'I suppose I just needed a friendly voice,' Anne continued. Sally was about to reassure her, promise Anne she could always confide in her, when the line crackled and Anne spoke again. 'Did you...? Have you seen my father since we left London?'

Sally's frown deepened. She sat down on the bed once more. 'Not really. I popped in to say hello the other day, but...' She trailed off, trying to recall the specifics of the encounter: the thump of the professor's cane, his usual bluster.

'How did he seem?'

'Well, he seemed fine. Excitable. Perhaps a little irritable, but that's not surprising. I don't think he wants to be in Scotland. Though now you come to mention it, there *was* something...' It came back to her in a flash, and she felt tremendously guilty for not giving it any thought before. She supposed she understood Anne's distress now.

'What was it?'

'Well, your father called me "Anne". Twice, in fact. I didn't have the heart to correct him, I assumed he was just tired... Oh, darling, I'd completely forgotten. I'm so sorry. This is what you've been worried about, isn't it?'

Anne confirmed it, telling Sally the issue had been on her mind for some time now. 'I think I first noticed back in... The end of May? Yes, shortly after all that business on Fang Rock. But now... Now it's not just simple absent-mindedness anymore, but real moments of confusion, even...' A long pause, as if she were struggling with the word. 'Dementia.'

Sally closed her eyes, aching sympathetically at the despair in her friend's voice.

'I rang him this evening,' Anne continued. 'To make sure he arrived at John o' Groats safely and he...' A strangled sound. Yes, Sally knew, she was crying now. Sally felt like crying herself, and her headache was threatening an encore.

'Oh, Anne, I'm so sorry.' It was the lamest response imaginable, but she couldn't seem to think of anything more practical to offer.

Anne got herself under control again. 'When he answered, I said hello, and… he immediately thought I was my mother. He got very angry, and insisted I come home at once and put dinner on the table.'

'But *he* wasn't even home, you just said.'

'I know.'

Sally sighed. She found herself thinking of her own mother, back home in Ashington. Whatever would she do were she to visit one day and find Matilda Wright's mind slipping away? How would she cope?

'What will you do?' she asked Anne gently. No immediate answer. Anne must be every bit as undone as Sally imagined she herself would be, her usual sensible efficacy eclipsed by panic, undone by helplessness. She must feel like a sailor long accustomed to calm seas who finds herself capsized by a rogue wave. Cast adrift in a typhoon. 'Will he see a doctor?' Sally asked, worried by Anne's continued silence.

There was a bitter laugh. 'Can you imagine a worse patient than Professor Edward Travers?' Sally heard her sigh and clear her throat. She imagined her friend wiping her eyes, gathering herself. The sailor adrift, clinging to a lash-up of wooden planks, fighting panic and taking stock of her practical options. 'I shouldn't have called you with my woes, Sally.'

'Don't be silly, Anne. We're friends, remember.'

'I know…' A further brightening of her tone. 'But you two are enjoying your first real holiday together since I've known you! Tell me, was your flight all right? Is New York wonderful?'

Sally thought of deep wounds in a dead man's flesh, and naked worry in the eyes of Ade Kramer, and she decided to lie to Anne. For now, anyway. 'New York is a dream,' she said, smiling. 'I'm just sorry you're not here to enjoy it with us. It looks like you could do with a break yourself.'

'Let me let you go. I'm just being a worrywart, as my mother used to say. Tell me all about it when you get back.'

'Don't be daft.' Sally wished she could give Anne a hug right now. She could do with one herself. 'I do hope everything's all right with your father. You mustn't assume the worst.'

'No, of course, you're right. Anyhow, I'll pursue it when he gets back, whether he likes it or not. Goodnight, Sally.'

'Goodbye, Anne. I'll bring you something wonderful for your birthday,' she promised. She heard the connection break as Anne rang off, and she returned the phone to its cradle, sitting there for a long moment, her thoughts bleak and black – holiday or no holiday.

She sighed and went back to the bathroom to dry her hair, unable to escape the shameful thought that occurred to her as she did so.

At least they needn't rely on Professor Travers' worrisome mental faculties on *this* ill-fated American holiday.

Lethbridge-Stewart stared at Travers across a table laden with plates and pints, worrying that the man was mad. That didn't explain his physical transformation, of course, but it was slightly more comforting than worrying that Lethbridge-Stewart *himself* was going mad. He certainly felt reason and logic sliding dangerously in his overtaxed mind: mental plates and pints threatening a quick, sharp crash.

He considered the number of times during the last eight months alone that his practical sensibilities had butted up against the impossible, the incomprehensible. *And you're supposed to be on holiday*, a small, needling voice reminded him. It wanted to sound like Sally's voice, but he rejected that. Unfair to her. Unfair to *them*.

The pub had filled up with patrons, most keeping to themselves or conversing quietly in twos and threes. Two elder gents produced darts for the well-pierced board near the back and began to debate where to draw the oche in the confined quarters. Lethbridge-Stewart and Kramer had ordered food from the impressively full menu – classic British pub food, the perfect complement to the décor and ambience of the place – and ate while Travers smoked and told his strange tale.

He told them about Det-Sen Monastery, and how that long nightmare had ended. Told them about chasing the Yeti up the mountainside and finding the cave. He recounted what had happened there. The voice. The wind. *The light.*

Here his recall broke down a bit. He paused, his face pale.

'Professor?' Lethbridge-Stewart said, encouragingly.

Travers' eyes cleared. 'I've had a lot of time to ponder what happened, and over the years I've come to believe that the power in the cave, some enduring part of the Great Intelligence we battled and threw down at Det-Sen, set its remaining forces a new mission. One designed to unfold at some later time. And unwilling or unable to wait for time to take its proper course, the Intelligence opened a door. A portal. And I was, inadvertently, pulled through.'

'To New York?' Lethbridge-Stewart asked. 'There were Yeti in New York City in 1965? London *wasn't* its first bridgehead in our time?'

Travers shook his head. 'Oh no. There's quite a bit more to it than that, sir.'

Lethbridge-Stewart cocked his head encouragingly. 'Please, go on.'

'When the light and the wind faded, I found myself on the ground just outside the cave. I stared up into the sky... and a... *jumbo jet* passed high overhead.' Travers spoke the phrase with a curious mix of awe and distaste, clearly awed and yet disapproving of this signifier of human progress.

'That must have been a sight,' Kramer said quietly.

'Frightened the bloody hell out of me, I can tell you! But I suppose I did the same for the two Norwegian hikers who happened upon me not long after. They dressed strangely, both immodest *and* impractical for a climb, I thought. But they spoke the Queen's English well enough, being foreigners. I quickly realised that my own attire was equally strange to them. I suppose they thought me mad.' Travers' voice meandered away, his hands curling around his pint glass. 'Good lads, though, eh? Good lads.'

'No sign of the Yeti inside the cave with you?' Lethbridge-Stewart asked.

Travers shook his head, sipping his bitter. 'None. I had been prepared for a confrontation with them, or at least the need to create some elaborate fiction regarding the mob of furry monsters I expected to see fleeing into the peaks, but they were nowhere about. Nor the unseen stranger in the cave. There weren't even any tracks! It seemed, upon some investigation, that I had come through alone.'

Travers paused. Distantly, darts thumped into the board, and the thrower grunted in satisfaction.

'How did you get home?' Kramer asked. 'Back to England, I mean?'

'My new Norse friends,' Travers went on. 'They kindly took me back to their camp. It didn't take long to realise where – when – I was, thanks to the radio and the newspapers they had brought with them. Once I was able to convince myself it was no delirium, my mind fairly reeled. I'd been flung headlong through *time itself!*'

He pounded the table for emphasis, eyes blazing. Tanya's head snapped up, sharp eyes looking about for trouble. Lethbridge-Stewart saw Kramer smile reassuringly at the barkeep, who offered no comment. Then the young lieutenant resumed staring at Travers like some new species of bug she'd never seen before.

Travers continued, fully warmed now to his subject matter. Lethbridge-Stewart supposed that made sense too; it must have been a long time since the man had been free to share his own improbable tale.

'It occurred to me that something must have gone awry, a failure of whatever magic or scientific skulduggery had been attempted in the cave,' Travers said. 'At first I surmised this misapplication, this paranormal or technological miscarriage, must have centred on the Yeti and their human colleague. Had they simply been consumed in the vortex, not just discorporated but disintegrated?'

'*You* survived,' Kramer interjected. 'Logic suggests they would too.'

Travers sighed. 'After what I'd seen at Det-Sen, I had cause to hope for their destruction. And despite my dislocation, my first thought was one of triumph. It might have cost me my own time and place, even my beloved Margaret, but if that was the cost of knowing for sure that the Intelligence's last minions had been destroyed, I would persevere.' His eyes twinkled. 'Keep a stiff upper lip, eh?'

'But they *did* come through alive,' Lethbridge-Stewart said grimly.

'Yes. I came to learn that, perhaps because my voyage

through the temporal rift came slightly later than theirs, even by mere seconds, I had simply arrived at a different point in time than the Yeti and the stranger. Perhaps there was an actual mechanism in the cave, a machine activated to open the temporal passage. Perhaps it broke down, or merely concluded its operation before I caught up with my fellow journeymen, ejecting me from the time tunnel too early. I should have investigated once I came to, but in my disorientation the notion never occurred to me.'

He fell silent. Kramer had to touch his hand to rouse him. 'Sorry! Sorry!' Travers sighed. 'As I said, that understanding would come later. At the time, though, no. There in that cosy encampment with my kindly new friends, drinking strong Norwegian *turkaffe* and reading news of a world gone decidedly mad. A murdered American president, this troubling business in Southeast Asia... And dear old spymaster Ian Fleming dead of a heart attack in Canterbury, bless him! But I remember thinking I had to be certain, one way or another. Had to get back to Det-Sen first, to ensure it wasn't under attack once more, and ascertain whether the Yeti had travelled on, preparing some dastardly new plot.'

His voice had taken on a note of dark pain, and when he looked up at Lethbridge-Stewart and Kramer again, his eyes were very old and very tired. 'I thought with a little luck, a little pluck, it might be a few days before I caught up with the blackguards. Maybe a week or two. But I've waited ever since,' he added quietly. 'Four long years.'

'I guess I should be getting back,' Owain said reluctantly.

Simon groaned, slinging a companionable arm across Owain's shoulders and shaking him. 'Forbidden. I forbid it. Just look around you, man!'

They were walking slowly along the broad thoroughfare of Times Square, burning off their delicious meal and still talking up a storm. Over Simon's protests, Owain had paid their dinner bill, using some of the crisp green US currency he'd traded pounds for at Heathrow before they left. He wanted to repay his new mate for saving his neck, and so Simon relented, thanking him with a chuckle for his *bourgeoisie* largesse. Laughing, they'd hit the street again.

They turned onto 42nd Street, and Owain stopped dead in spite of himself. There it was, laid out before them: Times Square. Simon swept his arms out grandly and announced (with a cynical humour that failed to mask his own awe and delight, Owain observed) that they stood at the hub of it all, the cultural nexus point of the planet. Blazing bright with neon and fluorescents, a dozen different beats pulsing from cars and clubs and cranked-open windows in the flats high above, alive with humanity everywhere you turned: hustlers, hookers, hippies and happy tourists alike.

Glowing signs threw cryptic terms at him, words made hieroglyphs, idolatry of the commerce gods: HAIG. Castro. Midori. International Electromatics. The Regal. And omnipresent, set highest in the neon pantheon, was the bastion of American soft-drinks, Fizzade, displayed so ubiquitously across the city that the letters lost all meaning, became totemic.

'I'm not saying I'm packing it in,' Owain told Simon, who was still giving him the occasional good-natured shake, trying to snap him out of his reticence. 'But I really should check up on Aunt Sally and Uncle Alistair.'

'You said they're enjoying an engagement holiday,' Simon countered. 'Are you sure you want to pop in and interrupt... whatever that enjoyment might entail?'

'Aw, sod off, mate!' Owain howled, laughing in shocked horror.

Simon laughed with him. He let go of Owain's shoulders, threw up his hands in mock surrender. 'All right, all right. If I can't stop you, I can't stop you. It's a free world.' He paused. 'You know what else is free tonight?' he asked slyly.

'What?'

'Music in Central Park.'

Owain felt a burst of excitement. He loved the idea of visiting Central Park at night, and what better excuse than a free concert? 'Who's playing?' he asked.

'No idea. But I saw Zeppelin there in July. *Incredible* night, man. A life-changer.'

'I've heard of them,' Owain said. 'Used to be The New Yardbirds, eh? I heard their drummer is absolutely mental. I heard he *ploughs.*'

Simon nodded. 'Those guys are going to change the world, mark my words.'

Owain mulled it over a bit longer. Capitulating, he gave Simon two thumbs up.

'All right!' Simon enthused. He clapped Owain on the shoulder. 'We're on our way, brother!' he hooted, and scrounged for his smokes, lighting up as they walked.

Owain, grinning back, went on basking in the riot of noise and colour all around them. He lifted his head, unable to get enough of the marvellous New York vista, especially the way it looked at night. All those buildings. All those brilliant squares of light and towering black angles in the sky, reaching for eternity.

All those souls within. All those dreams.

Walking beside him, putting his cigs and lighter back in his jacket pocket, Simon watched the Cornish youth closely for a moment, knowing Owain was too engrossed in the skyline to see the flash of cold calculation in his eyes.

CHAPTER SIX
Arrival of the Saara Kaithereeen

MANHATTAN PORT AUTHORITY and Coast Guard tracking stations picked up the big blip on various radar and secondary tracking systems as it was concluding its transatlantic passage just south of Long Island. The ship was travelling in the intercontinental cargo lanes, where the mightiest vessels in the world chugged back and forth from the Old World to the New, bringing over electronics, cheap textiles and Brit records, and exporting corn, cattle, Elvis Presley and junk steel from the US-of-A.

It was the ship's speed which first drew notice. Ships that size conventionally chugged along at twenty to twenty-five knots, doing no more than twenty-eight miles per hour. And they went more slowly still when the weather was winding up like it was right now. Sixteen knots... maybe eighteen.

This ship was doing thirty-five knots.

It was unheard of. A panamax-class cargo carrier, thundering along at forty miles per hour? With its standard load of twenty-foot cargo containers, or cans, it was impossible. Freakin' *impossible*.

The Coast Guard station monitor who first noticed the data called his floor administrator over. They talked quietly for a moment, agreeing enthusiastically that it was, indeed, freakin' impossible, then broke off when the ship suddenly changed course. It had been headed, presumably, to the crowded shipping ports on the Jersey shore, where swarthy men in loud suits often kept multiple sets of books, and sometimes mislaid whole cargo cans full of TVs or stereo systems.

It wasn't headed that way anymore.

The station monitor and the floor administrator rang for

their shift manager. There was more talk, less quiet now. The shift manager asked what the hell ship it was. The station monitor read off the fifteen-digit vessel tracking code, the international shipping industry's answer to Detroit's VIN codes, and the floor administrator ran to get his Big Blue Book. He found the corresponding VTC. She was the Indian container ship *Saara Kaithereen*, a nine-hundred-foot-long, ninety-thousand-tonne vessel eight days out of the Port of London. Beauty. And the shift manager knew its first mate, played poker with him now and again when he was in port. Good captain, good crew. So what the hell?

The ship initiated a starboard turn, sluggishly angling northwest, and started, blessedly, to slow. *Slow?* Readouts indicated she was reversing engines hard. It would take several minutes to reduce the massive vessel's speed to normal, but if she held the turn, she'd also end up nearly perpendicular to her previous course.

Putting the *Saara Kaithereen* on track to pass into the Upper Bay, heading north along the western Manhattan shore.

Cargo carriers didn't traverse those waters.

Seeing this, beginning to grasp the implications, the shift manager told the others to shut the hell up a minute. He picked up his red phone, and was immediately put through to Port Authority. Central security. The first-responder desk. He could scarcely believe the growing knot in his gut as he spoke rapidly to the voice on the other end of the line. This was the kind of thing airports had to worry about, right? Not ports and shipyards. Right? *Right?*

Freakin' *impossible.*

A solitary figure stood on the end of the long, concrete pier that was home to Manhattan Terminal, the dockside boarding facility on the Hudson River, where Circle Line ferries chugged and clustered during the day, honking and jockeying for position around the mammoth cruise ships like puppies demanding the attention of their brood-mothers. The big cruisers docked there no more than a couple of times a week, whisking patrons away on idyllic cruises along the eastern American seaboard, or taking them on decadent jaunts far out into the Atlantic itself. The ferries picked up and dropped off New York City tourists multiple times each day, conducting them on endless circuits around the city's majestic seaside, around Ellis Island where immigrants once crowded, coughing and jostling and dreaming of freedom, and Bedloe's Island, where those newcomers' icon stood proudly with book and torch, years of copper patination turning her crown and robes and face as green as the harbour swells sometimes turned the faces of the ferry riders.

There were no cruise ships docked tonight, and only a dozen or so ferries, all dark, the last having off-loaded their passengers only minutes before, sending them milling and babbling into the glass-enclosed terminal building that overlooked the docks, where many still lingered, not yet ready, perhaps, to break the ferry's sunset spell. They purchased last rounds of soft drinks and shaved ice, and browsed the souvenir shops while the gum-chewing counter-girls faked their smiles and gritted their teeth, clearly willing them to clear out so everyone could go home.

On the docks below the bright building, half a dozen workers were also finishing up: mopping decks, securing tie-downs, logging the day's fuel consumption. Business was done for the day; they would do it all over again tomorrow.

None of them, dockworkers or counter-girls, noticed the arrival of the small man in the tailored suit.

He stood for a time in the shadows directly below the terminal building, hands clasped behind him, a large satchel hanging over one shoulder, heavy but not uncomfortable. He looked out over the dark water and watched the last ferries empty. He watched the riders disembark, laughing and talking too loudly, their hearing dulled by the loud boat engines and the wash of the surf. He wanted to hate them – couples, families, happy vapid tourists without a trouble in the world – but the strongest feeling he could rouse in himself was a tepid mix of melancholy and contempt. He was very tired. His own life had been long, strange and mostly not of his own choosing, but he found he could not hate these loud, bright, silly Americans. They deserved what was coming no more than he himself deserved all he'd suffered.

But his master's will was far stronger than his own. He would obey.

Always, he obeyed.

Dockworkers shouted to one another, passing a joke between them that seemed to involve the maternal parentage of one or another of them. The little man's English was very good – he dimly remembered a teacher in his village, a Catholic priest who had come to evangelise but stayed to educate – but the idioms and inflections of these New Yorkers often still escaped him.

He tuned out the chatter but glanced about more often, realising he was nervous. He was a man of poise and equanimity, but he was used to moving less visibly through the city, mostly via the tubes and warrens of the subway system, his mighty 'Snow Bear', his Kabadom, always close by. He sometimes thought of Kabadom as his protector. Guardian. Friend, even. But the truth was never far from his mind: the Yeti was his jailer. He had accepted that long ago. So very, very long ago.

For some time, here in this city, he'd been able to set aside the truth. It had just been the two of them, after all. Four years now? Five? The work had been steady; the Master had kept him well occupied. And through Kabadom, his master had provided. He did not starve, nor truly wanted for much of anything. They lived almost invisibly in the great city, their passing all but unseen.

Until the detective...

The damnable detective, perhaps set on him by the red-faced old professor, perhaps by the clueless soldier woman. Kabadom had taken care of the detective, and he might have had to do the same with the other two as well.

But that was when *he* had arrived. Brigadier Lethbridge-Stewart, who had been present in London when the Master's trap had failed.

Too late, he thought, and the feeling that coursed through him was more exhausted relief than genuine triumph. *Too late to stop us now. All is in motion, and he will not stop us. Will not stop me.*

The Master would direct him against the English soldier in time, perhaps, and he in turn would send Kabadom, and all would be well. Their work would soon be completed, and perhaps things might even go back to the way they'd been. In time. Just him and his mighty protector. Safe at last. Perhaps he might even be permitted to take up toy-making again. Set aside the Master's work and become a carver of wood, a crafter of delight.

In the distance, on the dark water, a horn blared.

Below him, on the docks, the last few workers looked about curiously.

The little man shifted the bag on his shoulder. It had been waiting for him beneath a subway grate near the street entrance of the terminal building, left there by Kabadom at the Master's bidding. He had retrieved it wordlessly, attracting the attention of no one, and brought it here to wait.

The waiting was almost done.

He left the shadows and climbed the steps to enter the building overlooking the docks. It would not be prudent to stand here when the source of the horn arrived.

Travers brooded over his tale while Kramer called for another round of bitter and ordered cold roast beef sandwiches with chips. And as they fell to, Travers went on with his mad tale.

Thanking his new Norwegian friends, he said, he had journeyed to Det-Sen Monastery, where he found its generous people and welcoming halls virtually unchanged in the decades since his last visit. Brother Thonmi had become abbot, but he was away, ministering to children sickened by diphtheria in a nearby village. With some relief Travers found he recognised none of the others; better still, none recognised him. All was well. Nothing had shown up to threaten Det-Sen, it seemed.

Travers told them nothing of his 'corporeal translocation', as he termed it. He knew the brothers would delay him no more than the kindly hikers had done, but now that he knew the Yeti had not come here, he was eager to be off. Thanking his hosts, he took his leave and began the daunting task of returning home to England.

'A bloody tricky job it was,' he told his companions in *The Early Doors*. 'With only a fistful of Tibetan currency and a passport thirty years out of date!'

With some reluctance, he skipped over the months of strange adventures, chance encounters and fascinating new friends that highlighted his arduous journey, and instead picked up the thread of his tale in London, at his homecoming.

Professor Edward Travers stepped out of the terrace house that once belonged to his father, watched from the shadowy hedges of St James's Gardens by Professor Edward Travers.

The sun had nearly set; the weary traveller knew he was well concealed. He watched, mind reeling, as this stooped, grey version of himself tottered forward on his cane, first to investigate the flower beds, then the motorcar parked before the house. It was a ghastly, lime-coloured Citroën Estate. The younger Travers supposed the look on his elder self's face must have very nearly matched his own when he'd first arrived and seen that monstrosity.

He'd done a bit of research before coming, first visiting the county records office, then the local pub. He'd told himself it was purely meant to minimise the shock. He knew the passage of thirty years could have brought on unforeseen tragedy. War. Hardship. They'd seen their share of these, he and his Margaret. Perhaps she grieved, believing me dead, *he'd thought.* Perhaps, heaven forfend, she remarried.

With such dark notions in mind, he decided it was best to learn a bit more before he sprang this shock on his dear wife. And so he'd learned the truth – mostly in the pub, where two old duffers had been happy enough to share what they knew with 'cousin Arthur', in from the north country to visit his kin. Oh, the wonderful, terrible truths he'd learned. He had found himself the proud father of two healthy children, now grown.

And to find himself a widower. Oh, Margaret...

In front of him, the elder Travers abruptly turned back to the house. 'Anne!' he called impatiently. 'For heaven's sake, let's be off!'

She came out, slender and finely boned, lovely as her mother.

Hidden in the shrubbery, Travers' heart ached as if he were the thirty-years-on version. 'Ah, my dear,' he murmured. 'She looks so much like you.'

'You needn't shout like a ruffian, Father,' Anne chided the old man playfully, taking his arm. 'I'm not fourteen anymore, you know.'

A voice like cracked brittle: 'Would that it were so, my dear.'

Young Travers watched as Anne helped her father into the Citroën and slipped behind the wheel. He saw her lean toward her passenger, listening, then throw back her head, laughing brightly. Travers' heart skipped; so beautiful. And somewhere in the world she had an older brother. Alun. A good lad, the duffers in the local had said, and by all accounts quite successful.

Travers did not move until the car pulled out of the drive and sputtered away. Then he straightened, his cheeks burning, his chest constricted. A light rain had begun to fall. Travers gave the house a lingering look of guilt and grief, and turned away.

Kramer realised the food was gone. Tanya had collected their empty plates. Travers was gazing at his folded hands, cheeks flushed. Kramer met Lethbridge-Stewart's eyes. Quiet sympathy there, but no disbelief. She decided to let go of her lingering scepticism and meet Travers' incredible story the same way. Magic portals and all.

'I watched Anne for the next few days,' Travers said. 'Carefully. From a distance. I learned Alun teaches at Oxford. Oxford!' A brief swell of pride. Then he drew out a handkerchief and blew harshly. Kramer knew he was drawing up these memories from a deep well of pain. She was amazed that he'd hidden it so well all this time.

'They were small when they lost their mother, but they recovered. Both had Margaret's deep steel, Anne more so than Alun. For my part...' Travers sighed. 'I am not a man of deep steel. I fled England. History had been written. I could only try not to disrupt the future. So I got on with my pursuit of the displaced Yeti.'

Kramer looked doubtful. 'Hadn't it all gone pear-shaped already, Professor, thanks to whatever force dragged you out of the past?'

Travers gave her a keen look. 'Oh, my dear Adrienne. Don't you see?'

She glanced at Lethbridge-Stewart. *Do you?* He shook his head. It was beyond him, too.

'Had the timeline been irrevocably broken,' Travers said, 'I wouldn't have found my older self at home in London in 1965. Whatever bloody trials I've endured in the past five

71

years, it's clear they *will* come to an end. I *will* return to my own time. Margaret and I will be reunited, even if only for a few precious years. Alun will be born, and Anne. Do you understand now?'

Kramer chuckled, pinched together thumb and forefinger in a *this-much* gesture.

Travers nodded. 'The important thing was sussing out the Great Intelligence's plan. There was already one Travers in London to help face any new threat there. Bit shaky, yes, but still some fight left in the old dog. And he was *me*. Logic dictates he'd be cognisant of any threat. Knowledge of history previously acquired.'

'He'd know... because *you* know,' Lethbridge-Stewart said, eyes drifting.

'Sounds a little like cheating,' Kramer said with a chuckle.

'Needs must,' Travers said. 'Our enemy plays dirty, you'll recall.'

Kramer thought of the coma patients and nodded. *Plenty dirty*, she thought.

'Perhaps you played a little dirty yourself?' Lethbridge-Stewart asked Travers gently. 'In the Underground, hemmed in on every side by the Yeti and the Web... I don't recall you mentioning any foreknowledge of this time-travel scheme.'

Travers tipped him a wink. 'Likely my future self knows what I know. The future may be as delicate as tissue paper, its integrity best assured by the fewest possible handlers.' He pointed to Lethbridge-Stewart. 'It wouldn't have been a lack of trust, sir. It's only that we hadn't yet had the pleasure. As it turned out, when the London incident occurred, you were clearly the right chap in the right place at the right time.'

Lethbridge-Stewart dismissed the flattery. 'There was... other assistance,' he said, thinking about Knight and the rest, desperately fighting for their lives in the byzantine depths of the London Underground. 'I had an excellent team. Aided by our mutual acquaintance, that odd little fellow in the checked trousers.'

Travers hooted. 'Wonderful! What a delight to know that we'll be reunited! Oh, I wish it would happen again now, my grasp of temporal chronology be damned!'

Kramer leaned back in her chair, folding her arms. 'Sounds

like trouble tends to follow him around. I'm happy to forego the pleasure, thanks very much.'

Lethbridge-Stewart raised a brow, smiling.

'If you met the Doctor, you'd feel differently,' Travers said.

Kramer snorted. 'Perhaps I'll have the pleasure someday. But right now, Professor, and with all due respect, one time-travelling egghead is quite enough for this career army girl.'

Inside the Manhattan Terminal, the small Tibetan man walked past the souvenir shops, ignoring the family of portly, sunburned tourists spinning racks of t-shirts and postcards. He hefted the bag on his shoulder, chose a position about two-thirds of the way back from the big glass windows overlooking the docks and turned to regard the facility. There was a security guard, a fellow in his late fifties or early sixties. Probably a retired policeman, supplementing his pension, not expecting any excitement. The security guard glanced at the little man with the bag, sized him up, dismissed him.

And why not. I am five feet one inch tall. I am bent and wizened with age. I am no one's idea of a threat. His eyes went cold. He did not like to be underestimated. Dismissed.

He hefted the bag again, heard the heavy, metallic clink inside. The new spheres. He thought about what he had done to obtain them, and his eyes grew colder still.

Another heavy horn blast from outside, and what might have been excited shouts from the dockworkers. Now one of the counter-girls drifted away from her post, moving towards the big window, looking at something half-seen out there, beyond the reflective lights of the terminal's snack shop and souvenir stands.

'Miss,' one of the portly tourists harrumphed. 'Can I get some help over here?'

The little man watched the shadows shift and shiver in the glass. The counter-girl was turning to her colleague, eyes wide, mouth opening to speak. Or to scream.

Oh no, he thought. *Soon they will never underestimate me again.*

Travers got back on track with his account, emphasising the

facts that had launched his investigation. He recounted what he'd heard in the cave, the whispering voice saying *'must come'*, mentioning both London and New York.

'Do you see?' he asked them. 'Must *come*. It was commanding the stranger from his destination point. From the future.'

Kramer sighed. 'There isn't enough aspirin in the world, Professor. *Or* bourbon.'

Travers snorted. 'I knew the stranger from the cave was bound for New York. So that became my destination as well.'

'You never saw his face, never heard a name,' Kramer said wonderingly. 'How did you imagine you'd ever find this person?'

'My dear lady, I am well-versed in the intricacies of international customs.' Travers cleared his throat. 'I assumed I could bribe someone in the New York harbour authority to identify recently arrived ships carrying Tibetan cargo or passengers.' He paused. 'Alas, it was not that simple. I quickly ran out of "persuasion funds". Moreover, I learned the dangers of sharing the truth of my situation with various upstanding citizens whose first impulse would be to point me towards an American sanatorium. So I bided my time... and I found a job.'

Travers removed a pair of cards from his breast pocket, handed one to each of them. They read: 'EBON BOOKS. Ernest Ebon, Proprietor. Shop: 42nd and 10th. For Appointments: 212-555-1989.'

'Earns a pittance, and the fellow who runs the place is a rogue,' Travers scoffed. 'Meanwhile, I sought new avenues for my secondary occupation: finding the fellow from Tibet.' He fixed Kramer with a sympathetic gaze. 'Which led me to our late, mutual friend Detective Dawson, Lieutenant. I told him just enough to make him curious, and left out just enough to make him determined. He must finally have made the connection, found evidence of booked passage. And either confronted the scoundrel below-levels or chased him into a trap. I am deeply, deeply sorry.'

Kramer glared. 'All the times you avoided telling what you knew of the rats.'

'I was biding my time, waiting to be sure all these things

were connected,' Travers finished for her. 'But from what you'd shared about the coma patients, and given poor Mr Dawson's fate…' He struck the table again. 'But there were no Yeti here, I'd have staked my life on it!'

Lethbridge-Stewart spoke grimly, thinking of the wounds on Dawson's corpse. 'It would seem there was at least one.'

Kramer got up to pay their cheque, and to thank Tanya for her patience. Travers leaned toward Lethbridge-Stewart. 'I think I should see these coma patients at once.'

Kramer returned. 'We can arrange that. So, these Yeti?'

'It follows that their journey was much like my own. A leap through time, not space,' Travers said thoughtfully.

'But they *did* get to London somehow,' Lethbridge-Stewart said. He started to add that Travers, the *original* Travers, had secured passage for a sole, deactivated Yeti when he'd come back from Tibet. It was the one he'd sold to Emil Silverstein, and its eventual revival had led to the London Event itself. But that was too much to pile onto *this* Travers, Lethbridge-Stewart decided. It wasn't his fault, after all.

Travers pondered this. 'Maybe so. But Tibet to London is hard enough to fathom. Getting all the way to America without being noticed? How is *that* possible?'

None of them had an answer for that.

Port security and the Coast Guard scrambled six chase boats within four minutes of the big cargo ship's course change, but it was far too late. Just a few minutes after eight o'clock, the *Saara Kaithereen*, still doing almost thirty knots, punched through the Manhattan Terminal docks on a north-easterly approach. Most of its cargo – along with all but a skeleton crew, who cowered and quailed and did as their wordless 'guests' directed – had been dumped unceremoniously into the sea, so it was travelling far lighter than usual, but it still weighed almost seventy-eight thousand tonnes. The docks and four of the pony-sized ferries exploded beneath the charging-bull vessel, showering wood, metal and glass fifty feet in all directions. The biggest docks, directly beneath the glass-walled terminal overlooking the harbour, were concrete, intended to provide sturdier anchorage for the big cruise ships, and although these also cracked and shattered at the force of the impact, they also punched mortal wounds in the rusty old hide of the mammoth ship, impaling it so forcefully its seafaring days were instantly concluded.

The grinding, jagged stone piers slowed the cargo ship's runaway-freight speed drastically, preventing it from completely pulverising the terminal.

Even so, it struck the building at deck height, and the front half of the building was torn completely away in an instant. The unfortunate counter-girl who'd seen the ship coming never even got to complete her scream or warning or whatever words she'd been about to utter to the others. She simply vanished in a roaring hail of board fragments, mangled metal framework, broken bits of ceiling and flooring and glittering glass smashed nearly to dust, sparkling on the sudden breeze.

She was the only immediate casualty inside the building, though it would later be determined that three dock workers had been crushed on the piers below, unable to scramble clear of the titanic ship. Everyone else in the building was knocked off their feet, cut by flying glass and left sprawling on the buckled, black-tiled floor. Except the small Tibetan man, who had taken hold of a nearby column for support.

He shielded his face with his free arm, but came through the maelstrom utterly untouched. He smiled at this blessing from the Master.

Screams. Rending wood and metal. The ship, mortally wounded but not quite dead yet, ground another foot or two forward into the building, its heavy nose and front right flank filling the space where there'd been a serene seaside tableau just a moment earlier. Everything shook. The power went out, and the lights failed, plunging the room into a gloomy half-light. The screams grew louder. The *Saara Kaithereen* – the last half of the name now actually visible, the peeling red paint black as wet blood against the dusty, dented grey-white body of the ship – gave a final, lingering metallic groan, and then subsided, sliding downwards a foot or two as she gave up the fight, shredding more of the front half of the facility as she died.

Emergency klaxons pulsed in the night, and sirens from

oncoming police launches and Coast Guard skiffs grew louder.

Reddish security lights clicked on, only slightly improving visibility in the smashed facility, but it got them moving. The remaining counter-girl thrashed, found her feet and stood gaping at the ship. The portly tourist family were helping each other up, soothing crying children and attending to minor injuries, all of them too shocked yet to flee. The security guard went to the clerk, checking her for shock and serious wounds, but she appeared to have been protected by the big sales desk.

Ignoring them all, the little man walked forward, clutching his bag tightly and looked at the night sky above the ship wedged into the building. Twinkling stars were visible – despite the city lights – through the space where the ceiling had been, before the impact had simply ripped away twenty-five feet of it, hurling it off into the night.

He spoke, loudly and clearly, using his native tongue.

The others stopped nattering and sobbing and clucking at one another, and turned to look in his direction.

The man spoke again, louder still.

There was an answering roar from aboard the ship.

'What the unholy *frick*,' the security guard mumbled. The counter-girl grabbed instinctively for his hand, and he winced at how tightly she squeezed it.

Shapes appeared over the bent, twisted railing jutting out over the debris-covered floor of the building. Large shapes. Huge yellow eyes glowed fiercely in the gloom.

'Welcome,' said the little man. He removed the bag from his shoulder, held it up.

Six shapes now. Eight. Ten. And still they came. *So many*, he thought with satisfaction. Despite all the setbacks in England, his hard work and dedication had seen many of them through.

They leaped over the side of the ship and surrounded the little man, drawing shocked screams from the watching humans. He opened his bag, revealing the silver spheres inside: the new control units he had fashioned during the waiting time, here in New York. He had followed the Master's whispered orders the way he'd once followed the tutelage of the High Lama, Padmasambhava. Pouring hot metal. Patiently plying his craft. Delivering power sources similar to these.

Similar, he thought, *but not the same. No... not quite.* He remembered how he'd delighted in the lama's satisfaction, knowing even then, as the years stretched out beyond a natural human span, that there was more to his master than a simple man of the spirit. He'd known, even before the Master revealed himself, that Padmasambhava hid a second self. A secret self.

The memory was bitter indeed.

'Get out of there, mister,' he heard the security guard rasp weakly. 'Them things'll carve you like Christmas turkey.'

He ignored the fool. The Yeti began opening their chests, removing their old control spheres. They were lustreless, making almost no pinging sounds at all, their energy nearly gone. He passed out the new ones. These began to pulse with a deep, thrumming note unique to the new spheres. He knew what made them unique, but offered no word of explanation to the Yeti. They needed none.

As each new control sphere was socked snugly into place, transformation was instantaneous. The Yeti grew taller, their fur fuller, their claws longer and sleeker.

Outside, more sirens and horns, both from the lawmen arriving by boat and others beginning to draw near from the street out front.

'Mister!' the security guard shouted querulously at him. 'You've got to come away from there! The police is comin'! Don't be foolish!'

All the spheres passed out now, fifteen new and improved Yeti stood around him, growling. Humming. Awaiting his command. The little man turned and regarded the security guard and the other denizens of the building.

'Go now,' he said. 'You will not get a second chance.'

The tourists and the remaining counter-girl fled at once, banging through the hydraulic exit doors. Out there, red and blue lights flashed.

The security guard, sweating and shaking, was trying to draw his gun.

The Tibetan man looked at the Yeti clustered around him.

'I am Jemba-Wa,' he said. 'I am the most-humble servant of our Master Mahasamatman. He who seeks to brings all minds to the ultimate sphere of reality.'

'Mister!' the guard called again.

'It is time to begin,' Jemba-Wa said. He pointed at the security guard. 'Start with him, if he will not yield. There are more outside. None must interfere.'

Fifteen Yeti moved instantly.

The guard never got the gun clear of his holster. Never had time to scream.

Emotionlessly, Jemba-Wa, oldest servant of the Great Intelligence, followed his new army into the night.

CHAPTER SEVEN
Attack on the Subway

BY THE TIME they reached the hospital, Travers was dancing at the prospect of studying the coma patients. Distantly, they could hear the blast of sirens. Police and emergency vehicles both, and quite a lot, by the sound. Something big was happening somewhere.

Kramer and the professor hurried inside, leaving Lethbridge-Stewart standing for a moment at the top of the steps, listening to the chorus of klaxons and taking in the chilly night air. He could have done without the former – it only added to his unease – but the snap of cold was so very reminiscent of a brisk London night that he welcomed the feel of it on his face and neck.

He paused there long enough to draw the attention of the street people still lurking in the lee of the stone staircase, and politely as he could, he had to wave several of them away, apologising, telling them he was carrying no American funds.

Ah, New York, he thought morosely, and went inside to catch up with the others.

There were still a few nurses and orderlies about, but overall the hospital had transitioned to night service, and the front lobby was mostly empty. Perhaps the emergency services area on the far right side of the massive structure was still bustling, but here the cold tile, dimmed lights and rows of empty seats in the waiting area made the place feel more like a morgue than a busy metropolitan hospital.

'It's the new hospital over on 5th Avenue,' someone said, the voice echoing, nearly sexless, in the vast shadowy lobby. Lethbridge-Stewart looked around in surprise. There was a lone nurse, faded and colourless in her white smock and cap, seated at the main desk. She was so short he could barely make her out until he drew closer. Her nametag read *Joyner*.

'Beg your pardon?' he asked.

Nurse Joyner looked up at him, blinking owlishly behind enormous glasses, the lines around her eyes and mouth deepening as she responded. Her voice suggested multiple daily packs of cigarettes and likely a fair share of shouting. 'Midtown Med Centre,' she told him. 'It's the reason this place packs it in most nights, except your usual handful of drunks and gang-fight victims in the emergency centre. Midtown's got twice the budget and twice the staff, so naturally they pull the lion's share of the business.' She shrugged. 'We're mostly a research and training hospital these days. It's all right. Less blood on the floor, and you don't have to fight for the last cruller at the cafeteria in the mornings.' She looked about sharply, as if afraid she'd be overheard. 'Unless Spevins is on duty. You always gotta watch that Spevins.'

Lethbridge-Stewart nodded, mystified.

'You're with the lieutenant and her friend the British agent?' the nurse asked him.

British agent, Lethbridge-Stewart thought, bemused. 'I am.'

'I like that one,' Joyner said, grinning. Her teeth looked like Scrabble tiles, broad and stained a light brownish colour. 'He's got class. You know where you're headed?'

'I do,' Lethbridge-Stewart answered amiably, glancing at her desk. 'Would you mind if I used your telephone?'

Nurse Joyner studied him suspiciously a moment. Finally, she nodded and pushed the heavy desk phone toward him, rotating it to face him. 'Dial nine to get an outside line.' She rose, checking her watch. 'Time for my break. See if that Spevins is fooling round in the break room. *Again*.'

Lethbridge-Stewart nodded, hoping his expression suggested commiseration and well-wishes, and dialled the Algonquin Hotel as the woman's muted footfalls thumped away toward the stairs. By now, Travers would be leaning over one or another of the coma patients, he knew, likely babbling away in his excitement, hopefully ascertaining some clear link between the Great Intelligence, its hirsute minions and those oddly unresponsive, clearly ill souls in the quarantine chamber.

'Algonquin front desk,' said a clipped, business-like voice.

He asked the clerk to dial Sally's room. It rang four times before the clerk came back on the line to regretfully inform him there seemed to be no one available to answer. He tried Owain's room next. Again, no answer. Lethbridge-Stewart thanked the clerk, unable to quickly formulate a reasonable message for either party in his mind, and left none. He hung up, frowning.

The gnawing sense of dread and foreboding was back. It had hung itself around his shoulders ever since they'd seen the remains of the detective deep in the subway tunnel, and had only grown more insistent since the unexpected encounter with Travers. Nothing about the man himself struck Lethbridge-Stewart as particularly off; certainly he was disturbingly young and still dangerously naïve, not yet the cynical old gaffer now living in Edinburgh. But if the younger Travers was himself some sort of unwitting pawn of their enemy, it was a damned good ruse. His amiability, his enthusiasm over the case in hand...

No. Lethbridge-Stewart believed they had no reason to distrust Professor Edward Travers for the time being. And surely they would need his help, if there truly were Yeti loose in New York.

Lethbridge-Stewart drummed his fingers on the desk, looking at the telephone. *Where are you, Sally? And where's Owain?*

He didn't want to dwell on it, but if the Great Intelligence *was* at work here, his nephew might be in very great danger indeed.

Owain was struck by the similarities between New York's complex grid of subway tubes and stations and those he'd experienced in London. At the same time, he was appalled at the condition of this far more intricate underground transport system. He was a young man who enjoyed exploring the world and maintained no false expectations about its ugly underside, but bloody hell!

They'd been among the first to step onto the front car in the six-car line, just behind the driver's compartment. Owain found he could actually see the driver – his shoulder, at least

– through the small square of unbreakable glass in the door between them, and wondered how he could endure the stench all day long. Or perhaps one got used to it, even stopped smelling it at all after a certain amount of time? Owain fought back a mild queasiness, his pleasure over the grand meal they'd just enjoyed fading a bit.

Standing next to him, obviously unfazed at being jostled by the other embarking passengers, Simon chuckled. 'It does take some getting used to.'

Owain shook his head self-consciously as the train's doors slid shut. A bell gonged, and they abruptly slid into motion, the steady grinding racket beneath them forcing him to raise his voice a bit to be heard.

'It's great. I just—'

'Just didn't expect it to smell so much like a toilet?' Simon finished for him.

Owain shrugged amiably. Holding onto one of the overhead straps, he swayed with the motion of the train car, glancing around at their fellow commuters. It *was* still pretty great, the freedom this mass-transit system afforded the people who lived and worked in the city. He loved the notion of being freed from the need for a car of his own, being able to travel from meditation centre to music venue to university lecture hall and back again. It was cheap, it was efficient... It just needed a clean-up. Desperately. It occurred to him briefly that launching such an effort could be the sort of calling he'd been looking for ever since leaving Bledoe, and wondered what it would take to organise the Buddhist community here to pursue the idea. Perhaps enlisting the politically active but seemingly tetherless hippie kids he'd observed everywhere downtown? So many of them were clearly so angry over the Vietnam conflict and so discontented with the establishment. Perhaps they merely needed the same sort of motivational pursuit Owain himself dreamed of finding in the world? Certainly, turning all that energy and power towards a positive goal could do wonders to change things for them, for their city, for—

'Hey,' Simon murmured. 'Where'd you go, man?'

Owain blinked at him, smiled. 'Sorry. Caught me thinking.'

'Nothing wrong with that. Thinking's still free. Even in

this city.'

A fuzzy, almost mechanical voice burbled overhead, announcing they were nearing the next station. This was followed by a crackle of static and an even tinnier voice, coming from a small speaker of some kind perhaps halfway down the train car. Owain glanced in that direction and saw a pair of New York subway cops in their light blue, button-down shirts, heavy-collared dark coats and peaked hats, so markedly different from the custodian helmets more common to police back home. One of them had unclipped the portable radio from his shoulder and was speaking quietly into it. Owain noted the way the jammed riders parted wordlessly as the cops slowly made their way through the car; some things, at least, seemed universal.

Simon saw the cops too and groaned. 'World's greatest music scene or not, we're just a heartbeat away from living in a police state, brother,' he said grimly. 'Yet another reason to go see what's jumping in the park. Righteous set of people usually hanging out there. Our kind of cats, you'll see. I'll introduce you.'

Owain nodded, smiling, and was about to reply when the entire train car abruptly lurched. There was a scream of hydraulic brakes. Everyone in the car was thrown forward, most avoiding a bad fall purely due to the sardine-style packing of bodies into the enclosed space, others catching their neighbours by accident or design, clutching one another to avoid going down together. There were only a few shouts of protest or surprise, even as the train continued to grind to a stop.

In a flash, they were standing still in the tunnel, the train vibrating beneath them like a tense, frightened thing.

'What the hell?' Simon muttered.

Owain looked over at him wordlessly, then glanced outside. Nothing but darkness outside the train car on either side. They definitely hadn't reached the next station yet.

'Okay, everybody stay calm,' one of the cops shouted; unnecessarily, Owain thought, as no one was raising a fuss so far. 'This is just a temporary delay. Remain calm and we'll be underway again in a minute, I'm sure.'

His partner lifted his radio again to call in the problem,

when a muffled shout abruptly rose from the front of the car – *the driver*, Owain supposed – followed by a scream of surprise from the middle-aged woman standing nearest the driver's compartment door. She was trying to back away from it, pressing herself into the people directly behind her.

Owain and Simon had time to exchange a puzzled look.

Distantly, something roared; a guttural scream that most of the passengers likely mistook for the sound of another train. But Owain's blood suddenly froze in his veins, all the colour draining out of his face. He knew that sound.

'Not bloody possible,' he gasped.

Simon blinked at him. 'What—?'

Another muffled shout from the driver. They turned. The man had abandoned his seat and was now scrabbling at the door between them, bony face wild with terror, nicotine-stained fingers hooked into claws. His eyes locked with Owain's.

At that moment, something big smashed into the front of the subway train.

Everyone aboard was once more thrown about, staggering first to the left, then right. Numerous screams and shouts now, as even the most stolid New Yorkers' equanimity was rattled by this unexpected shock.

This was no train collision, Owain knew. That sound was no train.

Another crash of impact, and the train car shook wildly once more. Behind them, people were trying to evacuate into the second car, creating a stampede in their panic. The cops were shouting for calm, trying to organise and herd the passengers out of the quaking car, but there were still more screams signifying genuine pain, as the crowd became a crush.

Owain hauled up Simon, who had gone to his knees from the latest impact, and they joined the others in slowly shuffling backwards, following the herd. There was a harsh, metallic stench in the air now, part fried brakes, but that wasn't all of it.

Owain looked back at the front of the car, expecting to see the terrified driver's face still at the window, the bright light in the cab behind him turning him into a silhouette.

Instead, there was only darkness.

Owain stepped forward. The middle-aged *hausfrau*, the one who had screamed first, scuttled past him without a glance, sobbing in her terror.

'Owain!' It was Simon. 'Man, what are you doing?'

Crackles and sparks of electricity lit the black window a brilliant blue, making Owain pause a moment. When they had passed, he stepped forward again, leaning down and putting his face close to the streaked but unbroken glass. He felt a hand on his shoulder: Simon.

'What is it? What do you see?'

Owain shook his head, trying to penetrate the darkness out there, mostly staring at the reflection of his own, wide eyes. *You imagined it,* he told himself. *That roar. It was another train. It was some sort of siren, or—*

Something stepped out of the darkness, and Owain knew what he was seeing.

The entire driver's compartment, including the driver himself, had been torn away from the front of the train. Of the cab, and the hapless fellow who had inhabited it only a moment earlier, there was no sign. Only scattered metal wreckage.

This one's so strong, Owain mused.

What stepped into view, shuffling toward them through the shadowy subway tunnel, was a massive figure, easily eight feet tall, covered from head to toe in whitish fur, with great grey tufts around its fiercely glowing amber eyes. Its advance was lit intermittently, nightmarishly, by sparks and flares from the smashed electronics in the remnants of the driver's cab. Its unblinking eyes were fixed on the face of the young man staring back at it through the window of the train.

'What is *that*?' Simon barked, almost in Owain's ear.

Owain had no time to reply. As if it had recognised him, the Yeti let out an ear-splitting roar of fury, crouched and charged at the smashed train once more.

Sally switched off the fancy hair dryer she'd found in a bathroom drawer, tossing her lustrous hair back from her face, and only then realised the phone was ringing once more, its conservative warble perfectly masked by the noise of the blow dryer.

With a sigh, she set the bulky contraption on the sink and hurried into the main room. The phone stopped ringing the minute she put her hand on the receiver. She groaned and went back to the bathroom to finish drying off. *Let the front desk take a message*, she decided. She could call back once she had climbed into some fresh clothes.

Cool air sent the curtains billowing into the room; it felt great on her skin as she finished drying off and hunted up the moisturiser she had been sure to include in her travel kit. She listened to the traffic far below, the night music of the big city, not so very different from London when you got right down to it, though the occasional police sirens or ambulance klaxons had their own unique wails and warbles. Her headache was finally releasing its hold on her, and she smiled, hoping Alistair would soon put the afternoon's unexpected crisis behind him and join her.

She knew the cause of the continuing friction between them, and supposed she'd made it worse pressing for Dolerite Base and a seat at the table. She knew Alistair respected her career-mindedness, but she struggled to make him understand a deeper truth. Her goal wasn't just to be his wife, but to take part in work she believed in. Alongside others whom she believed in. That part wasn't about Alistair her fiancé, but Alistair the soldier. The patriot. She'd never met a man like him, and fervently believed that he would do great work. That he was destined to make history.

She wanted to do the same.

And, of course, there's no denying that his touch makes you tingle all the way down to the arches of your feet, she thought.

Grinning a little, Sally dressed quickly, choosing her favourite square-necked tan pullover and the new plaid skirt Anne had helped her pick out the week before they'd left. The skirt was scandalously short, she knew, rising almost to mid-thigh, but Twiggy had worn it in a recent *Look* fashion spread. And besides, Sally liked her legs. She knew Alistair liked them too.

She stepped into a pair of comfortable but sensible saddle shoes – perfect for a bit of wandering in this breathtaking city – and hunted for the room key, meaning to head downstairs to see if there was indeed a message for her. Perhaps it had been Alistair, letting her know he was on his way back. Or Owain, calling in to tell the old fogies not to wait up. She hoped Alistair's nephew was having a fine old time too; he deserved an adventure in New York every bit as much as she did.

The wind gusted behind her, causing the curtains to billow in once more. She paused at the door to the room, looking back, wondering if she should close the sliding glass door to the—

Something shifted out there, black on black. She squinted, frowning.

Her eyes widened.

Something was out there all right. Massive. Humped and towering. Silhouetted against the glow of the city below. It stepped forward, pushing through the curtains, ducking its enormous head to enter the room, its glowing lambent eyes fixed on the woman at the door.

Heart in her mouth, she scrabbled at the door handle, turned it and yanked it open.

There was a man in the doorway, clad in an expensive suit. He was no more than five feet tall, his deeply tanned face framed by long, snow-white hair, hands clasped behind his back. His almond eyes scrutinised Sally in a kindly way, and he favoured her with a curt bow and a smile. But that smile's warmth seemed utterly false to her.

On the night table, the phone rang again. She barely heard it.

'Good evening, Miss Wright,' said the little man, his accent thick but his words completely clear to her. 'It is very pleasurable to meet you.'

For the second time Lethbridge-Stewart told the desk clerk there was no message, and he hung up the phone on the nurse's station, frowning. Spotting Lieutenant Kramer coming down the hall with a uniformed officer and one of the hospital orderlies, he hailed her. She walked over. 'What's up?'

'Could you have someone check up on my fiancée at the hotel?'

Kramer frowned. 'What's wrong with Sally?'

Lethbridge-Stewart shook his head. 'Oh, probably nothing

88

whatsoever. I sent her back to deal with an oncoming headache. But she's not answering. It's not like her, that's all.'

Kramer put an understanding hand on his arm and turned, heading back to the uniformed cop. She conferred briefly with him. Lethbridge-Stewart started pacing, listening to the background buzz of the busy hospital as its day wound to an end. It was shift-change, apparently, a new set of nurses and orderlies arriving to take over from those exhausted souls ready to call it a day. Call-lights flickered above the doors to various sick rooms, and intercoms occasionally crackled with instructions or inquiries. Someone looking for a doctor. Someone else directing a nurse to a patient in need. All so normal. All so ordinary.

And yet nothing here seemed right to him. Not the muttering coma patients, not Kramer's lamentably dead detective, and most certainly not Edward Travers, bizarrely appearing out of the blue with his maddening tale of time tunnels. Enemies were gathering and dark forces were at work all around them.

Lethbridge-Stewart patted his hip and cursed. He wasn't even armed. He didn't like it. Didn't like it a bit.

That sense of confusion and dread – the pervasive feeling of being manoeuvred, *cornered* – only served to worsen his concern for Sally. He saw Kramer conclude her discussion with the policeman, who turned and headed back up the hall. Kramer glanced back and gave Lethbridge-Stewart a reassuring thumbs-up, mouthing the words, 'He's on his way now.' Lethbridge-Stewart nodded his thanks, and Kramer went back into the ward where Travers was studying the comatose patients.

Leaving him out here alone. Useless. Lethbridge-Stewart glanced about self-consciously. He was achieving nothing just standing here. Science was *not* his area of expertise after all. Best to leave it to Kramer and Travers. For now, anyway.

The cop was nearly to the end of the hall. Lethbridge-Stewart broke into a run to catch up. He would go back with the man, check on Sally himself.

At least there he would feel as if he were accomplishing *something*.

Owain leaped back from the window and turned to run, shoving Simon along ahead of him. More than half of the passengers had managed to exit the rear of the train car, either jumping to the tracks on either side or pushing through into the next car and continuing towards the rear. Owain and Simon made to follow them, running perhaps half a dozen steps down the nearly emptied aisle. There were still two or three stubborn souls huddled in seats, too terrified to move or refusing in bona fide New Yorker fashion to acknowledge this disruption of their daily commute.

Then the charging Yeti slammed into the front of the train car, throwing them to the dirty floor. The monster battered furiously at the exterior of the car, working its claws into the buckled frame and wrenching the connecting door off its hinges with an agonising shriek of metal.

The two young men climbed to their feet and whirled just in time to see the unearthly shape beginning to work its way through the opening, its bulk filling the compact space. Its glowing eyes seemed to fix on them with murderous intent.

'My God, Owain,' Simon breathed weakly. 'What is it?'

'It's a Yeti,' Owain heard himself reply, still hardly daring to believe it. The Yeti had been destroyed in Bledoe – all of them! But this one was different, it was—

The Yeti was all the way inside now, looking bigger than ever in the tight, enclosed compartment. It loosed another bone-rattling roar, eliciting shrieks of panic and terror from the remaining passengers. One of them, still between Owain and Simon and the Yeti, yipped in fright and rose, scuttling past them. Owain made room, pushing her toward the evacuating mob at the back of the car. He glanced at the two individuals still seated in front of them, a white-haired old man of perhaps seventy, and a teenager of no more than seventeen or eighteen, eyes hidden behind dark shades, transistor radio held, forgotten, to one ear below an impressive afro haircut. He just stared at the Yeti, not moving, not saying a word. The old man appeared to be praying, head down, eyes closed.

Owain lunged forward, hearing Simon croak a warning, unable to stop himself. He clutched at the old man, staring up at the Yeti. It still stood completely motionless, watching him.

The web will come now, he thought. *Any moment now it will pull out one of those strange web guns, and that will be the end. It'll kill me just like it killed Lewis.*

The old man shouted angrily, looking up at Owain with rolling, rheumy eyes. 'Vat you doink, boy?' he quavered in a thick accent, his voice gone reedy either from age or terror. 'Leggo! Leggo!' Incredibly, he was swatting at Owain with the newspaper he'd been reading. It made the young man feel like laughing in disbelief; it was the last reaction he'd expected.

'Don't you see what's happening?' he hissed.

'Man, he don't need you yankin' on him,' said the kid with the afro, still seated opposite the old man, his voice unbelievably calm despite the menacing thing standing just fifteen feet away. 'Thass Mr Padovani. Mr Padovani don't like nobody yankin' on him.'

'Please, Mr Padovani,' Owain gasped, dodging the rolled newspaper.

Simon was beside him now. 'Owain!'

Owain looked up again, and instantly saw what Simon meant. The Yeti still stood inside the shattered doorway. It was still staring at him, glowing eyes never moving, but it had begun to convulse, shuddering all over as if fevered.

'What the hell?' Owain murmured.

Something dropped from the rippling fur below the Yeti's massive left arm. It took Owain several seconds to register the shape. It was a large grey sewer rat, snout twitching, beady red eyes glittering unnaturally. It was at least eighteen inches long. It seemed to collect itself on the floor of the subway car, sitting up on its haunches and rubbing its forepaws together, almost seeming to stare at Owain the same way as the Yeti.

He felt Simon grab his arm, just as the rat let out a keening screech that made his teeth ache. Another dozen of the sleek, grey shapes dropped away from the shuddering Yeti, falling from the folds of its fur like magic tricks.

I'd have preferred rabbits from hats, Owain thought, dazed and repulsed.

Another screech and he raised his eyes. Sitting on the right shoulder of the Yeti, red eyes unblinking, was a mottled grey and white rat that had to be two feet long. It screeched again, and the rats on the floor of the car suddenly rushed at them.

Simon shouted in horror and yanked Owain backward, away from Mr Padovani and the kid with the big afro. 'No! Simon, we have to—'

But Simon didn't slow.

The Yeti hadn't fazed the youth with the transistor radio, but the sight of the rats caused him to leap up and step up onto his seat, looking for all the world like a housewife in a television advert, moments away from screaming, '*Raaaaat!*' Mr Padovani shut his eyes again and went back to his wordless prayers. The rats were on them in a flash. Owain watched, horrified, as both men beat helplessly at the leaping, snarling vermin. Moments later they collapsed in their seats, shivering, appearing to slip into unconsciousness.

Simon clutched at his shoulder again. 'Owain!'

Startled out of his daze, he glanced back at Simon. His friend's eyes were wide in terror. Behind him, the exodus had slowed, the panicked riders transfixed by the horrifying emergence of the monster's own small passengers. They would never be able to clear out before the attack came.

Owain looked back at the front of the train car to see the rats advancing, their first two victims already forgotten.

And behind them, the Yeti was starting forward too.

CHAPTER EIGHT
Assault on the Yeti

MAYBE IT was fear, adrenaline or irate fury at the thought of those filthy vermin, or maybe it was the anger over seeing the terror they inspired in the passengers all around him. The Yeti were one thing: unnatural, bizarre, impossible to tackle one-on-one. But *rats*! He found them disgusting, repulsive on a deep, instinctive level.

Owain remembered his brother Lewis, when they were about six, crying out in surprise and disgust one hot afternoon when they'd been mucking around in an old barn. They'd uncovered a nest of what they'd taken at first to be simple barn mice, but they'd quickly realised these were big, ugly brown rats, possibly having given up whatever urban den they'd previously occupied to take over this warm, cosy haymow. The reason was obvious; before them was a mama rat, lying on her side, swollen and hissing, with a whole writhing brood of small, squirming rat babies suckling and gnawing and cheeping at her. They were like small grey piglets, with none of the warmth and familiarity pigs engendered in the simple country boys they'd been.

Lewis's horror had been primal, atavistic. Owain had shared it ever since.

Thoughts of Lewis brought his death back too, swift and cruel, replaying in Owain's mind the way it always did, rapidly but still with bitterly complete clarity. He envisioned Lewis's face, left slack and emotionless in death. Remembered that long-ago mother rat, hissing up at them defiantly.

Rats and Yeti. Minions of the creature that had taken Lewis' life. *Damn them!*

And within Owain, something changed.

He felt it at first like a deep breath. His chest seemed to

swell with air, his brain to sing with extra oxygen. The air appeared to brighten around him; being inside the phenomenon, he could not see that he himself had taken on a bright, yellowish glow, one that seemed brightest in his eyes. He heard Simon gasp in surprise, and saw on his friend's face a mix of uncertainty, surprise, and sheer awe.

Owain didn't know what it was, but there was something familiar about it. Something he hadn't felt since that fateful day in Remington Manor; only this time it was stronger – so very *much* stronger! He felt compelled to move forward, to meet the rats and the Yeti. His fists clenched at his sides.

Seeing him coming, the Yeti, still shuffling forwards behind the skittering rats, let out its loudest, most triumphant roar yet. And then the roar seemed to die in the monstrosity's throat. It cocked its head, looking at him in puzzlement.

'Stop,' he told it.

The Yeti stopped.

Owain looked down at the rats, which had almost reached his feet.

'Stop,' he told them.

They stopped too. Several were actually hurled backwards, screeching. They writhed, regained their feet and fled to the safety of the Yeti's massive paws. Some began to scale the furry brute in their newfound panic.

Behind him, Owain could hear Simon hurriedly escorting the last of the passengers out of the car, telling them to run up the tunnel to the next station. That was good. The people were safe.

But then Owain got a good look at the kid with the afro. At Mr Padovani. Both were still slumped in their seats, unconscious or dead.

The brightness all about him seemed to waver. A grunt of satisfaction from the Yeti, and it took a step forward.

'*Back!*' Owain bellowed, suddenly overwhelmed with rage. The light glowed fiercely; the yellow energy he was somehow channelling became a physical force he could actually see. Somehow *aiming* his mind – his will? – at the creatures, he sent angry pulses of power towards the Yeti and the rats, sending the lot of them staggering and running back the way they had come.

'Out!' Owain yelled. 'Get out! Be gone!'

The rats emptied from the shattered end of the train car, disappearing into the tunnel beyond. Hunched in the doorway, the Yeti turned its great, glowing eyes back to Owain once more, marking him, seeming to promise a reckoning.

'Yeah, yeah, yeah,' Owain said defiantly, 'this isn't over, just wait until the Master hears about this. Get the hell out of here. Tell your boss he doesn't own me yet. I'll do whatever I have to do to stop him. And you.'

The Yeti roared bitterly, turned and fled the train car, rats leaping onto its furry hide as it shambled away. Owain watched until it was invisible in the distant gloom, and with a breath of relief, the energy dissipated around him.

It was here. Somehow the Great Intelligence was here. Owain felt his hands trembling. He was so sure he had escaped its influence.

Simon touched his arm. 'Owain. Hey, man. Let's get out of here. Let's boogie.'

Nodding, Owain followed his friend through the doors at the back of the wrecked train car, no longer sure there was any escape for him.

The hotel was in an uproar.

Lethbridge-Stewart stepped out of the taxi and saw a scatter of blue police vehicles around the entrance, blocking half the street. He broke into a dead run at once. A pair of skinny, arm-waving cops tried to block his entry into the hotel, but he dodged them and pushed through the revolving door.

The lobby was full of more cops, harried employees and curious guests, many in dressing gowns and slippers, more than a few protesting at having been turned out over what was surely none of their concern. Before long, Lethbridge-Stewart spotted the young desk clerk who had been on duty when they checked in. He pushed through the crowd and braced the man, whose face had gone a waxy colour in shock and confusion. Perhaps it was that, or perhaps Lethbridge-Stewart's accent and military bearing, but the young man had no problem spilling everything he knew.

'Jerry Mallard and one of the janitors, Jorge, I think… They're *dead.*'

Lethbridge-Stewart took him firmly by the shoulders, forcing direct eye contact. 'Where?'

'Eleventh floor.'

Lethbridge-Stewart let him go and headed for the lifts, shouting over his shoulder for the man to send security and the police to Miss Wright's room on the double.

When he got upstairs, they were already there.

Her room wasn't in terrible disarray, but a desk chair had been overturned, the phone ripped out of the wall and hurled across the room. The chief of security informed him the front door to the suite had been found standing wide open.

'Blast it all!' Lethbridge-Stewart snapped. 'Didn't anybody see anything, man?'

The chief, a burly fellow with a Clark Gable moustache that did nothing to improve his features, glowered. 'My man Jerry saw something, I'd wager, and one of the custodians too. They look like they ran into a buzz-saw.'

Lethbridge-Stewart nodded. 'Of course, sir, my sympathies.' He glanced at the shredded telephone wires protruding from the wall below the writing desk. 'Can someone contact Lieutenant Adrienne Kramer, put her in the picture? She's our UN liaison. We're here supporting—'

'Uncle!'

Lethbridge-Stewart whirled to see Owain and a youth in a denim jacket and bell bottoms burst into the room.

Owain looked wild, shell-shocked. 'Sally?' he asked, eyes widening.

Lethbridge-Stewart shook his head. 'We don't know yet. I hate to say it, but it looks rather like—'

'It's the Yeti, Uncle. They're here. In New York. I've *seen* one.'

Lethbridge-Stewart immediately led him toward the rear of the room, drawing him away from the cops and security agents. He noted that Owain's friend stayed close, listening intently. He seemed to be glancing warily at the clustered lawmen.

'What happened?' Lethbridge-Stewart asked Owain.

'What did you see?'

As quickly as he could, with his friend interjecting the occasional titbit, Owain recounted what had happened in the subway train. When he finished, Lethbridge-Stewart whirled and shouted for the security chief. The man rumbled over.

'We must get Kramer at once,' Lethbridge-Stewart told him. 'She has to seek authorisation for a special forces assault on the source of this attack and another which occurred only minutes ago on a subway train not far from here. These young men can point you in the right direction.'

The security chief paled. He looked past Lethbridge-Stewart, no doubt only seeing a pair of shaggy hippie kids. 'You can't be serious,' he rasped.

'Sir, I have never been more serious. Now *move!*'

The burly man's eyes widened at the timbre of the command. He hustled away. Lethbridge-Stewart followed at his heels, still issuing directives.

Sally Wright looked for the tenth or twelfth time at the nearly bare room where she'd been left to sit, tied to a chair, alone with her whirling thoughts. She knew her makeup had streaked and run with frightened tears when she was first taken by the hulking monstrosity – *one of Alistair's Yeti, I'm sure of it* – but she swore now she was done with crying.

Don't let them see you're scared, she told herself. *Don't give them the satisfaction.*

She looked around again, seeking some means of escape, but could see nothing to help her. There was a small wooden table against the far wall, next to the closed – and surely locked – door, but otherwise, the chair she was tied to was the only item in the room. Bare wood floors, no loose nails that she could see. Nothing on the walls, no old picture hooks or loose mouldings. The chair itself? Perhaps she could tip it over, break the legs, use one to pry loose the ropes securing her limbs.

The door opened. She blinked, staring hard at the widening gap. It was the small Tibetan man again. He entered, followed once more by the massive Yeti.

He called it Kabadom, she thought. *Treats it like a servant, or a pet.* Maybe that was something she could use.

The man regarded her studiously. 'You are comfortable? You are unharmed?'

'Are you mad? Of course I'm not comfortable! Where am I? Why have you brought me here? Who are you?'

He ignored her questions, glancing at the Yeti, then walked further in. Kabadom remained in the doorway. The Tibetan clasped his hands together, smiling at her.

'I do apologise for all this, Miss Wright,' he said slowly and evenly. 'You are the unfortunate bait on the hook. If there were any other way to achieve my goals, believe me, I would pursue them.'

'Okay,' she said huskily. 'Let's say for the sake of argument I do believe you. Why don't you untie me, and we can seek those alternative means?'

He chuckled. 'You're a very clever woman, very brave. I admire that. But I simply do not have the luxury of time. All is in motion now, and we must play the roles we are destined to play. It is the will of my master. And my will too.'

'And you are…?'

He gave her a bow. 'Jemba-Wa. Builder of my master's living tools of judgment.'

'Tools of…?'

Jemba-Wa narrowed his eyes. 'The Yeti, of course.'

The scene outside the subway station was growing busier and more carnival-like all the time. The arrival of police vehicles and various emergency response crews – and especially the heavy, urban response vehicle carrying the assault team in their armoured gear, weapons already in hand – drew a curious crowd of onlookers, who cat-called and shouted questions that generally turned the atmosphere a bit ridiculous. Someone produced an enormous, battery-powered radio, and Kool and the Gang's *The Gang's Back Again* began to pulse out over the scene. Some kids started dancing. Older folks continued to bark indignant questions. Inconvenienced traffic honked ceaselessly.

Lethbridge-Stewart glowered, wondering why the officers in charge didn't send them all packing. He shrugged off his impulse to control the moment. At least the officials seemed to be willing to listen; first to him, then to Kramer, whom they'd reached via police channels. With her help the police were now assembling the heavy response team to go down and reconnoitre.

She walked over to him now, nodding in thanks or acknowledgment, he wasn't sure which.

'I'd like to go in with the team,' he told her.

Kramer shook her head. 'Absolutely not, sir. You're a guest here, and I can't put you into harm's way.'

'Lieutenant, no one here is as familiar as I am with your targets, if indeed they're still down there. I won't engage. I'll merely advise. But a more knowledgeable advisor you could not find.'

Kramer considered for a moment and nodded. She pointed at the lead officer in the heavy response unit. 'That's Kresal. Captain Kresal. You follow his lead, do as he says, and hang back when he tells you. Yes?'

Lethbridge-Stewart nodded briskly. As Kramer turned to relay further instructions to the nearby officers, he started toward Kresal, a squat cinderblock of a man whose countenance brooked no argument. *Right,* Lethbridge-Stewart thought. *Here's a chap I can relate to.*

Someone grabbed his arm. Lethbridge-Stewart turned to see Owain standing there. He'd slipped under one of the barricades the police were finally throwing up. Beyond Owain, he saw the lad's new friend protesting as he was shoved back behind one of the yellow sawhorses. Lethbridge-Stewart started to say something, but Owain was speaking rapidly, and he frowned in surprise.

'—want to go with you,' Owain finished saying.

'Absolutely not,' Lethbridge-Stewart said. 'I can't put you in harm's way.'

'Listen, Uncle, you don't know. I—' Owain broke off, struggling to find the right words. 'Something happened to me on the train. I can help you. There was this—'

Lethbridge-Stewart clapped a hand on his shoulder, thinking about Owain's brother Lewis, and the devastation the last Yeti incident had wrought on his family.

'I understand your feelings here,' Lethbridge-Stewart said. 'I know these particular abominations carry an added weight for you.'

Owain shook his head. 'No, it's not that. On the train, there was an energy. I... *did* something. I backed it off. The Yeti. I faced it down, and it fled.'

Lethbridge-Stewart hesitated, then resumed shaking his head no, despite Owain's crestfallen face. He knew there was more to the young man than a free spirit and strong will, but he couldn't let Owain risk his life in an effort to come to terms with his perceived destiny, his kinship with the malevolent, bodiless Intelligence.

'I'm sorry, Owain,' Lethbridge-Stewart said tersely. 'The answer remains no.' He spun and walked away fast, heading for the response team and the subway entrance, leaving Owain fuming helplessly.

'All right!' Kramer shouted, following Lethbridge-Stewart. 'Let's get started!'

Jemba-Wa opened his mouth to say something else, then abruptly stopped, closing his eyes and cocking his head in an almost dog-like fashion. After a moment, his eyes opened again.

Sally recoiled. The eyes were a yellowish-grey colour.

Jemba-Wa blinked, and came back to himself. The strange colour was gone. He turned to the Yeti. 'Kabadom,' he said, 'time to begin our primary task.' He continued for a moment in another language – Tibetan, Sally supposed – then, as the hulking brute nodded and turned to go, he stopped it with a hand on its furred arm. 'Four should do,' he added. 'Quickly. Get them in place.'

The Yeti left, straining once more to get through the door. Jemba-Wa smiled at Sally, merely standing now and observing her. 'A busy day,' he said.

Sally only stared defiantly at him.

'Owain! Hey, Owain!'

He turned to see Simon stuck behind the barricade, held back by the police with the rest of the onlookers. Owain hurried over, still frustrated that Uncle Alistair had cut him off the way he'd done. Owain wished he was with them, wished he could do something.

A policeman saw him coming, sneered at Owain for some

reason he didn't quite understand, and turned to glare at Simon. 'Nobody crosses,' the cop snapped, returning Simon's withering stare with a smug smile. 'You want to make something of it, you hippie punk?' When Simon didn't move or respond, the cop put out a gloved hand and shoved him back from the yellow-and-black-striped barrier. This earned him angry shouts from a number of the bystanders, many of them Simon and Owain's age or younger. Kool and the Gang continued to thump and beat over the scene, still lending it that weird circus-like feel.

But there was something else in the air, Owain sensed. Something bad.

The cop snorted at the protesters, thumbed his nose and turned imperiously away. Owain went over to the cop squaring off with Simon.

'It's all right!' he said. 'He's with us.'

The officer just snorted, sizing him up briefly, the look in his eyes revealing his thoughts: *You're a hippie punk too, no matter who vouches for you.* Owain forced himself to let it go.

'Please, sir,' he said. 'This man is—'

'Give me a break,' the cop said bluntly, cutting him off. 'No more civilians across the barricade!'

More barks of anger from the increasingly restless crowd. They were New Yorkers through and through, Owain guessed, almost no tourists here, and they clearly didn't like the way this officer of the law was treating one of their own.

Simon merely groaned in frustration, waving a dismissive hand at the policeman. 'Never mind. Look, what's happening?'

Owain and Simon huddled, moving away from the haughty cop. He stared after them for a moment, his cold eyes suggesting, *I know punks like you, oh yeah. I do.*

Letting the crowd noise overshadow their conversation, Owain quickly updated Simon on the SWAT team's plan, and Alistair's involvement.

'Left you out of it, did he?' Simon grunted.

Owain nodded. 'I just want to help.'

'What you did on the train,' Simon said. 'You tapped into something, didn't you? You found your inner eye and tapped in.'

'I don't *know* what it was. Well, not exactly. I have an idea, but... I've never done anything like it before.'

'But you definitely *can* do something. Open yourself to the power, man. Find your inner eye again. Open your mind. *See.*'

Owain just looked at him for a moment, puzzled, uncertain how to even attempt such a thing. He recalled the Yeti tearing its way into the train car and remembered the surge of adrenalin that had electrified his whole body, the way some mechanism in his head seemed to click into operation, humming into life, throbbing behind his eyes and temples. He looked briefly at the wet street, the crowd of humanity craning to glimpse a bit of carnage, the flashing police lights, the flock of blue uniforms.

He looked back at Simon, who stared earnestly at him, nodding his encouragement.

Owain closed his eyes. Slowed his breathing. Shut out the noise and the odours. Sweat abruptly beaded on his forehead and upper lip.

By the time the Yeti returned, Jemba-Wa had asked Sally the same half a dozen questions three times, seeking to learn more about Lethbridge-Stewart, about their trip to New York, about their connections with some British man working with the police and the detective who'd been following him. 'Until Kabadom was finally forced to put paid to his foolish curiosity,' Jemba-Wa told her, his face strangely sad. 'Pity. But it became unavoidable.'

She regarded him imperiously. 'You're a monster.'

He shook his head, eyes steadily fixed on her own. He pointed at the Yeti standing behind him, unmoving. '*That* is a monster, or so you people insist. And unless you want me to order it to do something... distasteful... I suggest you start answering my quest—'

He broke off suddenly, hands rising to the sides of his head as if suddenly afflicted with a terrible headache. His eyes widened, widened further, glowing a penetrating amber colour. Sally drew in a shocked breath at the sight.

'*Power,*' he said with a choke.

But the voice that emerged was, Sally was certain, not remotely his own.

*

Screeching. Chittering. A flash of claws, and sheeting redness.

Owain reeled, wiping at his face like he'd been hit with something hot and wet. He choked back a cry of horror.

Simon leaned across the barricade and caught him before he could topple over backward. 'Owain!' he shouted. 'What? What did you see?'

Panting, pale as a sheet, Owain looked at Simon with wild, panicked eyes. 'It's a trap,' he gasped. 'They're all going to die down there.'

In the empty room, Jemba-Wa gathered himself, staring stonily at Sally. There were no more questions. She was about to ask one herself, to enquire what had happened, when he whirled, touching the broad arm of the Yeti. They both left the room. She heard the key turn in the lock, the murmur of Jemba-Wa's voice as he gave new orders to his unnatural ally.

Then she was fully alone once more.

She cursed, wrenching at her bonds helplessly.

The Metropolitan Transportation Authority had been directed once more to shut down power to the lethal third rail, enabling the eight-man heavy response team to descend quickly into the station and onto the tracks themselves. Sergeant Talbot was in the lead, with Captain Kresal and Lethbridge-Stewart bringing up the rear. The latter admired the disciplined advance. The team's boots made almost no sound as they hustled along. All of their weapons were up and trained to the left or right of the column.

There was a sizzling pop, and a deep red glow bloomed to Lethbridge-Stewart's left. He saw Kresal drop the guttering red flare he'd ignited, marking their way.

They moved fast, single-file, through the rubbish-strewn tunnel and reconnoitred the smashed train. It yielded nothing of import. They turned off the main track line, descending into another, older section of the vast underground network. Kresal popped a couple more flares, left them hissing on the tunnel floor as they passed.

Talbot suddenly held up a closed fist. The column froze at once. Kresal went forward, conferred with the sergeant and returned to Lethbridge-Stewart. Talbot himself scrambled away in the darkness, leaving the rest to await his report.

'The tunnel opens up into a sort of junction ahead,' Kresal told Lethbridge-Stewart. 'A crossing point for several old track lines, maybe even some kind of roundhouse for the train cars once upon a time. Higher ceilings, wide platform. Talbot's on recon.'

'It's strange that so much of the system is disused,' Lethbridge-Stewart said.

'Progress,' the captain replied, the word coming out like a curse. 'It's all about streamlining, moving Citizen A to Destination B as fast as possible, and renewing the infrastructure faster than John Q Public can wear it out. MTA does all right, honestly, cos let me tell you... In New York? We wear it out *fast.*'

'How old is this section?' Lethbridge-Stewart asked, studying their surroundings.

'Started building right after the turn of the century, building *deep*, like they knew they were gonna overhaul it every twenty/thirty years. They've been revising and rebuilding ever since, stacking up new components of the subway and the city, rebuilding on the bones of the past. It's a freaking warren down here, hundreds of miles of abandoned tunnels. You got sections seventy feet below street level, forgotten places the bums and skells have turned into hidey-holes for themselves.' Kresal grunted in displeasure. 'The mind boggles at how some folks are forced to live. At how some are *willing* to live.'

Lethbridge-Stewart shook his head. 'Some of it must be below sea level.'

Kresal nodded. 'Almost all of it, matter-a-fact. Built right into the bedrock of the island. They've got a staff of sixty who do nothing but mind the pumps and filters, pushing the water back out as fast as it tries to creep in. Don't kid yourselves, they're the real miracle-workers in this city. Whole thing would be flooded right up to the subway entrances if it weren't for those crazy—'

Talbot returned, causing his boss to break off. The sergeant slipped past the other men, snapped to attention in front of Kresal. 'Four targets, sir,' he said quietly. 'Right up ahead, in the open, neat as you please.'

'What are they doing, Sergeant?'

Talbot shrugged. 'Just standing there, sir. Maybe waiting for us. But they're facing the other way, every one of them. If it's an ambush they're doing it backward.' He chuckled.

Kresal nodded, and Talbot returned to the front of the column. Kresal gestured to Lethbridge-Stewart. They spoke in low tones, though Kresal's first words sent Lethbridge-Stewart's blood pressure soaring.

'We're going in. You hang back here.'

'Absolutely not!'

'I have to insist, Brigadier,' Captain Kresal said patiently. 'You're a civilian here, and I won't cause an international incident by putting you in harm's way.'

'Captain, you don't understand, I—'

'Begging your pardon, sir,' Kresal interrupted. 'But I understand very well. We are about to put a righteous hurting on these mutts. I don't care who they are, I don't care what their beef is. I understand from Lieutenant Kramer that you may have dealt with something similar back home in London, but they picked the wrong city to muck around with this time. So please, for your sake and mine, wait here and let us show you how we do things here in Gotham City, USA. I'll call you forward when it's done.'

Lethbridge-Stewart shook his head, adamant. 'But—'

Kresal cut him off, smiling. 'Cigars on me, Mister Stewart. Afterward.'

Lethbridge-Stewart groaned inwardly. The captain probably imagined he was being rakishly cool, putting this interloping Limey in his place. *'Gotham City' indeed.* He had to make the man understand. But Captain Kresal had already turned away, and was ordering his men forwards in an assault formation. Lethbridge-Stewart heard automatic rifles readied, safeties disarmed. He found his hand drifting down to his own belt, where the comforting weight of his service revolver was missing. *No comfort there*, he thought grimly.

'Americans,' he grunted.

The policeman who had been shoving Simon back and sneering at the crowd had moved further down the barricade line to deal with another over-eager gawker, a wild-haired street preacher bellowing about the End Times. Seeing that the cop's attention was fully engaged with this new troublemaker, Owain took the chance to shove one of the sawhorses aside. He beckoned Simon forward.

'I've got to get to Uncle Alistair,' he said. 'He's in terrible trouble, they all are!'

Simon nodded. He glanced over at the knot of blue uniforms clustered at the subway entrance, waiting on word from inside, then looked at their friendly cop friend monitoring the barricade. He had unfolded his arms at last and was now holding his truncheon in one of them, tapping it against his leg in a manner that surely would have quieted anyone other than the distressed old man in the tattered surplice. Other onlookers were shouting at the cop again, recognising the threat of the club and telling him to leave the crazy old man alone.

'Yeah, this will be so worth it,' Simon muttered.

'What?' Owain asked him.

Simon only clapped him on the shoulder. 'Get ready to run,' he shouted in his friend's ear, fighting to make himself heard over the din.

'What are you going to do?'

Simon didn't bother to answer. He ducked under the barricade, keeping Owain between himself and the sharp eyes of the cop as he did so. Once he was on the cop's blind side, he cut sharply back and began to hurry towards the man.

'Oh no,' Owain breathed.

Simon reached the cop, who was once more shouting at the street preacher to pack up his craziness and call it a night, and thumped the uniformed officer hard on one shoulder.

The cop turned and sized him up indignantly. 'Now whaddya think you're—'

Simon didn't answer. Owain saw his hands close into balled fists, and Simon laid out the policeman with a surprisingly hard right to the jaw.

There was a brief silence, and the stunned crowd abruptly roared its approval. The street preacher began backing away, eyes wide, open hands raised in a peace-making gesture. He turned and shoved his way into the seething crowd.

Wringing his hand, Simon turned, scanning the cheering

mob quickly until his eyes met Owain's. 'Go!' he shouted, gesturing towards the station entrance.

Still stunned, Owain saw the rest of the cops point and shout, identifying the source of the ruckus, which had grown into a full-scale tumult of waving fists and bellowing voices. To a man, the blue uniforms swarmed into action, lunging towards the hippie youth standing over their fallen comrade, who lay there rubbing his jaw and trying to regain his senses. Billy clubs were unslung.

Pandemonium greeted this sight. As if they'd been waiting for such a signal, the crowd exploded through the barricades, charging to meet the oncoming policemen.

Simon abruptly collapsed to the pavement, covering his head with his hands and assumed a foetal pose.

Simon drags me clear of a potential punch-up back at the hotel and I repay him by getting him in such a fix he takes a swing at a bloody cop to help me, Owain chastised himself. *You're really living the code, brother.*

The cops and the civilians slammed together all about him. Fists flew, men bellowed and cursed, clubs whistled down to crack on knees and forearms and skulls, and some of the bellows and curses turned to shrieks of pain and outrage.

Amid all this, Owain saw to his astonishment that Simon's diversion had worked. The steps leading to the subway were clear.

Not wanting to waste the chance, he dodged struggling knots of kicking, punching, spitting human beings, unable to see if Simon lay targeted and suffering at the centre of them, and ran for the stairs leading down.

Kresal, Talbot and the rest of the response team crouched at the point where the tunnel opened into the wider chamber, perhaps twenty yards further down the tunnel from where they'd left Lethbridge-Stewart holding the rear guard position.

It was no brighter in there, and the smell was as rank as ever. Many of the disused tracks lay in puddles of greenish-black water, and everywhere was the stench of human waste. Slimy moss clung to the walls like clotted fish netting. More hung down, in some places almost dragging on the floor, from the tangled nest of overhead pipes disappearing upwards into shadow. The hanging moss seemed to shudder in place, drifting minutely: gaunt, wasted spectres floating on the foul-smelling wind from distant subway trains. The faint metallic screech of those passing cars became the spectres' voices, haunted and ghostly.

In the foetid darkness stood four massive, shaggy figures. As Talbot had said, they appeared to be facing away from Kresal's team, their eyes fixed on a different entry point on the opposite side of the roundhouse.

Kresal did a quick recce of his own, leaning silently away from the curved lip of their tunnel's entry point into that spacious chamber.

The four hirsute figures were spread out across the spacious area, almost like stone obelisks draped in some strange flora. Kresal frowned as he studied them, wondering what they were doing here, what they might be guarding or hiding down here in these abandoned underground spaces. And why they, like the hanging moss all around them, appeared to be shuddering slightly.

Despite the questions running through his mind, despite the deep unease the sight of the hulking shapes raised in his gut, he observed his targets coldly, his sense of wonder overruled by the cold calculations of rank and duty. He set aside his scepticism over the strange appearance and unfathomable purpose of this enemy and simply readied himself for the task in hand. It didn't take long; he was an unimaginative man by nature, and when faced with the inexplicable, he always retreated into discipline and routine, leaving the bigger questions to the officers and the big brains in the labs. Let *them* figure out what the hell these things were. After Kresal and his team had filled them with lead and dragged their bloody carcasses out of the subway tunnels, that was.

For a moment, he pondered the admonitions of the British officer he'd left watching their backs. Then he shrugged off that thought.

This is America, pal, he mused mirthlessly. *Trains got to run on time.*

*

Owain crashed down the subway stairs, somehow avoiding slipping on the old newspapers and other rubbish strewn there and breaking his neck in the process. He hit the platform below at a dead run, seeing the guttering flare still lying on the tracks of the right-hand tunnel. *There.*

He had no torch, no weapon, nothing at all that could help Uncle Alistair and the police team down there.

Nothing but total awareness of the danger awaiting them.

In his mind's eye he saw it again: *Blood spraying in a fan, sheeting across stone and hanging moss, gleaming wetly as the screams of the dying echoed back and forth in the gloom.*

He leaped over the turnstiles, dropped to the filthy dirt between the big metal train tracks, and hurtled past the dying flare, running for all he was worth.

If only he could get there in time.

Captain Kresal turned his attention back to the mission. He scanned the rest of the chamber where the four furry creatures lurked, assessing the ground, the walls, the hanging moss, as carefully as he could, for tripwires or other traps. He didn't like all that hanging moss, didn't like the deep shadows far back in the three or four other tunnel mouths he could see from here. But in the end, it wouldn't matter. He leaned back, addressing Talbot.

'You check infrared?'

'Yes sir. Four targets, weird damned things, definitely biologicals—'

'Don't waste time telling me what I already know, Sergeant,' Kresal snapped, his voice never rising but his tone silencing his subordinate regardless. 'You identify hardware? Explosive ordnance? Anything that gives you pause?'

Talbot shook his head. 'Negative, sir. I don't think there's a weapon among them.'

Kresal glanced over his shoulder at the brigadier, crouched in the distance, unable to hear any of their conversation. 'Animals,' he snorted. 'Fur-covered killer machines. Right. This is four morons in fur coats, maybe terrorists, maybe just home-grown wackos. Either way, we're taking them.' He smiled. 'They don't get to have *all* the fun out in Los Angeles, boys. Go weapons hot.'

The whole team moved at once, flipping the safeties off their MP5s and crouching, ready to spring into the roundhouse. They knew the plan. They would fan out by twos, each pair flanking one of the creatures in the tunnel, waiting just long enough for the captain to give the wackos fair warning. If the wackos showed the slightest sign of attacking, they'd drop all four of them.

'Quicker than Cassius Clay laid out Sonny Liston down in Florida,' the captain had told them earlier. 'I lost a C-note on that fight. But I wouldn't bet against us today.' He was smiling.

No one was smiling now.

'*Go!*' Kresal hissed.

Behind him, Lethbridge-Stewart heard running footfalls. He whirled, going into a fighting crouch, abruptly sure a new enemy was closing on them from behind.

'Wait!' a ragged voice called from the black depths of the tunnel. 'Uncle, wait!'

'Owain?' Lethbridge-Stewart gasped, thunderstruck.

If Captain Kresal heard the young man's shout, it didn't slow him. He, Talbot and the others swept into the spacious junction area, pairing up wordlessly, each duo advancing like silent doom on one of the towering, furry shapes. Eight weapons trained, unwavering, on the unnatural figures, ready to ruin their day. Permanently.

As they drew close, however, it seemed to Kresal that the slight shuddering he'd seen earlier among their targets had grown more pronounced. The four humped shapes were standing still but... *quivering*, as if frightened or fevered, the fur covering their bodies now very visibly rippling. And, he also fancied, as they drew closer, that he could *hear* something. A sort of chittering vibration, like... teeth clicking together, was it? Chattering in the mouths of their quarry as if they were... cold?

But it wasn't cold in here; quite the contrary, it was brutally, explosively hot. Jungle-hot. Even with that faint, stinking breeze drifting in from the far-off trains, it was as close and steamy in the dark tunnel as mid-August in a Hell's

Kitchen tenement with no air conditioning. Kresal could feel the sweat running down the small of his back, could see the wet sheen of it on the face of Talbot, five feet to his right. If his number two was uncomfortable, it didn't show. As they approached the nearest figure in perfect tandem, the sergeant's face was implacable, his weapon trained unerringly on the spot at the base of its enormous, misshapen head where the spine met the brain, where a single shot would disconnect that most crucial junction and switch off the wacko in the fur coat like a thrown breaker in a fuse box.

Just as they reached optimal position and Kresal raised a clenched fist, causing the team to freeze with their weapons ready, he heard a commotion behind him.

'Wait! Kresal, hold on!' It was Lethbridge-Stewart.

Fool, he thought, muttering a particularly blue epithet. Instead of responding, he addressed their targets. 'This is the New York Police Department!' he bellowed. 'Do not move, or you will be fired upon! Throw down your weapons and lay down flat on the floor! *Do it now!*'

The four figures did not respond, but they did react. The shuddering grew stronger. All four swayed in place, jerking and juddering like epileptics launching into a seizure, or zealots of some strange religion overcome with spiritual fervour.

Only now, as the creature nearest him started to topple over, did the simplest, most rational question occur to the captain: What sort of wackos, terrorists or otherwise, deck themselves out in stifling fur coats before pulling *any* kind of job?

He never got to pursue the question further.

The towering figure he and Talbot were covering fell over on its face, directly away from them. The other three immediately collapsed as well, limbs flailing in all directions. The four figures hit the ground and exploded outward in a screeching, writhing mass. Of rats.

Kresal's eyes went wide. He could scarcely register what he was seeing: Hundreds of the vermin, thousands maybe, some as large and fat as housecats. They came boiling out of the deflating fur coats which had been packed with them, so crammed with living, writhing rats they'd managed to hold the furry skins taut, standing more or less upright like the real deal. The Yeti's heavy fur pelts, keys to completing their unearthly disguises, were now nothing but castoffs. The rats streamed from torn seams in the legs, the arms, the heads; seemed to wriggle up out of the thick fur itself in some places, like repulsive newborns emerging from monstrous wombs.

To Kresal's right, one of his men screamed.

He blinked at the high, terrified sound, looking numbly in that direction. It was Carpenter, staggering backwards, beating at the swarm of wriggling, chittering rodents climbing up his legs, leaping at his face and chest. Their glowing red eyes burned like garnets in the gloom as they shrieked their tiny, monstrous fury.

Another desperate cry to his left. Talbot now, kicking at the oncoming swarm, cursing in a wild, rattling voice totally unlike his own, surprise giving way to panic almost immediately as the rats poured out of their fallen quarry and charged him relentlessly.

Still more screams. Gunfire exploded in the darkness. 'Hold fire! Hold fire!' Kresal shouted, but it was too late. One of the others – he thought it might be Kelly, the youngest, recruited just six weeks earlier – tried to back away and tripped, perhaps stepping on one of the rats. He was down and already covered with them, shrieking, convulsively triggering his weapon. Kresal saw bullets strafe left, kicking chunks of old stone out of the tunnel wall, punching into Brock's lower back, Carpenter's belly and thigh with puffs of pink mist. Brock went down, hard, and did not move again. Carpenter slumped to his knees, groaning in disbelief. The rats swarmed him and pulled him down.

Rats. It's just rats, *for crying out loud*, Kresal thought indignantly, turning to see Talbot on his knees, screaming and beating at his own face, at the trio of writhing vermin that had leaped on him, yanking his goggles down, spitting, clawing, *biting*.

'Kresal! Pull them out!'

He knew it was Lethbridge-Stewart, but as he turned to look behind him – perhaps to call for help, perhaps merely to give the man an apologetic look for disregarding his advice – more of the rats with the strange ruby-red eyes came for him too, came *en masse*, and engulfed him. He did the only thing he could think to do; he threw his own weapon as hard as he could, watching it pitch end over end and land just twenty feet or so short of the crouched British officer.

Finally, the *coup de grâce*. Four robot Yeti dropped from the shadowy bristle of piping overhead, landing with a thunderous crash like doom itself.

Captain Kresal never saw them.

CHAPTER NINE
Manhattan Under Attack

LETHBRIDGE-STEWART and Owain watched in horror as the rats took down the entire response team. 'Too late,' Owain croaked miserably, fighting for breath after his mad dash through the subway tunnel. 'I was too late, Uncle.'

Lethbridge-Stewart didn't reply. From their vantage point at the mouth of the tunnel, it was obvious that only one or two of the police specialists were dead, and those only because they'd been caught in their compatriot's panicked, reflexive gunfire. The rest were on the ground, too, but very much alive, writhing helplessly beneath the assault of the rats or trying in vain to crawl away, each one shivering and gagging from the effects of multiple bites.

One by one, they went limp and still.

They were entering the same comatose state as the hospital patients far overhead. Soon the skin of the surviving response-team members would begin to turn waxy and yellow-grey, their eyes turning a pulsing amber beneath jittering lids.

But *why?*

Lethbridge-Stewart hadn't a clue. At least there was no question about the source of the affliction anymore, he concluded, watching in mute horror as Captain Kresal disappeared beneath a writhing carpet of grey vermin. The rats were undeniably the vector for... whatever it was. Infection. Alien plague. *Something.* Regardless, the threat was undeniable. If mere hundreds could do this much damage to a squad of highly trained heavy response police officers in a matter of moments... If the carriers began to emerge in numbers into the world above.

It will spread like wildfire, he realised.

Sick with dread, furious at his inability to talk Kresal out of this foolish assault, Lethbridge-Stewart turned to his nephew to share some of his suspicions, to tell him they had to get word back to Kramer and Professor Travers, had to turn on an international response and *fast* before—

Four massive shapes plummeted from the overhead pipes near the centre of the chamber. They crashed down with deep, metallic *gongs* of impact, punctuating their landings with titanic roars of triumph.

The Yeti stood there, stolidly observing the work of the rats with their piercing yellow eyes. Massive clawed feet splayed. Arms thrown wide for balance. They regarded the prone policemen, saucer-like eyes never narrowing or changing expression in any way but somehow conveying deep satisfaction just the same.

Lethbridge-Stewart and Owain gaped in astonishment.

The Yeti were naked, furless.

'It's a trap,' Owain said.

'Yes, so I see,' Lethbridge-Stewart agreed, sardonically.

Without their furs, the creatures were unimaginably strange to the eyes. Only the artificial, elephantine legs and the spear-fisher talons curving from club-like paws sustained the illusion of a brute animal. The rest was pure robot. Lethbridge-Stewart, regaining himself after the initial shock, realised it was the first time he'd ever seen one fully exposed this way. There had been postmortems done on the destroyed Yeti from the London Event and those found in the Vault's underground bunker, and he had seen files documenting the findings, but these were no inert, lifeless hulks on autopsy slabs, their fur sheared away in long sections to permit examination of the undercarriage.

He thought at first that each Yeti must have been cobbled together from a fabulous collection of junk, so motley and segmented were the scores of unpolished metal pieces that comprised them. Some of the pieces were solid, thickly cast and sensibly interrelated, almost in the manner of human bone structure and musculature, but composed and arranged to create much wider and more powerful-looking chest structures, forearms and thighs, like robotic interpretations of trolls. Demented nightmare constructs indeed.

Other sections included metal constructs that were far more delicate and sophisticated. Many of these had been socketed together at weird angles, positioned without clear evidence of purpose or relationship to the whole. Some were overlaid with hard protective plating, forming rings and fans of metal, concentric circles which shifted and flexed organically.

And in the centre of its abdomen – the yellow glow there pulsing with ominous regularity – was the control sphere. The source of all that mechanical might. The core of the Yeti's power.

They don't even clank, Lethbridge-Stewart noticed with numb fascination. Sure, they made crashing sounds when they stomped, and he supposed blows from those massive clawed fists would echo like thunder if they connected with metal or other unyielding surfaces. *But for all of its complex, mechanical inner workings, they don't make a sound. Blast them.*

They were also marvels of engineering. Much of that workmanship had confounded the examination teams when studied close up. But even they never learned much about the Yeti's physical mysteries. Each was a bizarre concatenation of a thousand working parts.

And now, watching the four furless Yeti moving carefully among the fallen policemen, their ungainly, tree-trunk legs delicately avoiding the rats, Lethbridge-Stewart was amazed to consider the idea that all those elements had been hand-crafted decades or maybe centuries ago in the rural highlands of Tibet.

'Uncle!' Owain hissed.

Lethbridge-Stewart was yanked out of his reverie by the sight of the nearest Yeti, just thirty feet away, turning and regarding the two of them with mute curiosity. The thing grunted, gesturing to its cohorts. Below it, dozens of rats abandoned their victims and swarmed up its body, leaping and hopping, twining through various recesses and crannies in the metal giant. Several perched on its shoulders, chittering, regarding Lethbridge-Stewart and Owain with their shining red eyes.

Lethbridge-Stewart saw Kresal's automatic weapon laying on the floor where the man had pitched it. It was close, no more than six or eight long strides away. He hoped.

The Yeti and the rats were coming their way. Not hurrying.

Lethbridge-Stewart whirled, shoving Owain towards the tunnel behind them, his face calm but commanding.

'Alistair!' Owain cried sharply, intuiting what his uncle meant to do.

'Run, Owain. Tell Kramer what's happened. Go!' He pushed the young man towards the tunnel again, then whirled and sprinted for the gun. He heard Owain comply, his footfalls gaining speed and beginning to echo more loudly as the lad dashed away into the darkness.

The closest Yeti had halved the distance, those spear-tipped claws outstretched to enfold or skewer him, when Lethbridge-Stewart bent on the run and dove into a fluid forward roll. He came up with the MP5 in his hands, crouched almost directly beneath the furless monstrosity. It stopped, glowering uncertainly at him, the rats clinging to its shoulders and arms squeaking angrily. The rest of the pests filling the chamber, easily a thousand strong now, took up the noise, screeching in unison as they streamed forward to circle the lead Yeti defensively.

They also encircled Lethbridge-Stewart, cutting off his escape route. If they had seen Owain's departure and intended to pursue him, they gave no sign. That was *something* in their favour, he supposed. He had no illusions about his own chances, caught here in a circle of sick vermin with four of the Yeti ready to fall on him.

As if reading the flow of his thoughts, all four of the robotic creatures loosed triumphant, bloodcurdling screams, drowning out the cries of the rats.

They also drowned out the sound of Lethbridge-Stewart thumbing the MP5's safety off, and the blue epithet he spat at them as he tipped the barrel back, aimed it dead-centre of the lead Yeti's chest and opened fire.

Owain stumbled out of the tunnel and hauled himself onto the grimy platform, where two uniformed policemen in flak jackets grabbed him and hustled him up the exit stairs. His feet barely touched the concrete floor as the wired-tight cops

117

manhandled him out of the danger area, barking questions at him. Owain didn't respond to these; neither did he complain about the way they hauled him bodily away from the entrance. Exhausted and very nearly in shock, legs throbbing from running on hard stone and tile, he was distantly grateful for the free lift.

Outside, he gulped clean, cold night air in relief, feeling his sweaty skin contract at the abrupt dip in temperature. It had been hot down there. Hot and horrible. But the particulars of it… They were fading, blurring in his mind. He looked about himself dully, puzzled but unable to muster real, emotional concern. Was this shock? Was he going into shock?

The riot that had broken out as he dashed inside – mere minutes ago, though it felt like hours – had been brought under control. He saw that there were far fewer gawkers clustered at the barricades now. Fewer idling police cruisers, too. Owain guessed the rest had been used to haul away handcuffed combatants, more than a few cursing, weeping or bleeding. It didn't pay to take on angry cops already tensed up for action. Owain supposed the few remaining onlookers had learned that lesson the hard way. Those still here were subdued, but everywhere he saw angry eyes, resentful glares directed towards New York's Finest. Despite the biting cold, the night was a stew of furious, barely contained energy, the hot friction of rage.

And of his friend Simon, there was no sign at all.

'Owain! Hey, Owain Vine!'

Hearing his name, he glanced around again, still slightly dazed by what had happened underground. Lieutenant Kramer was hurrying towards him, making her way through the logjam of emergency vehicles, trailed by various city officials now as well as the chiefs of police and fire. She passed a parked medical vehicle, where a heavyset Latino ambulanceman was bandaging a minor scalp wound on a surly-looking officer. Owain saw his lip was also split and swollen, and recognised him with a minor jolt. It was the cop Simon had decked to help him get into the subway. If he recognised Owain in turn, he gave no sign.

Giving Owain another appraising look, Kramer leaned in the open rear doors of the ambulance, ignoring the chirp of protest from the ambulanceman, and lifted out a heavy woollen blanket. She brought it to the shivering youth, shook it out and draped it over his shoulders. He pulled it close, slumping down on the trunk of one of the city vehicles.

'Thanks,' he said.

Kramer nodded, and looked around. 'Where is your uncle? And the assault team?'

Owain shook his head numbly, uncertain how to answer.

Kramer blinked in disbelief. 'Are they alive, Owain?' she asked urgently.

'It was a trap. Ambush. The Yeti... The rats... Alistair was observing at a distance. He—'

Owain broke off, fighting the sob that tried to well up his throat, furious with himself at his fright, his helplessness, at having run away, even with Uncle Alistair having commanded he do so. He felt Kramer draw close, putting a comforting hand on his shoulder. He supposed she could tell by his distress that things had gone badly in the tunnels below. He knew she needed to hear everything, was practically bursting with frustration, but he was grateful she didn't press him.

Owain looked up at her. Kramer's gaze had gone once more to the ambulance, where the ambulanceman had finished with the cop. The pompous git rose and stalked away, stewing under his bandages, probably plotting to find some skulls to crack in payback. *Let him*, Owain thought dully. *None of it makes any difference anyway.*

Simon's face rose to the front of his mind again, laughing in the diner, gesturing at the bright lights of the city, and Owain wondered gloomily if he'd slipped away clean or if they'd carted him off to jail.

'Come on,' Kramer said to him, her voice still surprisingly gentle. 'Let's have the ambo attendants give you a quick once-over.'

He rose at her bidding, and followed her towards the heavyset paramedic, his mind roiling with shock and guilt and confusion.

Travers returned to the coma ward and studied the chart for Ingrid Hagerstrom, the oldest of the victims. She was eighty-one. Her chest rose and fell regularly between her waxy yellow arms, which lay folded atop the blanket. Some kindly nurse or family member had carefully clasped her liver-spotted hands as if in prayer.

He recalled reading about her case. She'd been out for a walk in her Hell's Kitchen neighbourhood just before dawn, clad in shawl and slippers, to let Grendel, her equally aged Pekinese, do his business. Bin men had found her curled up on the pavement (not far from a wide sewer mouth, Travers later confirmed for himself). She'd been breathing steadily but was otherwise completely unresponsive. The scrawny little dog, eyes milky with cataracts, had sat patiently by her side, ostensibly waiting for her to rouse herself and lead the way home.

Travers shook his head, marvelling. He'd been living in New York for almost four years, and he supposed Mrs Hagerstrom to be slightly mad, walking alone *anywhere* in the city at that hour, at her age. Gang violence in Hell's Kitchen had dwindled in recent years, he'd gleaned from the papers, but there were still plenty of hoodlums. The old dear might as well have carried a sign: *Please Mug Me.*

Of course, it had turned out to have nothing at all to do with an ordinary mugging.

Ingrid Hagerstrom suddenly grunted. The other sixteen patients did the same, in perfect unison. Travers jumped at the flurry of guttural croaks. He whirled, almost dropping the chart, to study each of them in turn. They were all breathing rapidly now, very nearly locomotoring, like women in the grip of powerful labour.

They began to chant.

Travers felt his jaw unhinge. He bent over Mrs Hagerstrom, checking her vitals. Her heartbeat was fast, but there was no change in her temperature, and everything else seemed normal. Her eyes did not open, but moved ceaselessly under their lids. She gave no other reaction, merely babbling those strange words. Rapping them urgently, almost spitting them.

He leaned closer still, trying to make sense of what she was saying. Was it... Tibetan? He believed it might be, but it was too low and fast for him to catch any real sense of it.

120

All through the darkened room, all the other comatose patients were doing the same thing. Chanting in a language he guessed that most had never even heard used aloud, let alone spoke fluently themselves. The words spilled out *fast*, desperately fast.

Travers ran for the door. He had to find a telephone.

Assuring herself that Owain was not going into shock, but still concerned that his numb reaction meant he'd witnessed not just the death of members of the assault team but possibly that of Brigadier Lethbridge-Stewart as well, Lieutenant Kramer pulled herself away and forced herself to focus on the task in hand.

She led a team back to the subway entrance, listening to the various departments argue about secondary responses, sealing tunnels and evacuating the area. It was a circus. They were scared, they were at their wit's end over this incredible business and, most troubling of all, they were mad as hell, ready to seize on any scapegoat they could find. Kramer dearly hoped they wouldn't decide she was the choice target, but she knew the conventional human mindset in situations like this one. Moreover, she knew how things tended to go in a line-up that included twelve middle-aged white men and one young, relatively inexperienced black woman.

You got to dance now, Ade, she told herself with steely resignation. *Dance like you've never done before. Even if it means dancing on the head of one or more of these blustering fools.*

She was surprised to discover how much the idea of the dance – and the bizarre circumstances that made it necessary – appealed to her. She was ready for this. *Wanted* this. She'd accepted a great many impossible things tonight. Some of them alarmed her, but she had to admit she also *liked* the feeling. Liked being out here on the edge, where it turned out the world was a whole lot bigger and stranger and more exhilarating than army life ever tended to demonstrate.

If this was the life Lethbridge-Stewart led, she wanted in.

Thunder boomed. The storm that had been threatening all evening was almost upon them. *Great*, Kramer thought. *Add insult to injury, why don't you?*

She prepared to cut off the arguing voices. She meant to

go through the assembled leads one by one, ask each for input, then simply tell them what the hell she intended them to do next.

What stopped her was a deep, reverberating roar from far below them.

Everyone shut up at once.

The noise went on and on, rolling out of the square of dim yellow light at the bottom of the subway stairs like a bestial avalanche, a throaty scream of unalloyed fury. The crowd of cops at the top of the stairs looked at one another and shuffled their feet uneasily. Kramer, frowning, raised placatory hands.

'Okay, nobody go off half-cocked, we've—'

The roar had barely begun to dwindle away when it was overwhelmed by another, louder bellow. Multiple voices, shrieking together, promising all the damnation in all the hells in one sustained blast of organic noise. The glass in the windows of the vehicles clogging the scene seemed to hum and shiver. Distantly, still sitting in the back of the ambulance, Owain lifted his head, and Kramer saw him looking over at her. She couldn't make out his eyes from here.

The titanic roar rolled on and on. Thunder boomed in counterpoint.

The crowd behind the barricades began to back away, murmuring uncertainly.

Well, this isn't good, Kramer thought grimly.

The sound began to fade, replaced by... what? She could make out a low, thready muttering, strange and unnatural, like many dry hands being rubbed together in an empty room. Maybe it was wind. Or water. She wondered if the tunnels were flooding.

'What the hell *is* that?' the fire chief asked in a weak voice. He too had taken a step back. He wasn't the only one. More shuffling feet. More uneasy murmurs.

The sandy whisper of those rubbing, rubbing hands grew louder. Louder still.

And audible above that hellish noise – footfalls. Human ones. Running.

Kramer looked down, eyes tracking the dirty stone steps. At the bottom, there was a blank tile wall, sticky with gum and the residue of glue or tape used once upon a time to post signs there. A hard right turn brought you to a long, descending stone ramp that led to the subway platform proper. They'd left three cops armed with shotguns patrolling the area down there, ready to raise the alarm if there was any sign that the response team's targets were headed this way.

Now two of the cops – the source of the running feet – crashed through the entryway, clambering up the stairs. Both were white as ghosts, eyes hollow and horrible. One was babbling and gobbling in shock; later Kramer would learn he was speaking the names of his three daughters, over and over again: *Anna Sandra Rose-Marie Anna Sandra Rose-Marie Anna Sandra Rose-Marie...*

He had lost his shotgun.

'What in the name of—?' Kramer began breathlessly. Lightning split the sky, and thunder crashed. And from below: a terrible, agonised scream.

The third patrolling cop.

The cry was choked off, becoming a wet gurgle. It was lost beneath that uncanny, rasping hiss. The screamer's two comrades never even looked back. They crashed into the crowd of officers and supervisors, shoving through wordlessly, eyes rolling like panicked horses. A police captain grabbed one of them, shaking him, shouting his name. The cop punched him in the mouth and ran, never looking back.

Kramer, hearing all this, was still looking down the stairs, where the rasping noise was still rising. She felt the first raindrops on her face and the backs of her hands, but barely registered them.

The dim yellow light down there was fading. Something was beginning to block it out.

'Weapons,' she said. 'Draw weapons.' Her voice sounded strange and far off. She doubted anyone had heard her. She was about to try again, when the doorway below went dark. At the same moment, the storm cut loose and rain began to sheet down.

A massive shape burst through the doorway below.

It was not a single entity.

It was rats. Rats by the *thousands.*

Obscured by the downpour, the rat sea boiled forth,

running up the stairs at them.

'Weapons hot!' Kramer shouted, drawing her own and flicking off the safety in one smooth motion. The cops around her did the same, spreading out instinctively.

Behind them, civilians screamed and fled, deciding they'd had enough excitement for one night. Kramer turned her head for one quick look, seeing Owain at the back of the ambulance. He'd risen to his feet, the blanket dropping away from his shoulders. His eyes met hers for a scant moment, and she was turning back to the oncoming nightmare.

The rats were halfway up the tunnel now. They began to shriek as well, answering the screams from the crowd with their own. Horrid little voices rose in fury, blending with the whispery *scritch-scratch* of all those clawed feet, the dragging rasp of all those revolting pink tails.

All around her, weapon muzzles rose. There were at least four service revolvers, a couple of .38s and one shotgun; the precinct supervisor had yanked it away from one of the fleeing subway patrolmen. The tubby fire chief, unarmed, soaked to the skin as they all were, fell backwards on his rump and scuttled away like a crab, desperate to get out of the line of fire.

Knowing it wouldn't be enough, but helpless in the face of this mad, oncoming army to do anything else, Kramer shouted, 'Fire! Fire! Fire!'

The weapons opened up, deafening, before she'd even finished the first word.

Rats shrieked. Civilians screamed. Guns thundered.

Total mayhem.

Professor Travers spun in place, looking at the chanting patients as their voices grew in volume, in urgency, until they were all fairly shouting the same rapid-fire muddle of nonsense words. Not Tibetan, he realised in astonishment. Something older.

Something *alien*.

Closest to him, Mrs Hagerstrom's eyes snapped open, staring straight up. Her head lifted slowly, smoothly from the pillow. The steady flow of arcane language never paused or changed.

All of them were wide-eyed now. Wide-eyed and unseeing. Heads rose, then shoulders. They were sitting up in their beds, chanting, the fierce yellow glow in their eyes brightening, pushing back the darkness of the room. Soon all seventeen were sitting straight up, staring directly ahead, eyes like amber torches punching through the gloom. It made Travers wince and shield his own gaze from them, clapping his hands to his head, suddenly fearful for his own mind, his own self-control.

He cried out, the sound lost in the clamour of their voices.

'Alistair! *Alistair!*'

Someone was calling his name. He rather wished they'd leave off.

'*Alist*— Oh sod it! *Brigadier Lethbridge-Stewart!*'

He mentally snapped to attention at that, discipline and muscle memory overtaking inertia and confusion. But it was only a mental snap-to; he was still woozy, disorientated, and his limbs seemed to be constricted in some manner. His head thumped painfully, but when he recalled the last thing he'd seen – the gleaming metal hulks of the Yeti converging on him – he was mildly relieved to find he still *had* a head, sore or not. He tried to extend his range of consciousness, found he was cramped into a nearly foetal position.

Reason and understanding flooded back. He shook his head, clearing it a little, and looked up, craning his neck a little to do so.

Everything was sideways. He was in a room, small, nearly bare of furnishings, and he was staring at a woman seated in a chair. No, *tied* to a chair. He knew her.

It was Sally.

Sally. Smiling at him below wet, worried eyes.

'Hello, darling,' he said blearily. 'Been waiting long?'

'You're tied too,' she said, ignoring his poor attempt at humour. 'They brought you in and dropped you there. For a moment, I thought you were de—' The word caught in her throat. She swallowed, regaining her composure via sheer will.

Despite the pain in his head, Lethbridge-Stewart was pleased. There was hidden steel in Sally. It was an aspect of her character that he admired deeply. Loved, even.

Shaking his head again, he shuffled himself into a hunched, sitting position, inspecting the rope knots at his wrists and ankles. Yeti hadn't done that; they lacked the dexterity.

'Did they hurt you?' he asked Sally.

'No. Not at all. They merely seemed to want me out of the way, took me to bait a trap.' She sighed. 'And here you are. Sorry.'

'Not your fault, dear.'

'There this little man...'

'What little man?' Lethbridge-Stewart frowned.

'Jemba-Wa, he said his name w—'

As if she'd summoned him, the door abruptly opened, and the man himself walked in, bringing a second wooden chair with him. He placed it carefully on the floor not far from Lethbridge-Stewart, then stood looking down at the bound soldier thoughtfully. Finally, he bowed deeply at the waist.

'Brigadier Lethbridge-Stewart,' he said in precise English. 'I am Jemba-Wa, servant of the most revered Master Mahasamatman.' When he straightened, his eyes were a fierce, blazing yellow. 'It is a pleasure to make your acquaintance properly this time,' hissed a familiar whispery voice.

It was the Great Intelligence.

The door closed, unassisted, behind their captor.

CHAPTER TEN
Prisoners of the Great Intelligence

FOR A MOMENT, Lethbridge-Stewart expected Jemba-Wa to help him into the empty chair his captor had brought into the room, but those terrible burning eyes negated the idea. Instead the small, immaculate figure seated himself in it, hands folded in his lap, long fingers interlaced. Those yellow eyes never left Lethbridge-Stewart.

'What do you want?' he asked as coolly as possible, despite his aching head.

'Just a quick look at you, actually; a reminder of what you cost me in the London Underground,' the voice rasped, full of dark humour. 'But there is no time to waste on pleasantries. There is other, much more important business to which I must attend tonight.'

The door opened, once more of its own accord, and Lethbridge-Stewart and Sally saw the shaggy, whitish form of a Yeti standing there patiently.

The hollow voice of the Intelligence growled, 'To the tunnels. Direct the others to their assigned places. Go at once.' The burly Yeti turned and began tromping away, heavy footfalls echoing loudly. The door closed again, and Jemba-Wa bowed his head, almost reverently.

'Are you quite finished?' Lethbridge-Stewart asked caustically.

Jemba-Wa's head lifted; the yellow light was gone. His eyes were once more his own, tiny black ice chips sunk deep in the lines and crevices of his face.

'Ah. Not the master but the help,' Lethbridge-Stewart continued smoothly. 'No matter. Would you mind very much telling us what this is all about?'

Jemba-Wa blinked at him, but whether he had been put off

by his prisoner's bluntness or by the apparent departure of the being possessing him, Lethbridge-Stewart could not be sure. In truth, he was both relieved and alarmed at the Intelligence's abrupt exit – if indeed it was truly gone. This wasn't like it had been with Staff Sergeant Arnold, the unfortunate vessel used by the Intelligence first in life, during their desperate struggle beneath London, and later in death, spreading its poison to Bledoe, seeking to destroy or devastate Lethbridge-Stewart himself.

Only the Great Intelligence encountered in Bledoe had been left to die, fading away like a whisper in Remington Manor. Lethbridge-Stewart was still a little unclear on the details, but as he understood it the Intelligence he'd last met in Bledoe was from the distant future... which must mean the Intelligence in New York had to be the same one defeated in London back in February, a much younger version of the evolved bodiless being.

'You're not from here,' Lethbridge-Stewart said to Jemba-Wa, thinking back on the story Travers had told him earlier.

A smirk. 'Very astute.'

'I don't mean New York or America,' Lethbridge-Stewart retorted. 'You're not from this *time*. You came here from the mid-1930s. You're the time traveller who brought the Yeti forward thirty years, enabling the Great Intelligence to set its trap in London.'

He'd chosen his words carefully. His mocking tone, as well as the expressly stated knowledge, had the desired effect. Jemba-Wa's mouth fell open, and he blinked rapidly, leaning back in his chair, unable to conceal his shock. From the corner of his eye, Lethbridge-Stewart could see Sally staring at him with surprise almost as total as their captor's.

The man's wizened old face relaxed. He chuckled. 'I see you are acquainted with Lieutenant Kramer's informer, the irksome meddler who dogged me from Tibet to London to New York. Master Mahasamatman has long suspected that interloper was not of this time, that he somehow...' Jemba-Wa muttered in his own tongue, then resumed. 'As they say here, "hitched a ride". Yes, hitched a ride from 1935 to the present. A freeloader and a parasite. He has been a thorn ever since.' He waved a dismissive hand. 'It is no matter.'

'If it's no matter, why kill the detective?' Sally asked quietly.

Jemba-Wa did not answer.

'Your master sent the Yeti into the tunnels,' Lethbridge-Stewart said slowly, still uncertain of the big picture but becoming more and more certain of its launching point. 'The police ambush also took place down there, not far from where Dawson's body turned up. You killed Dawson.'

'Not I.'

Lethbridge-Stewart continued undaunted. 'You killed Dawson because he was too close to something.'

Jemba-Wa stood up smoothly and began to pace, hands clasped behind his back. 'Master Mahasamatman warned me that you would be clever.'

'How would he... *it*... know? We barely met in London.'

'Indeed, but a future aspect of the master briefly appeared in London, and they made contact. Not for long, but enough for my master to learn of you before his future aspect vanished to who-knows-where.'

Lethbridge-Stewart remained silent. He knew where; the future Intelligence had gone back to 1938, to Bledoe, and its eventual, final defeat. Before it had died, the future Intelligence had intimated that they had encountered each other many times after London.

'You'll find that I, too, am clever,' Jemba-Wa continued. 'Surely you understand that, given what you have seen of my creations.'

Lethbridge-Stewart frowned. 'Do you mean the robotic Yeti? I was given to believe the high lama of Det-Sen Monastery was the architect of their design.'

Jemba-Wa bridled, his steady pace around the room faltering. 'Padmasambhava was my patron.'

'He was your fellow prisoner, slave to the Intelligence.'

'He was a just and noble man,' Jemba-Wa said, anger flashing in his eyes. 'I know to whom he was sworn, and I am sworn to him as well.' He resumed pacing, but his eyes darted about self-consciously.

Lethbridge-Stewart pressed further. 'That's as may be, but do you know what it is, this master of yours? What it *really* is?'

129

'I know my faithful service will be rewarded in time,' Jemba-Wa retorted.

'In *time?*' Lethbridge-Stewart echoed. 'That thing has ripped you *from* your time, sir. Dropped you here to do its dirty work, and when it's finished, success or failure, it will abandon you to your fate. I have seen it happen more than once.'

'My Master seeks nothing less than the grand enlightenment of all people.'

'Good God, man, you're as deaf as you are blind!' Lethbridge-Stewart roared, shifting in his ropes to rise to his knees. 'Your master seeks the enslavement of all humankind! The eventual melding of every human mind into a single, gestalt consciousness. His path to enlightenment is drenched in the blood of good men and women.'

Jemba-Wa suddenly looked very old and frail indeed. 'I have been promised,' he said in a quiet voice.

'The Intelligence won't honour its promises to a mere human.'

Jemba-Wa's eyes grew more perturbed still.

Owain was completely lost.

First hearing, then seeing the rats boiling up from the subway entrance, like a living grey wave of teeth and glittering red eyes, had started him forward, wanting to help. But he was stopped cold by the thunder of all those guns and the fact that it did almost nothing to slow the oncoming horde. He saw Kramer and several others fall back, reloading, but at least three of the cops, misgauging the speed of the approaching multitude, failed to clear the top of the steps and were engulfed and dragged under. People began running for their lives, and Owain followed suit. He aimed for Times Square, or to his best estimate of where Times Square would be, but as more rats began to pour from sewer grates and drainage points in the street, he gave up on direction and purpose and simply ran. And ran.

He stumbled from alley to alley, darted across side streets, dodged the glare of sodium street lights to avoid making a target of himself. Drenched to the skin, the sheeting rain still obscuring his vision, he was certain every pool of darkness and clot of shadow held a new menace, and he found himself unable to control that base impulse: run. Run. *Run.*

Now the rain seemed to be letting up a bit, enough for him to make out the height of the buildings around him as he fled down another dark alley, his footfalls mostly lost in the thrumming rain. He glanced behind him, saw nothing in pursuit, and finally permitted himself to slow to a fast walk, chest heaving. He scooped his sodden hair out of his face, swept it back, and made to wipe his wet hands on his jeans... then laughed at himself as he realised they were even wetter than his palms.

If you manage to get through this night without being turned into a shambling drone of the Great Intelligence, it'll be a miracle, he chided himself. *Or if you can do it without being torn limb from limb.*

He emerged from the alley, looking about in confusion. No one on the street; just cars whizzing past, mostly taxis. Owain could still hear the din of honking horns in the distance behind him, and assumed the gridlock and chaos back there might soon begin to affect the surrounding streets, if it hadn't already done so.

Had he lost his pursuers?

Owain looked behind him again, and realised he could see nothing of the alley from which he'd emerged beyond a patch of yellow light reaching ten or fifteen feet in.

Somewhere ahead of him, there was a deep, animal grunt.

Owain snapped his head up, his eyes widening. He looked up and down the street. Nothing. Closed shops, passing yellow cabs, another shadowy alleyway opposite him, providing passage between what looked like a hole-in-the-wall record shop and a tattoo parlour. All his senses strained forward, but the sound was not repeated.

It was a car, shifting gears or something.

Something moved in the alley on the opposite side of the street.

Owain gasped, staggering where he stood.

It was one of the furless robot Yeti. Its massive, clawed feet struck the paving – *clud! clud! clud!* – as it stepped forward into the light, savage foreclaws clicking together. Its massive head seemed to cock to one side as it observed him from across the street, marking him. Claws clicked convulsively. One heavy leg twitched, seemed to paw the ground like a bull preparing to charge.

A flood of red-eyed rats swarmed out of the alley behind the Yeti. They crept and curled about its feet like cats seeking affection. Some climbed the massive metal shape the way their cousins had done with the Yeti underground. Owain could hear the repulsive things keening as they climbed swiftly and perched on the Yeti's shoulders, chest and forearms. He stiffened, intending to flee back into the alley from which he'd come.

But before he could move, the Yeti dropped to all fours and charged.

Owain just stood there, dumbfounded. He could see gleaming metal shifting like muscles, what appeared to be sophisticated hydraulic pistons whooshing as they powered its ungainly bulk. Its mighty claws chewed stone chunks out of the kerb as the Yeti leaped off the sidewalk's edge and into the street.

Roaring in triumph, it would close the distance between them in four great leaps.

Its roar was lost in the explosive shriek of air brakes.

The Yeti was in the middle of the street when the oncoming city bus – no timetable delays for *this* municipal worker – struck it sidelong. There was a crunch of metal, a boom of shattering glass, and the Yeti and its shrieking rat passengers were flung away into the rain. The behemoth flew forty feet, limbs windmilling, and slammed into the side of a parked car, which was lifted off its tyres by the impact, the windows blowing out in a glittering spray.

Owain blinked, stunned. The bus was still sliding to a stop, and he could see the shocked driver leaning up and over the smashed windscreen, trying to figure out what the hell he'd just slammed into. Some of the passengers were also on their feet, shouting in surprise. No injuries, as far as Owain could see, just indignation at having their ride home delayed. A pair of yellow taxis sped past the bus without slowing, horns blaring, one of the drivers, astonishingly, shaking a disgruntled fist as he blew past. Both cabs sent sprays of rainwater sheeting up and over the huddled shape of the Yeti, but neither stopped; never mind that they'd just witnessed a major traffic accident.

Ahh, New York, Owain thought, echoing his uncle's wryly cynical viewpoint. Then: *Why are you still standing here?*

He wiped rain from his face again. He started to turn right and head down the street, seeking some familiar sign that would lead him back to his friends, when a hand fell on his shoulder. Owain shouted and whirled, fists rising in defence.

It was Kramer.

'Oh my god!' he shouted. 'Are you trying to give me a bloody heart attack?'

She shook her head, looking past him at the idling, smashed bus – from which the driver was now emerging, hands on hips, shaking his head in exasperation – and at the motionless shape of the Yeti against the battered car.

'Is it dead?' Owain asked.

'I don't have the slightest idea,' Kramer said. 'What happened to you?'

Owain pointed back the way he'd come. 'Did you see my uncle?'

'Nothing else came out of the subway but rats.' Kramer gestured at the Yeti. 'And more of those. I shot my weapon empty and retreated to reload. We couldn't do anything, really. A handful of guns against thousands of rats? And a half-dozen metal monstrosities?' She gave a short, barking laugh with absolutely no humour in it. 'There was a time, you know, when I believed the worst thing we were dealing with was some kind of infectious plague.'

'It's a plague, all right,' Owain said quietly. 'Can you get us to the hospital from here?'

Kramer nodded. 'But you never did tell me about the team in the tunnel.'

Owain looked back at the crumpled shape in the street. 'You said nothing else came out but rats and Yeti. That should tell you everything you need to know.'

'But were they dead?'

Owain sighed. 'All right. I'll catch you up on the way. But let's go. It's not safe out here.'

Kramer started to say something else, but a scream interrupted her. Both of them whirled.

The bus driver was thrashing about, convulsing as if in the grip of a seizure, and Owain and Kramer saw to their horror that he was standing in a shifting, shivering mass of rats. The rest of the pack that had followed the Yeti out of the alley across the street. The sleek grey rodents swarmed up the man's legs and bit at his flailing hands as he hopped and shrieked and tried to knock them away.

He gave a final weak scream and fell over, twitching.

'Like the coma patients,' Kramer realised.

'Like the assault team,' Owain added.

More screams from the bus. Now they could see rats leaping up the steps and swarming inside, attacking the passengers.

'Come on,' Owain said. 'Before they decide we're next.' He began to run up the street. Kramer quickly fell in beside him.

As they passed the unmoving Yeti – which was surrounded by six or eight dead, smashed rats, Owain now saw – Kramer unholstered her pistol, keeping it ready. He was grateful to see it, but reflected on what she'd said before. He wondered how many rounds she could still have on hand.

And how many thousands of red-eyed vermin would be left once she ran out.

Before Lethbridge-Stewart could press his advantage, Jemba-Wa retook his seat in the wooden chair, facing his prisoners. He had regained his composure and regarded Sally and Lethbridge-Stewart coldly, hands folded in his lap.

Lethbridge-Stewart settled back as well. He sat with his bound ankles stretched out in front of him, flexing his tied hands behind his back. He'd realised when he lurched upright in anger that those knots weren't quite as tight as he'd initially imagined. He wondered if the old man himself had tied them up, those weary, gnarled fingers perhaps not quite up to the task.

He kept his eyes locked on Jemba-Wa, continuing to twist his wrists, further loosening the ropes binding them.

Careful, Sally mouthed.

But if the man was wilfully giving them this opening, Lethbridge-Stewart was determined to take it. Behind him, his wrists twisted and flexed, twisted and flexed. He was beginning to sweat, mainly from the effort involved in holding most of his body rigid as he worked on the ropes. It also made his head pound worse than ever.

'So,' he said gruffly, trying to stay focused. 'The last act of the Great Intelligence in 1935 was to push his surviving Tibetan forces forwards in time for another attempt?'

'Master Mahasamatman was silenced in Tibet,' Jemba-Wa said quietly. 'But in his eternal power, his older self, over thirty years hence, called out and brought us here to aid him once more.'

Thirty years hence, Lethbridge-Stewart considered as he continued to work at the rope. So, not the Intelligence encountered in Bledoe, but rather the one in the present. Why had it taken over thirty years to come back? Lethbridge-Stewart didn't know. Maybe it was important, maybe it wasn't.

Jemba-Wa leaned forward, eyes narrowing. 'Are you uncomfortable, or—?'

Lethbridge-Stewart's hands froze. He faltered. 'I—'

'So,' Sally said helpfully, 'the Great Intelligence opened the vortex here? Now? Well, before February at least.'

Jemba-Wa leaned back, looking at her, and shook his head. 'Preparing for what you call the London Event, assessing all potential outcomes, all possible futures, my Master called forth all the remaining Yeti I had created for Lama Padmasambhava, to emerge where and when needed. He was able to modify the Yeti brought from Tibet by Travers, but one Yeti was not enough, so more were needed from the past. A second force was safely hidden away until all was prepared here.' There was something else behind that smile, an old dark pain. 'And here we are.'

'Because the Great Intelligence knew it was destined to fail in London,' Lethbridge-Stewart said disdainfully.

'No, he—'

'It *was* defeated,' Lethbridge-Stewart pressed on. 'You may have missed the outcome, fleeing to America as you were, but I assure you, it was cast out. Control units smashed, web routed. Most of your lovingly crafted Yeti were destroyed in Cornwall, leaving you almost nothing for this latest doomed endeavour. A handful of Yeti? What can you do with that?'

'Perhaps you forget what happened to your attack force,' Jemba-Wa growled.

'Oh, yes. Cowardly ambush tactics may have worked once, but the forces now rallying against you are sure to be swift, relentless and overwhelming. Your master, lurking in you, will enjoy nothing but another defeat. That's a promise.'

A gold glint of fury blazed in their captor's eyes. He leaned forward with a low snarl, and backhanded Lethbridge-Stewart hard across the mouth.

Lethbridge-Stewart momentarily forgot all about freeing his hands. Frail or not, Jemba-Wa's hands worked well enough for certain tasks, it seemed. Lethbridge-Stewart blinked to clear his watering eyes, felt wetness on his chin; the blow had split his lower lip. It was swelling already. From the corner of his eye, he could see Sally straining against her bonds, furious even in her renewed fright. He nodded reassuringly to her, but didn't smile for fear of splitting the wounded lip further.

Jemba-Wa stared fixedly at him. 'You will come to regret your mockery,' he said. He rose, trembling. He was cradling his right hand, the one he'd used to strike his blow, in his left. Lethbridge-Stewart didn't think his split lip was the sole injury that blow had caused.

He is old indeed, he thought. *Older than he looks.* He decided to press a little further. 'If it could call creatures through time at will, it would have left you there, in comparative safety, to continue to do its bidding, turning out new Yeti and sending them through the vortex to fill its ranks. But it hasn't that kind of power anymore, has it?'

'His power has never been greater,' Jemba-Wa countered. His hands fell to his side, curling into fists.

'Alistair,' Sally gasped. Lethbridge-Stewart glanced at her, saw her shaking her head. She mouthed two words at him: *No more.*

Jemba-Wa abruptly turned away, seeming to gather himself. He started for the door, back straight, fingers uncurling. 'Enjoy your stay,' he called over his shoulder. 'When New York falls, Master Mahasamatman will be most pleased to show you the folly of your arrogance.'

When New York falls, Lethbridge-Stewart thought. He

believed he was beginning to understand, at least in part, what was happening here, though *how* it was being accomplished still confounded him. He risked one more question.

'Why New York, sir? Why here and now?'

Jemba-Wa put a hand on the doorknob. *No mystical power this time*, Lethbridge-Stewart noted. *Perhaps there are times when his master truly departs from him.*

Jemba-Wa looked back at them. Perhaps it was the deferential 'sir' that did it. Perhaps something else.

'Here I found what my Master needed.' He opened the door. The hallway beyond was empty. 'What we *both* needed,' he added.

He gave Sally a stiff bow, and departed without further comment, closing the door behind him. They heard it lock, heard his footfalls moving away.

Lethbridge-Stewart allowed himself to lean back and close his eyes. He blew frustrated air through his teeth, offered his fiancée a small smile. 'All right, darling?'

'Alistair, you nearly pushed him too far,' Sally said anxiously. 'He's clearly unbalanced.'

'Actually, I think the chap wants to unburden himself,' Lethbridge-Stewart pointed out. 'I think he's here against his will. Perhaps has *always* been held against his will. But being drawn out of his own time, brought here to this strange city…' He trailed off, recalling the discussion at *The Early Doors*. 'Travers did say he heard the stranger in the cave protest when the vortex caught him. *Screamed* in protest, in fact.'

'Travers?' Sally asked, puzzled. 'But he's in John o' Groats. Did you ring him there?'

Lethbridge-Stewart gave her a small smile. 'Not quite. I've quite a lot to catch you up on.' He hauled himself up once more and began to knee-walk over to her. 'I'll talk; you work on my bonds.'

CHAPTER ELEVEN
In Pursuit of Answers

BY THE TIME Owain and Kramer reached Manhattan General, it seemed as if all of New York City had run mad. Even through the steady rainfall, the acrid stench of fire-smoke lingered in the air. Distant screams and the occasional gunshot punctuated the discordant choir of alarms, which seemed to come from everywhere: police, fire, ambulances, emergency klaxons, car alarms. At least half a dozen crashed vehicles – among them taxis, an overturned panel truck and one gutted police car – were scattered outside the hospital's entrance. Fire licked up from a trashcan below and to the right of the stone staircase, but the homeless who had sheltered there were nowhere to be seen.

There were two dead bodies in the rain-puddled street.

Owain and Kramer were on the opposite side of the street from the hospital, huddled in a shadowy alley not far north of the hospital entrance. Kramer finished her recon, leaned back into the alley. She wiped rain from her face with her free hand, while the other still held her handgun.

Owain, close behind her, found a length of metal piping with a heavy copper fixture rusted in place at one end; it made a serviceable weapon. He was relieved he hadn't had use for arms yet. The swarms of rats had spread outwards from Times Square and Hell's Kitchen like locusts, and Yeti appeared to be moving to strategic points across the city – why, neither of them could say – but so far they'd made their trek without being accosted. Even the handful of opportunistic looters they encountered, already hard at work in the early hours of this strange invasion, relieving various businesses of their goods and merchandise, left the two of them alone. Owain supposed it was Kramer's gun more than his pipe that led them to that wise course of action.

'Maybe the emergency room entrance is drawing folks,' Kramer told him. 'But over on this side, it looks like the place is shut up tight.'

'Any rats?' he asked in a low voice, spitting rainwater. 'Yeti?'

Kramer shook her head. 'Not yet anyway. Or more likely they've been and gone.' She studied his drawn features cautiously. 'I do see a couple of bodies out there, though. Can you handle it?'

Owain nodded dismissively. 'I've seen bodies before.'

Kramer nodded, took another quick look around the corner, and led him into the street. They moved fast, but Owain had ample time to observe the nearest corpse, and to regret his defiant tone. It had been a woman, perhaps thirty, her face wracked with pain, her body twisted at a cruel angle. There was blood, but not as much as he would have expected, given that terrible, broken form. She lay between a pair of seared black tire marks which raked the paving for twenty unbroken yards. The car that had made them, clearly unable to stop before or after striking her, had skidded into the building near the alley from which they'd emerged. There it had burned, despite the rainstorm. Thin smoke still curled up. Staring at it, Owain realised the driver's mostly incinerated remains were trapped behind the wheel. And were those small, charred lumps on the exposed dash and crumpled hood burned rats? The smell, even from here, was pungent and sickly sweet. He shuddered, turned away.

The other body in the street wasn't actually a corpse. He was a boy of twelve or fourteen, sprawled in the gutter below the hospital steps, jeans and anorak sodden, galoshes pointing at the sky. He was unconscious, his breathing shallow to the point of imperceptibility, and rat-bit several times on the hands and face. Rainwater had pooled in the hollow of his throat where his sodden shirt had come unbuttoned, and more was collecting in the sunken orbits of his closed eyes.

Kramer went past, glancing down to assess the kid for herself. She grunted unhappily, indicated the yellow-grey pallor already visible in the coffee-coloured skin of the lad's face and hands, and told Owain that it was common to all the infected. There was a reluctant note in her voice, but still she hardly paused before mounting the steps to the big doors. There she waited for Owain, turning in a slow half-circle, gun at the ready, her dark eyes moving, always moving.

Trying to decide if she was cold by nature or just practical-minded, like Uncle Alistair, Owain stooped and gathered the child into his arms, lugging his dead weight up the wet steps. When Owain reached her, Kramer's penetrating eyes were on his, and that small, winning smile was back on her lips. *Just practical-minded*, he decided. He was glad. He liked Adrienne Kramer.

'You're a good man, Owain Vine,' she said quietly, as if she'd been reading his mind. He flushed, wondering if she'd been testing him, waiting to see whether he'd abandon the injured boy or see to his care. She put a hand on the right door's heavy push-bar. 'Now let's get inside before—'

From somewhere south of them there came the sonorous roar of a Yeti and the rapid cough of automatic weapons fire. A moment of quiet, then another lingering roar, louder still. It echoed across the deserted, rain-swept battleground below them, which had been an everyday Manhattan thoroughfare less than an hour earlier.

They traded a look. 'Come on,' Kramer hissed. She pushed, and the big door – blessedly unlocked – swung inward. Hefting the child, Owain followed her inside.

Behind them, the rain continued to pour down, and the city continued its descent into chaos.

Sally worked on Alistair's tied hands. She was getting closer, and she sensed him biting back the urge to tell her again to hurry. The ache in his head had subsided a bit, he'd assured her, as had the throbbing of his lip where Jemba-Wa had struck him, but she could hear the tension in his voice, clamping down on his words like a vice. She knew, as he did, that time might be very short indeed.

She shook her head in wonder at the story he'd shared with her.

'I'd say it's unimaginable, but when one has been kidnapped from a lush Manhattan hotel room by an eight-foot Yeti, it's no longer quite so difficult to grasp such things,' she said. 'Alistair, there's still something more to this. Our arrival was too coincidental. It can't just be about taking revenge.'

Alistair nodded. 'No, you're right. Whatever scheme the Intelligence is pursuing in New York, our arrival was just bad luck. For it, I mean. I only hope we've forced its hand, made it set its plan into motion before it was fully prepared.'

'Prepared for what?'

'I'm not sure yet, but I'd wager it all comes back to Lieutenant Kramer's coma victims. They seem to be acting as some sort of...'

'Stored energy system?' Sally suggested.

'Yes, I think you're right. Human batteries, from which the Intelligence may draw power and enact its will.'

'Why not do the same to Londoners *en masse* when it attacked the Underground?'

'It must have something to do with available resources,' Alistair said. 'Something besides the people. Something about the *place*. Something it had access to during this endeavour which it didn't have when it attacked London. I think the Intelligence found something here, or its man Jemba-Wa did anyway.'

'Damn!' Sally said, startling him, as the loosened rope slithered through her increasingly numb fingers. 'I'm sorry, Alistair. This is difficult to do one-handed.'

Alistair chuckled. 'No worries, my dear. It's only the safety of the free world at stake.'

She gave him a mock-glare he couldn't see from his position, and redoubled her efforts. A few moments later, she peeled back a fingernail all the way to the quick. It drew blood to the tender surface and tears to her eyes, but she blinked back the latter and said nothing of it. Instead, she pondered Jemba-Wa again, and found herself sympathising with the angry, imprisoned soul.

'That poor man was forced to come all this way,' she murmured.

Alistair grunted in agreement. 'Halfway around the planet, down an unimaginable channel of years. It's up to us to discover why.'

'Ah!' Sally exclaimed in relief and delight. 'Well, now's our chance.' He craned to look. Sally lifted the cord, pulling the loops free of his left hand. 'Be a love and undo the rest of your knots,' she said demurely, 'and then see about a lady's bonds, would you?'

In spite of the deceptive ghost-town quality of the street outside, there was no shortage of activity inside Manhattan General Hospital, Kramer was initially relieved to see. But as she and Owain stepped in, dripping on the already rain-spattered floor – and as Kramer holstered her weapon to avoid frightening those inside – her relief quickly turned to dismay as she grasped what a tumult of terror and confusion tonight's strange business had unleashed on the city.

Nurses, doctors and orderlies attended dozens of injured civilians. Doctor Supravhal and Nurse Joyner, both frazzled but still all business, were among those working briskly to set broken limbs, treat minor and major burns, and assess the condition of numerous unresponsive patients brought in by frantic family members and friends. At least four of these, Kramer could see, were comatose; more victims of attacks by the infected rats.

Lordy, she thought, *how big* is *this disaster?*

The broad foyer and crowded waiting area rang with shouted orders and cries of pain and distress. Overhead, the intercom crackled and buzzed nonstop, the white noise occasionally interrupted by blaring medical codes or exhortations for various specialists to come to different surgical bays or hospital rooms. It was sheer bedlam.

Kramer headed for the information desk, watching Owain carry the unconscious boy over to a bustling station beneath a big red 'Intake/Admissions' sign. He spoke quietly to a nurse, who called over a heavyset orderly. This bearded giant gently took the boy from Owain's arms, asking the young man a series of questions that Kramer couldn't hear and suspected Owain couldn't answer.

She did her best to persuade the flustered woman at the information desk to ascertain whether Lethbridge-Stewart or anyone else had left them a message. The harried woman, one phone receiver clamped between her chin and shoulder, another clenched in her hand and serving as an impromptu conductor's baton, waved Kramer off impatiently, bluntly suggesting she had more important things to do than handle *messages*.

Snorting in irritation, Kramer gave up. She caught Owain's eye and beckoned to him. Raising a finger to the orderly, he hurried over to her.

'They want the kid's contact information,' he said, bemused. 'I said I had no idea, so they asked for *my* contact information. I told them we're on holiday, and gave them the number at the hotel.'

'They probably want to bill you,' Kramer said.

'What?' Owain shook his head with a sigh. 'Oh, right. No NHS here.'

'We'll get it taken care of.' Kramer pointed at a door marked 'No Admittance'. 'Come on. There's someone upstairs we need to put in the picture.'

Owain began to follow Kramer, when someone whistled sharply. He looked around, braced for further hassle. It was the big orderly, all right, but to Owain's surprise the bearded man had settled the kid onto a wheeled gurney, clearly preparing to take him on to Receiving – and now he was smiling at Owain and holding up a pair of plush, pale-green towels. He winked and tossed them to Owain, who caught them nimbly, nodded his thanks, and pushed through the doors to find Kramer.

She was halfway up a flight of stairs, waiting for him. He hurried up the steps after her and handed her one of the towels.

'Thanks,' she said and began to scrub gratefully at her hair with it as she led him through another series of doors, all marked with the same 'No Admittance' label.

'Where are we going?' Owain asked, towelling rainwater from his own hair as he followed her. He was aware they were still leaving wet footprints as they went, but at least his head was warm for the first time in what felt like ages.

'Intensive care,' she said. 'Professor Travers should still be studying the first coma patients.'

'Anne's father is here? Why did he—' Owain stopped.

The end of his echoing footfalls made her turn back.

143

'Owain? Are you all right?'

'What are we going to do about Uncle Alistair and Aunt Sally?' he asked her abruptly.

Kramer put a hand briefly to his cheek. 'Don't worry. For one thing, it won't do any good. For another, your uncle can take care of himself; I've seen that for myself today. And I know Sally Wright. Right now, I'd wager whoever took her is wishing they'd broken into a different hotel room.' She curled her hands into cat claws, giving him a broad smile. He returned it gratefully. 'They'll be fine,' she finished. 'You with me?'

He told her yes, and she led him through the big doors into ICU.

Their ropes lay in coils on the floor, amid pieces of the disassembled wooden table that had previously stood empty by one wall of their cell.

Lethbridge-Stewart hefted one of the heavy wooden table legs. He handed another to Sally, whose knuckles went white as she raised it defensively. They had listened at the door leading to the hall for almost five minutes before deciding there was no one guarding them – it was just too quiet for man or Yeti out there – and they'd come to the shared conclusion that it hardly mattered anyway. They had to get out of here and put a stop to the Great Intelligence's deadly campaign. Either they'd succeed in making a run for it or they wouldn't, but standing there behind a locked door, doing nothing, only guaranteed they would fail.

Now Lethbridge-Stewart bade her get behind him. In one smooth motion he stepped forward and kicked out hard with one booted foot. There was a grinding snap. The entire door jumped and swung wide on protesting hinges, pieces of the cut-rate lock and handle mechanism flying.

Steeling himself for a response to the splintering crash, Lethbridge-Stewart planted both feet, raising the bat. He sensed Sally doing the same to his right.

Nothing. No noise in the hallway beyond. They were alone.

They traded hopeful glances and slipped out.

The hall extended away in both directions, empty. There were several more closed doors on their side, opposite a series of high, panelled windows. The latter were filthy, scummed over nearly to the point of opacity, but as Lethbridge-Stewart studied them, a flick of light briefly lit the smudged glass. He thought it was a wash of passing headlights, until the distant boom of thunder reached them. Outside, he realised, the rainstorm had finally come.

There were no other indicators in the hall of where they might be, no signs or familiar-looking furnishings, but as Lethbridge-Stewart turned right and began to move quietly down the corridor, Sally behind him and covering their backs, he found himself almost certain this was some kind of warehouse. The windows suggested it; they looked like the kissing cousins of those he'd seen in every other storehouse and large-scale cargo facility he'd ever had reason to visit.

He turned the knob on the next door down, yanked it open and moved swiftly into the darkened room, the table leg raised and ready to bludgeon any enemy he encountered. Once again, he felt Sally behind him, watching his blind side. Except the darkness in here was so nearly complete that *every* side was his blind side.

Well done, old boy, he chided himself silently. *You've already been ambushed in one dark room today. Try not to make a regular thing of it, eh?*

He groped, found a wall switch and flipped it – whatever it was used for, the place still had electricity – and saw they were in a business office of some kind, probably a paper-pushing middle manager's den judging from the rows of old filing cabinets crammed against every wall. There was a large, u-shaped antique desk centred in the back half of the room, a red leather chair tucked into its kneehole. The chair listed on old springs, its stuffing bursting in numerous places, and the desktop was empty and thickly coated with dust. The place was derelict.

A perfect place to stow away one's captives.

'Alistair,' Sally said quietly from the doorway.

He turned, followed her back into the hall. There were large double doors at the near end, the big swinging kind on pistons, designed to enable workers to easily push through in either direction, pushing heavy carts or bearing armloads of goods.

He and Sally exchanged a 'ready-steady-go' look, and pushed them open together. A hiss from the old hydraulic pistons, and they were standing all alone on a vast, concrete warehouse floor. High fluorescent beams lit the space in a series of tight circles, leaving cones of shadow that dotted the floor in regular dusky swatches. Enormous orange girders reached thirty feet overhead, anchoring a criss-crossed mesh of gantries, dolly cranes and automated lifts. The sprawling bay was empty except for a dozen or so shipping crates – large, rectangular metal cargo containers of the type Lethbridge-Stewart knew American dock workers called 'cans'. They'd been stacked three high against the far wall, which was nearly a hundred yards across the empty floor from where they stood. The roll-up door beside which the shipping crates were stacked was firmly closed.

'Abandoned,' Lethbridge-Stewart murmured. 'Damn.'

Thunder crashed down again, muted by the heavy walls and thick glass above and behind them. He became aware of the steady beat of the rain, a low, rapid-fire thrumming on the metal roof of the enormous building, its ominous underscore filling the air all around them.

'Where do you suppose we are?' Sally asked him.

'From what little I gleaned from the maps and city guide, it could be the Meatpacking District, southwest of Times Square,' Lethbridge-Stewart explained. 'But Hell's Kitchen seemed to be the centre of activity for the rats, and it's also where Detective Dawson was killed, so that's another likely possibility.' He shrugged. 'But it's a damned big city, and I'm sure there's no shortage of warehouses from one end to the other, so...'

Sally had just started to say something else, when she was interrupted by a grinding metal creak.

The bay door on the far side of the warehouse floor had begun to roll up in its track.

Lethbridge-Stewart touched Sally's arm. Wordlessly, the two of them darted back through the swinging doors, crouching there in the hallway. He caught the doors, stopping their slow, back-and-forth sway, and gently pushed the right one open a crack. Just enough to see the distant bay door complete its motion.

It was a pair of Yeti, standing in the broad entryway, silhouetted by some exterior security light. They were clearly rain-soaked, their fur hanging low and streaming water. It did not appear to affect them in any way; their big golden eyes glowed impassively as they tromped inside.

'Are they coming this way?' Sally asked anxiously. Her knuckles were paper-white as she clutched the table leg.

Lethbridge-Stewart frowned. 'Actually, they're not,' he whispered back.

The two Yeti walked perhaps a dozen paces inside. They stopped abruptly, leaned close as if conferring, and headed towards the stacked shipping crates. The nearer of the two reached out, pulling open one container's heavy metal door.

The resulting screech of old hinges made the huddled observers wince even from their distant hiding spot.

'What the devil—?' Lethbridge-Stewart breathed.

The Yeti walked into the shipping crate. Its claws re-emerged, grasping the edge of the container door, and pulled it most of the way shut again.

Distant thumps and bangs inside the metal container. Then silence once more.

Lethbridge-Stewart straightened up. He waited another moment, afraid this might be some sort of trap, then pushed through the doors. Sally followed. They hurried across the warehouse floor, trying their best to muffle their echoing footfalls, but were almost running when they reached the open roll-up bay door. Through it, they could see steady rainfall shimmering in the security light.

'Where did they go?' Sally asked.

Lethbridge-Stewart stepped up to the wall by the door and peered out.

It was a quayside warehouse, all right. More of the stacked crates towered over the water's edge. A small forklift was parked beside them, deep furrows of rust and the generally poor condition of the machine suggesting this wasn't the first time it had been forgotten in such a downpour. Beyond the containers was a barge of some kind – a garbage hauler, by the drifting stench – moored parallel to the wharf. It too appeared to be unattended, lit only by the security lights. In either direction, nothing else moved on the docks as far as he could see.

Beyond the barge, he could dimly make out a few ships gliding across the shivering surface of the river. Was it the Hudson? The East River? He could make out no landmarks on either side.

He cast a rueful eye upward. With the rain, he couldn't even get a fix on the stars. 'So much for all that Scouts orientation training,' he murmured wryly. 'One bloody rainstorm and we're lost in the deepest, darkest jungles of America. Complete with dangerous wildlife.'

Lethbridge-Stewart gave Sally a smile as he said this last, meaning it to sound off-handed, humorous, but she was too keyed up to respond in kind.

'We should get out of here, look for a way back downtown,' she urged him. 'From what Jemba-Wa told us, all hell could be breaking loose.'

'Quite.' Lethbridge-Stewart nodded, glancing beyond her at the stack of crates against the warehouse wall. 'One moment, darling,' he added, and moved quietly to the row of containers. The door the Yeti had entered still hung open a few inches, and he leaned forward, peering inside. 'Well, I'll be damned!' He pulled the door open, wincing at the groan of metal. It wasn't as loud as it had been when the Yeti tugged the door open – it hadn't been trying to muffle its actions – but it still caused Sally to let out a breath of shocked air. 'Sorry,' he offered. 'Come and take a look.'

She crossed to him, peered inside. Gasped.

There was a small, low-watt light affixed to the back wall of the container, throwing enough dim light out to clearly show them the large, ragged hole in the bottom of the crate about two-thirds of the way towards the back. It had been peeled upwards like tissue paper, with no thought given to finesse. The ragged edges had been stamped nearly flat to permit easier passage. Below the semi-circular gap, the diameter of which was easily half as wide again as the largest Yeti they'd seen, the stone floor of the warehouse had also been gouged away... and the rock and earth beneath that as well. The crate now hid a very large hole leading downwards. The head of a sturdy metal ladder protruded from it.

Wherever the two Yeti had come from, patrolling the

wharf or pursuing some new action on behalf of their disembodied master, they had gone down that ladder into the depths below.

'Alistair,' Sally breathed. 'Where do you suppose it goes?'

'Back to the subway line, I'd wager,' he said briskly. 'And I think that's pretty fair evidence we're still on Manhattan Island, likely not too far from our Tibetan friend's primary operations beneath Hell's Kitchen.' He loosened his belt as he spoke, and stuck the heavy table leg into it. It protruded at a funny angle, and for a moment made him look like the world's oldest play-acting boy, his pretend sword sheathed at his waist.

'Alistair, what—?' Sally began, already fearing she knew what was coming next.

He took her by the shoulders and kissed her. Deeply. When he released her, she blinked at him, smiling in spite of her consternation. 'I'm sorry I didn't do that when we first got free,' Lethbridge-Stewart said earnestly. 'Forgive me, Sally. It's sometimes hard for me, even in the best of circumstances, to put the soldier at ease and call up the husband-to-be, as it were. Nobody knows that better than you, I'm afraid, and I'm sorry for it.' She started to respond, but he shook his head. 'Listen, in case there's not much time. I'm going to follow the Yeti—'

'*No*, Alistair!'

'—and I want you to get out, stick to the shadows until you get a sense of where you are, then run for it. Find a police station or firehouse, if you can, or hail a taxi and get to the hospital, Manhattan General. Find Travers in intensive care there; I'm sure he'll still be on hand, studying the coma patients, unless something's drawn him away. And get in touch with Kramer and the police.'

To her credit, there were no tears, not even a glint of them. Dry-eyed but still visibly upset, she said in an even tone, 'I want to go with you.'

'It makes more sense to split up. I may be able to learn the Yeti's purpose underground, perhaps find out what drew them here in the first place. You can get to a phone, find Kramer, and very probably save lives.'

'Alistair—'

'Don't make me pull rank, Corporal.'

Sally's mouth snapped shut. Opened. Shut again. Colour flew into her cheeks and her eyes – still dry – now blazed. He could see her struggling with a number of possible retorts, waited silently to see which she'd settle on. Deep down, he regretted making such a blunt remark to the woman he'd pledged to marry, but first and foremost she was an NCO in the British Army, and he was her commanding officer. He would have used the same head-clearing tactic with any of his people back home – Bishop, for example, or even Samson or Dougie, both of whom had been friends of his for many long years. Fiancée or not, Sally was still a subordinate officer, still under his leadership, just like Lieutenant Bishop and Colonel Douglas. And this was no time to permit their personal relationship to interfere with their duty.

And underneath it all, there was the other, unspoken thing, the part he could not say aloud: *I will not risk her life.* No, he wouldn't. Not like he was about to risk his own, going into the hidden tunnel to pursue the Yeti. He knew it flew in the face of the very duty he'd just used to enforce his will with her. Knew it was biased and unfair.

But he was very fond of her, in his complex and difficult way. And he would not see her fall to these wretched miscreations the way so many had fallen before.

Here, he mused regretfully, *is a perfect example of why couples should not serve together.*

Sally acquiesced without another word of protest, but when she leaned forward to kiss him once again – to kiss him goodbye, perhaps – her mouth was cold on his. There was no anger in her eyes now. Only worry.

CHAPTER TWELVE
Danger Above, Danger Below

ONCE THEY'D determined there was no movement outside, no sign of Yeti waiting to ambush unsuspecting human trespassers, Sally darted away into the downpour. Lethbridge-Stewart permitted himself to linger in the doorway only a moment, looking after his fiancée until the darkness and the rain swallowed her up. He went back to the cargo container and slipped inside, the improvised bludgeon in his belt thumping against his left arm.

He stood over the hole leading down, considering, and assured himself he could hear nothing grunting or shifting in its shadowy depths. He descended swiftly.

The ladder went down twenty-five feet, where it was anchored to the flat wood top of a painter's rig. This descended another twenty-five feet via another ladder to the floor of the old tubular channel. There was no track at all in the shaft, and the accumulated bed of damp, compacted trash he stepped down on suggested it had been years, perhaps decades, since this tunnel had been used for any purpose at all. If it had ever served as a subway line at all, that time was long past.

Even so, emergency lights gleamed high on the curved walls every fifteen or twenty feet in either direction, their soft yellow glow revealing damp walls splotched with mildew and speckled with thick growths of fungus. Lethbridge-Stewart realised he could hear the steady drip of water, too; the relentless encroachment of the nearby river, he supposed. Colonies of bugs teemed on the walls and floor. Mostly fat black beetles, and occasional nests of large, brass-coloured cockroaches which fluttered their stiff, useless wings as he drew near. Not all of them scattered at his approach, either, clearly having forgotten any lingering fear of men. He stamped viciously at the most brazen of them, revolted. A few nasty crunches later and the roaches fled before his boot heels. Lesson learned.

To his left, the tunnel stretched away into the distance, running straight as far as Lethbridge-Stewart's eyes could discern in the hazy half-light. To his right, it continued just forty or fifty feet before curving sharply back to the right. He assumed it must double back there, perhaps cutting across this unnamed warehouse district and finishing up in another of those wide roundhouse chambers, like the one where Kresal's team had been ambushed.

Remembering that horrific scene, Lethbridge-Stewart took the heavy table leg from his belt. He considered a moment, and decided he would go left. He still had no sense of where he was in relation to the parts of the city he'd become familiar with, and he hoped his temporarily faulty sense of direction would soon improve thanks to some external aid or landmark. Until it did, he would have to rely solely on his keen instincts.

There was a distant, murine chittering and a flurry of faraway claws on metal. It seemed to come from beyond the sharp curve in the tunnel. It didn't sound like a lot of rats necessarily, but rats it definitely was, and the sound deepened his resolve. Left-hand channel it would be.

He started off at a brisk pace, swinging the improvised bat and staying attentive to the distant rodent noises. The screeching grew faint, and disappeared completely. He wasn't sorry about that.

He was, however, surprised there weren't *more* of the repugnant vermin around. He remembered how they'd poured into the roundhouse, engulfing the assault team, dropping off the attacking Yeti like parasites. Their role as vector for the infection was obvious, but there were still many unanswered questions.

Once more, he was caught up in a deadly, supernatural onslaught he wasn't properly equipped to deal with. Once more, good men had fallen while he stood helplessly by, fists clenched.

Once more, this callous, ruthless enemy had outfoxed him.

'For the moment,' Lethbridge-Stewart murmured. 'Only for the moment.'

There were no cabs. No cops. No one. The city that never sleeps may have still been awake, but as Sally Wright ran for her life, for *all* their lives, New York's human population was nowhere to be seen. She supposed people were huddled behind locked doors, waiting out the thunderstorm and the pestilent, screeching nightmare that had materialised with it. She envied them. She wished she could squirrel herself away too, somewhere safe and dry, until this was all over.

But that wasn't the British Army way, or the English way. It wasn't *her* way.

And Alistair was counting on her.

Running pell-mell through the rain, she'd discovered they were indeed in the Meatpacking District, in an area dotted with huge, mostly disused warehouses. She'd orientated herself, certain that at any moment she'd hear a protesting shout of alarm – or an inhuman, bestial roar – and set off southeast, aiming for the nearest cross streets where she could turn north toward Times Square. No one shouted for her to stop; no monstrous shapes loomed out of the rain to bar her way.

Sally ran and ran, silently thankful that her kidnappers had let her slip on her comfy plimsolls earlier, rather than the snappy new heels she'd bought expressly for this holiday.

Holiday. Oh yes, what a holiday.

He heard the Yeti before he saw them.

There was a rumbling howl from somewhere up the line in front of him. Lethbridge-Stewart froze, listening. The trickle of water had ceased, and there were no more rat sounds echoing back from the walls around him, but something was happening up ahead. The tunnel sloped downwards and to the left, obscuring his view. Whatever awaited him remained out of sight. For the moment.

There was a bitter, smoky tang on the air – old, hot machinery pushed too hard for too long – and below it another scent, cloying and sickly sweet. This second odour wasn't as thick as the acrid smoke, but it had its own stomach-turning metallic tinge. Lethbridge-Stewart's jaw clenched; he recognised the smell. He gripped the table leg tighter.

It was blood.

The empty taxi on the first main street she came to, keys still in the ignition, was a godsend. Less than ten minutes later, Sally left it parked among the scattered vehicles outside Manhattan General and raced inside. She pleaded with Nurse Joyner until the woman agreed to take her up to the coma ward.

Now she stood next to Owain in the small antechamber off the ICU, part utility access, part observation room. The heavy towel someone had given Sally to dry her hair was still draped around her shoulders. She crossed her arms, watching Professor Travers through the one-way glass as he assisted another nurse with the hourly check of the coma victims' vital signs.

Each patient lay staring upwards in the dimly lit room, their murmured chanting going on and on. The nurse went to each one, applied a blood pressure cuff and slipped a thermometer into his or her armpit. Travers took down the resulting data, writing each notation on the bedside clipboard of each respective victim.

Sally studied Travers' ruddy cheeks and mostly lineless, unshaven face, still fighting her disbelief. This healthy, middle-aged fellow had none of the tremors of the old man she knew from the UK, none of his absent-mindedness. His eyes were bright, his thick hair not yet faded to the colourless grey mop it would be reduced to over the course of years, his beard dark but short. Amazing. She dreaded the inevitable day when they had to explain it all to Anne; she could barely wrap her own head around the idea. Two versions of the same man. Anne's beloved father. One travelling his proper timeline and losing his mind, the other hale and hearty but… a paradox.

An enigma.

Adrienne came back into the small observation room, bringing two steaming cups of coffee. Nodding to Lieutenant Kramer, Owain excused himself, closing the antechamber door behind himself.

Sally gratefully accepted one of the warm coffee cups. She sipped, feeling the welcome jolt of sugar and caffeine, and smiled at her old friend. 'Thank you, Ade.'

Adrienne smiled. They drank in silence for a long moment, watching Travers and the nurse work.

'I've called the governor's office and my UN chief of security,' Adrienne explained. 'They're moving things along faster than I can do from here. We'll shortly have three battalions of regular Army and National Guard here from Fort Drum. They're also scrambling two special response companies from Fort Hamilton.'

A nod from Sally, her eyes far away. She'd stopped shivering from the ceaseless, drilling cold of the rain, but still felt chilled to the bone. The coffee was beginning to cut through it, though.

'So!' Adrienne said brightly, eyes flashing. 'When's the big day?'

Sally laughed. Her friend joined in briefly. 'Sorry,' Sally said. 'It's hard to remember to focus on such things when our lives seem to be nothing but this sort of madness anymore.' She cupped the coffee tightly in both hands, warming her fingers. 'We've talked about the spring, perhaps after the first thaw.' Her smile faded. She was thinking of Alistair's kiss in the warehouse, the one that had felt dangerously like a farewell.

Adrienne stepped closer. 'Hey. He'll be all right. He's going to come bursting in any minute. You wait and see.'

Sally laughed, tasting tears in her throat, and stubbornly forced them away again.

'Come on,' her friend said, pointing to chairs near the back of the room, tucked under a small, utilitarian table. 'Let's sit down for a few minutes. We'll be called back to saving the world soon enough. For now, I want to hear about your dress, your vows, the works.'

Smiling, knowing Adrienne was trying to take her mind off Alistair's rash journey under the city and welcoming her friend's thoughtfulness, Sally followed her.

Lethbridge-Stewart found the source of the smoky, bloody

stench. As the steep tunnel floor began to level off, he followed the echoing grunts and barks of the Yeti – soon joined by those of a second robotic giant and perhaps a third – and discovered a few hundred yards later that he was now walking in shallow water. The odours on the faint breeze also grew more unpleasant, and now he could see thin drifts of hazy blue smoke creeping upwards past him.

He slowed further, trying to minimize the splashing sound of his footsteps, and shortly found himself moving at a bare crawl around a gentle left curve in the tunnel as the visible, jointed bars of the tracks first grew narrow and glistening in the dark water and then disappeared altogether, submerged by the rising run-off.

Shortly, the water was calf-deep.

Then it was knee-deep.

Lethbridge-Stewart waded slowly around the curve, the water lapping at the sodden knees of his trousers, his free hand cupped over his nose and mouth to lessen the acrid taste of the smoky air. He realised, looking down at himself, that some darker, viscous fluid was also staining the material of his trousers. He briefly took it for oil, and then remembered the other stench in the air. That sharp, coppery smell.

A moment later, reaching the end of the long curve, he found the first two bodies.

They floated face-down in the water, which was nearly to mid-thigh. Two men in torn, blue-grey overalls stamped *M. T. A.* across the backs. Their flesh was ripped open in numerous places as well, leaving the water dark with spilled blood. Lethbridge-Stewart could see it through the floating blond hair of the nearest of the two bodies, dyed a temporary shade of red by the tainted water. The other still wore his regulation hard hat, its pale light creating a murky reddish glow around his bobbing corpse.

Lethbridge-Stewart was relieved he could not see their faces. They were civilians, but there were no infectious rat bites for these poor chaps. The agents of the Intelligence had merely cut them down as if *they* were the vermin in the system.

He raised his head. The tunnel continued into the distance, but the smoke obscured it some thirty or forty feet down. Halfway to that point stood a recessed area in the tunnel's right wall containing a double-wide doorway. The door was smashed open, and the smoke in the tunnel was wafting lazily out of this chamber.

He carefully skirted the two dead MTA workers, wading purposefully towards the doorway. There was another dead man half-in and half-out of it, brutally slashed and thrown aside like his co-workers, a curving fan of his blood arcing up the length of the broad, dented door like a primitive work of sanguinary modern art. The sight of it made Lethbridge-Stewart bite back a snarl of rage. Beneath the blood spray, a metal sign bolted to the door identified the chamber as 'Primary Hydropump Station 6M West Hudson'. Another, smaller sign beneath that one denoted the facility was under MTA authority. Authorised personnel only.

Careful not to audibly splash the bloody, swirling water, already certain that what he would find inside the pump station would hardly constitute authorised personnel, Lethbridge-Stewart reached the door and peered around the edge.

Inside the chamber, perhaps ten or fifteen feet away from the door, with their backs to it, water a third of the way up their legs, were two of the furless Yeti. They appeared to be surveying the damage they had wrought. Their massive claws had made short work of the pumping machinery just as they'd done the workers monitoring it. The banks of equipment were smoking ruins, the massive sump baskets and intricate switching mechanisms wrenched free of their connectors and dashed to pieces against the stone walls. Sparks flew, and smoke continued to laze its way upwards, meandering out the door. The sound of trickling water grew louder still, becoming a steady stream.

Recognising the electrocution risk, Lethbridge-Stewart wondered briefly why they hadn't moved on once the damage was done; then he realised that they must serve a second purpose here: guarding the water-evacuation station in case other city workers detected the loss to the system and sent backup crews to effect repairs. Or sent security teams to deal with the saboteurs. The Yeti could effectively guard both the entryway where he was now crouched and the heavy, wrought-iron ladder he could now make out in an alcove beyond the smashed and smoking machines.

Lethbridge-Stewart's eyes lingered there, on the alcove and the ladder. 'Emergency Exit', the sign beside the ladder said. 'No street egress without keys'.

He briefly wondered which of the unfortunate workers had possessed the key. Much good it had done him. Lethbridge-Stewart looked down at the table leg in his hands, knowing it wasn't remotely what he needed to deal with these murderous trespassers. Perhaps he could draw them away, make a run for one of the subway platforms and lead them out where they'd encounter armed responders.

No, damn it. He couldn't count on what was happening in the city overhead, and certainly couldn't count on stumbling across the right exit and finding them ready to tackle the Yeti menace. At most, he'd stumble into cops pulling no-entry duty outside a subway entrance, and he'd surely just get them killed.

All that was moot anyway. The water here was far too deep to gain any running speed. They'd be on him before he made it fifty yards. *Damn it all!*

His train of thought was interrupted by a distant klaxon – surely a response to the rising water in the subway line. He ducked back around the corner of the tunnel wall as the Yeti, alerted by the noise, turned to look towards the open door. Wincing, Lethbridge-Stewart briefly closed his eyes, wondering if it had all come to nothing. He raised the crude club once more, waiting for the Yeti to appear in the doorway.

'Oh, no, no, no,' said a voice behind him. 'This is not right at all.'

He whirled.

Jemba-Wa stood there, pointing a compact silver handgun at him. He'd clearly used the sound of the running water and the distant klaxons to his advantage, sneaking up behind Lethbridge-Stewart.

'They were only supposed to secure the facility, not destroy it outright,' Jemba-Wa continued in dismay, stepping closer but wisely keeping out of Lethbridge-Stewart's reach. 'We don't want the city permanently ruined, after all. Hands up, please.'

Lethbridge-Stewart raised his hands, gripping the table

leg in both of them like a rifle he wanted to keep clear of the rising flood. He frowned as more pieces fell into place. 'The Yeti are shutting down or destroying all the pumps beneath Manhattan. The tunnels will flood, like Kresal said, right up to the subway entrances.'

Jemba-Wa nodded. 'Within twenty-four hours the subways will be completely underwater, driving an estimated four to six million rats into the city above.' He shrugged. 'I wonder how many of them are infected. Ten percent? Twenty?'

Lethbridge-Stewart went pale. Four hundred thousand toxic rats about to attack. Maybe *six* hundred thousand. The thought enraged him. 'Think of the pump workers, man, not to mention the poor devils who *live* down here! You can't—'

As if in answer, the long metal claws of a Yeti settled on his shoulder. It clamped down. Hard. He winced as the nerves cried out and then went numb. The table leg dropped from his hands, splashing into the bloody water.

'Unavoidable casualties,' Jemba-Wa said, coldly eyeing the silent Yeti behind Lethbridge-Stewart. 'Means to an end.'

But as Jemba-Wa spoke, Lethbridge-Stewart saw his eyes flutter and dart to the left. *Classic indicators of deception or equivocation*, he thought.

'You're a maniac,' Lethbridge-Stewart growled.

Jemba-Wa blinked in surprise and shook his head, hiding whatever guilt he might harbour beneath a stubborn pride that sickened Lethbridge-Stewart.

'I am my Master's good and faithful servant,' Jemba-Wa said. 'Let's take a walk, shall we? It won't be long before this entire tunnel is submerged, and I suggest we continue on to our next stop before that happens.'

Both Yeti crowded close behind him now, and Lethbridge-Stewart realised he had no choice. He was once more a prisoner of the Great Intelligence.

Travers looked around in dismay at the ceaselessly murmuring sleepers in their ICU beds. He glanced at the tray of hypodermic needles on the night table next to Mrs Hagerstrom's bed. He hoped the chanting wouldn't continue so long they'd have to resort to sedating the lot of them. Who knew what a sedative might do to them in their current condition?

He bent over Mrs Hagerstrom, whose voice had deteriorated to a mere whisper. 'Hold on, my dear,' he said thoughtfully. 'We'll see what we can do about that dry throat.'

Wondering if she might accept a sip of water, he started to cross to the back of the room, knowing there would be a small, ice-choked water jug and a stack of paper cups sitting on the long counter. And that was the first time he noticed Owain Vine, standing in the shadows near the ICU's door, watching him mutely.

'Goodness!' Travers gasped, jerking to a halt. 'When did you come in, my boy?'

Owain walked forward, hands in his pockets, head cocked as he peered around at the chanting sleepers. 'Is it true you were brought here from 1935?' he asked.

Travers opened his mouth. Closed it again. *Where had* that *come from?*

'Uncle Alistair told me,' Owain said. 'It's fascinating, really. I know your daughter, a little. I met your uncle once, well sort of. Ben Travers.'

'Ben...?' Travers thought on that for a moment. 'Now steady on, my uncle Ben died when I was a child. How did...?'

'Time travel, of a type.' Owain glanced over at the big mirror, behind which Travers imagined Lieutenant Kramer and Sally were still catching up.

Owain turned back to Travers. Travers cleared his throat. 'Yes, well, time travel makes for a long, strange journey, but I sense it's coming to an end,' he said.

The young man nodded, and moved toward the bed next to Mrs Hagerstrom's. Travers watched his head turn slowly, taking in the full contingent of chanting, staring patients.

'So many of them,' Owain said.

Travers murmured noncommittally, but did not elaborate. Owain's gaze fell on a twenty-year-old bicycle messenger in the bed next to the old woman. His chart identified him as Pat Damiani. Pat glared at the ceiling, eyes unfocused, chattering in that alien tongue as if he'd spoken it all his life. Owain shook his head in dismay.

Travers nodded sympathetically. The nurse had told him

young Pat's father had begged to see him every day for the first two weeks after he'd been brought in. The poor man had been rebuffed time and again by hospital security. Eventually, he'd settled for having his son's favourite bedside lamp placed on his night table, alongside a framed photograph of the Damiani family; his sister Rachael, and their mother Sarah. The man had pleaded so insistently that the hospital staff finally relented.

There was some small hope the items might spark a reaction, the nurse told Travers, but so far, that hadn't happened. No one had ever plugged in the lamp, a heavy brass thing with a tall cream lampshade, its faux-copper base carved to depict a Wild West scene: cowboys twirling lariats, stampeding horses.

The father's gesture had touched Travers, making him think of the son he'd not yet brought into the world. From his point of view, at least.

All around them, the urgent, tuneless rhythm of the chant continued.

'Do you know what's happening to them?' Owain asked. 'What this chanting means?'

Travers shook his head. 'How I wish I understood,' he admitted. 'Lieutenant Kramer is right about the source of their malady; each has been the victim of at least one deep bite, all bearing the characteristics of a rat or rodent.' He gave a deep sigh. 'Alas, for all my studies tonight, I don't yet know enough to alleviate their condition, let alone help Kramer and Lethbridge-Stewart thwart the plans of the Great Intelligence, whatever they may prove to be. This just isn't my field. I was always planning to expand my scientific studies beyond anthropology upon returning to England, but things haven't quite worked out that way.'

As Travers spoke, Owain stepped quietly around the side of Pat Damiani's bed, drawing closer to the man. Wholly caught up in his observations, Travers stood with his back turned, seemingly oblivious to Owain's advance. One of the professor's hands came out of his pocket and gestured briefly. Then he rested it on Mrs Hagerstrom's bed table, fingers drumming restlessly.

Owain hardly noticed this. His head was a maelstrom of noise. The noise told him what to do next.

He reached out, wrapping his right hand around the shaft of the unplugged lamp on the Damiani youth's bed table. He took another silent half-step toward Travers.

The chanting suddenly increased in volume.

Owain winced as if struck with sudden agony. He put his left hand to his temple, while its mate shakily returned the lamp to the night stand. He opened his mouth and drew a shuddering breath, as if his sinuses had abruptly been plugged, his airway restricted. The noise. The pain. This all-encompassing *pain*...

When he opened his eyes again, Professor Travers had turned to face him, regarding him with cautious, perhaps suspicious, eyes.

'Are you all right, young man?'

Owain shook his head. 'I– I don't—' The noise had departed. He found he was hardly able to recall how it had felt, or what it had compelled him to do.

He realised his hand was still hovering near the lamp – what in God's name had he intended to do with *that*? – and he jerked it away as if the lamp were scalding hot. Travers' eyes flicked to the lamp. Back to Owain's face.

'Is everything okay in here?'

Owain turned to see Kramer and Sally enter. The two of them were looking at him with the same inquiring concern as Travers.

'Fine,' Owain said huskily. 'Why are you looking at me like—'

And that was when Travers, who had covertly lifted one of the hypodermics from the tray by Mrs Hagerstrom's bed, stepped up behind Owain and sank the sharp needle into the side of his neck.

CHAPTER THIRTEEN
I Want Your Minds

SALLY WATCHED pensively as Adrienne helped Professor Travers secure the moaning, semi-conscious Owain onto a gurney in the coma patients' room. 'I'm glad you were watching him through that window, Adrienne,' she said.

Adrienne's eyes were wide with shock and confusion. 'I don't understand,' she said, stepping back. 'Is he... possessed?'

'A crude term for an ability we simply don't know much about yet,' Travers said. 'And if he *was* being controlled, it wasn't total. Owain could have done me considerable damage when he first came in, before I suspected something was... off. But he didn't. It's almost as if he's struggling with whatever influence is fighting to control him. Consciously or unconsciously.' He considered for a moment. 'Or perhaps the control itself is unfocused. Whatever power is being channelled through him, maybe its source isn't aware that young Owain is a conduit.'

Sally thought about what Alistair had told her about Owain's history (or was that destiny?) with the Great Intelligence, and wondered if that last notion was even possible. She wrestled with what to share with the others about Owain's past, and *whether* to share it with them. She didn't want to permanently colour their opinion of the young man, who meant so much to her fiancé. Once again, she wished mightily that he'd walk in and take charge, if only to make uncomfortable decisions like this one himself.

Together, Travers and Adrienne quickly looked Owain over, checking his bare skin front and back, rolling up the sleeves and legs of his scrubs.

No rat bites.

As they finished, Owain's eyes suddenly snapped open, and they all gasped. His eyes had turned the same glowing, yellow colour as those of the other patients. He moaned. After a moment, his eyes slipped shut again, cutting off that malevolent glow. The three of them exchanged a look.

'I don't believe it's the same condition, despite some superficial similarities,' Travers pronounced. 'Owain's not a victim of infection.'

'How long will that shot you gave him keep him incapacitated?' Sally asked.

'Not long. The nurses were keeping those hypodermics handy with a fast-acting sedative in case the patients grew violent, but I think it'll wear off fairly... fairly...' Travers looked around, eyes wide. 'Fairly quickly,' he finished.

Sally and Adrienne looked at each other, puzzled. Then they too saw it.

All seventeen of the coma patients were sitting up in their beds, heads swivelling on their necks, their glowing yellow eyes staring raptly at Owain.

They moved steadily along, and came across a subtle rise in the tracks which left the swirling water behind them, making it easier for Lethbridge-Stewart to move. The water was still rising, he knew; he could see evidence of that all around him in shining trickles on walls and small, moving streams on the tunnel floor. He thought of the water running in freely from the Hudson and East Rivers, no longer held at bay by the pump systems. He was no expert but had spent more time in the London Underground than he would have liked, and he could well imagine how much worse it would be in a city the size of New York. The water would continue to rise, flooding the tunnels beneath the city. He shuddered at the thought, and hoped anyone caught underground would be able to escape in time.

Water streamed down their lower legs as the Yeti marched, and that heavy *clud! clud! clud!* sound of their passing had returned as they stomped across the damp but mostly bare tracks at this point. There was a twittering hum from their control spheres, glowing brightly in the centre of their abdomens. They turned to one another, seeming to commune wordlessly, then dropped to all fours, galloping away through the tunnel like great, metal panthers. Their speed was astounding, the pistoning metal-works strangely beautiful as they gathered speed and bulleted away.

Lethbridge-Stewart imagined this latest iteration of the Yeti would prove the deadliest yet in direct combat. His heart sank further. He hoped Sally had made it to safety from where they'd been held, but now regretted the heavily one-sided fight that was sure to come if she and Kramer called up military and police responders.

There had to be something else he could do to warn or aid them. He knew under the right circumstances he could easily disarm Jemba-Wa; the Tibetan was bright-eyed and fairly agile for his apparent age, but he was still just one man, and Lethbridge-Stewart had trained exhaustively in such tactics over the years.

But the little man was no fool, either. He kept the gun trained unwaveringly on Lethbridge-Stewart and kept at least a body's length between the two of them, making it well-nigh on impossible for Lethbridge-Stewart to dart at him and wrest the gun away without catching a bullet in the lung or liver for his trouble.

So he walked on in the direction Jemba-Wa indicated. And watched for a chance.

Keep him talking, he thought. *He seemed willing to share information before.*

'Not a lot of water moving through here yet. You may need to adjust your timetable, old chap,' he said in his usual brisk, cheerful tone.

'Do not concern yourself,' Jemba-Wa said. 'All twelve primary pumping stations will soon be under my master's control. As will Manhattan's population, once the rats pour forth. They will invade homes, businesses, places of worship. There will be no sanctuary. Even those not yet infected will be threats, disease-carriers.' He paused, swallowed as if tasting something distasteful. 'And they will be *hungry*. But the infected ones, they are the real purpose here.'

Lethbridge-Stewart slowed, turned to face Jemba-Wa, wanting to implore him to see reason. Jemba-Wa halted as well, raising the gun, eyes narrowing sharply. Lethbridge-Stewart sighed, putting his hands out, palms up, to show he intended no assault, and continued walking. The other lingered for a moment, letting the gap between them increase marginally, and then followed.

They moved past a side tunnel, where the tracks diverged and a second line curved away into the distance, descending as it went. It was no doubt already partly submerged. Lethbridge-Stewart thought he could already hear the distant splash of rising water down there. A moment later, the triumphant roar of a Yeti from down there was unmistakable. He winced.

Hold steady, old man, he thought. *Keep him talking.*

'You know, it didn't escape my attention earlier that you're very keen to return home,' he said, once more trying for that jocular, old-men-telling-war-stories-in-the-pub tone. 'Can't say as I blame you. It's a bit too much city for my taste as well.'

No response, but Lethbridge-Stewart fancied he could feel the old man watching him cautiously. And he was sure the gun was still trained at his midsection.

There was a rustling sound. Lethbridge-Stewart looked around for its source. His gaze dropped to the tracks, and he couldn't help but start in surprise and revulsion.

Hundreds upon hundreds of rats, some mere kits, some full-grown adults eighteen inches in length, had begun passing on either side of them, running as fast as their tiny legs would go. The tunnel floor was abruptly swarming with them. The mass of vermin ignored the two humans, steering well clear of their striding legs, but neither did they seem the least bit afraid. Most seemed to have ordinary pink-red eyes, but Lethbridge-Stewart couldn't be sure about the whole pack, or swarm, or whatever the collective noun for rats was. He supposed there must be at least some among them that harboured the infection. Whatever the case, they hurried on, streaming away into the next side tunnel like their own lethal flood.

After a moment that whispering sound diminished. Died out altogether.

My god, Lethbridge-Stewart thought, trying to control his

breathing. *That's happening all over the subway system.* The *stink* of them, and the proximity.

He wanted to pant. Wanted to spit.

Thousands, he thought. *Hundreds of thousands. Filthy with disease, and every one of them seeking a way out. A way* up.

Lethbridge-Stewart could sense Jemba-Wa's mocking smile behind him. He refused to look at the old man. Cold sweat was beading on his forehead, but he resisted the urge to wipe it away. He wouldn't give his captor the satisfaction.

Instead, he went back to his previous line of inquiry, forcing his mind away from the rats and back to those pub stools, the pint mugs. He felt the smile come back into his own voice as he said, 'Yes indeed, a bit too much city for men of refinement, eh? Men of class and civility. How you must long for your home. Your people.'

Silence from Jemba-Wa. Lethbridge-Stewart knew the old man's scornful grin would be fading away, and he took savage satisfaction in it. 'But I say, old chap,' he went on, 'it occurs to me you never did get to elaborate on what it was that brought you here. Before, I mean. During our chat in the warehouse. You told my fiancée and me that you found what you needed in the city.'

'What my Master needed,' Jemba-Wa shot back hoarsely.

'I believe you said it was something you *both* needed. Running a little game of your own, eh? Setting aside something for retirement?'

Silence behind him as Jemba-Wa seemed to struggle with an answer. Lethbridge-Stewart merely walked on. Around them, more subway lines split off from the main tunnel, arteries to carry the Yeti, the rats and the relentless, rising water across Manhattan. Locking down the city. Rendering it helpless to the coming attack.

Behind him, voice fraught with pain, Jemba-Wa murmured, 'I just want to go home.'

Lethbridge-Stewart stopped, regarding his captor with as much sympathy as he could muster. Jemba-Wa halted too, eyes narrowing suspiciously, the gun pointed unwaveringly at his enemy's sternum. Ignoring it, eyes steady on the old man's face, Lethbridge-Stewart calculated. There was still a six-foot gap between them. Too far to try for the weapon.

'We can find a way to get you home,' he said evenly.

'No, you can't. What do you know of time travel? No, you cannot, but I can.'

Lethbridge-Stewart knew there were ways; he'd witnessed a couple. 'Believe it or not, time travel isn't completely outside my experience,' he said. 'There are means. We can pursue avenues of research to get you back to your own time.'

Jemba-Wa abruptly waved the gun around the tunnel. 'This is how I go home!' he shouted, eyes blazing – but not blazing yellow, Lethbridge-Stewart saw. 'I regret what must be done, but I was promised! *Promised!* And I… am going… home!'

Lethbridge-Stewart raised his open hands once more, trying to calm the man. 'If you regret it, can't you accept our help in pursuing an alternative path?'

'It is beyond my control.'

'Beyond your control?' Lethbridge-Stewart scoffed. 'I doubt that. But even so, it is well within your responsibility, sir. You are a human being, not a puppet. You made the Yeti, you said. You helped guide them here. You powered them in a new way, updating the control spheres that altered their physical forms once again. You are responsible, man!'

Jemba-Wa's jaw twitched. His face sagged with exhaustion. Perhaps even guilt.

'Let us help you,' Lethbridge-Stewart repeated. 'It isn't out of the realm of possibility for us to return you to 1935. You could live out your days in—'

Jemba-Wa laughed bitterly. 'What makes you so certain 1935 is my objective?'

Lethbridge-Stewart began to respond, but closed his mouth again.

'I was just nineteen when Master Mahasamatman found me, tending sheep near my village in the Nyainqêntanglha mountain range. The outside world was like a dream to us there. It was the year 1706, and when my work for the Master is finished, that is where and when I will ask him to send me. As my reward.'

The coma patients abruptly sank back in their sets, their preternatural awareness fading once more. The chanting ceased for the time being.

And Owain opened his eyes.

Sally, standing over him, gasped. No yellow. 'Professor!' she called.

Adrienne and Travers joined Sally, who started stroking the young man's damp forehead. They traded a stunned look.

'What happened?' Owain asked weakly. He glanced down at himself. 'Am I tied…? Why am I tied to this bed?' He went limp, eyes going to the ceiling. 'Oh my god,' he murmured. 'Professor, I am so sorry!'

'Nonsense, my boy,' Travers said dismissively. 'You cannot be held responsible for—'

'You're wrong,' Owain said bitterly. 'I think I *am* responsible.'

'What do you mean?' Adrienne asked.

He told them quickly about his adventure that had led him to the hospital. 'I was trying to help Uncle Alistair,' he added. 'Only I think I alerted something else to my being here. I think I made a connection with the Great Intelligence.'

Sally swallowed, and considered the dumbfounded looks on Adrienne and Travers' faces. She couldn't blame them.

Lethbridge-Stewart was stunned by Jemba-Wa's revelation, and his longevity. 'What's done is done,' he told the old man in an even voice. 'You don't have to remain its tool. Its slave.'

Jemba-Wa blinked at him.

'Tell me what it's doing,' Lethbridge-Stewart tried again. 'The Great Intelligence survived its downfall in London. And now it's using completely different means in its quest for power. What is it *doing* here?'

Jemba-Wa looked away. He seemed to be searching himself, perhaps weighing the truth against the rancour of the Intelligence for telling it. *Or maybe he's trying to ascertain the proximity and external engagement of the Intelligence itself,* Lethbridge-Stewart thought, remembering how the future Intelligence had been weakened by spreading its influence too widely in Cornwall. *Wondering whether it can hear him in its currently occupied state. Whether it can* punish *him.*

'Talk to me, sir,' Lethbridge-Stewart said. 'We are running out of time.'

Jemba-Wa sighed. All the long centuries of futility and lonely isolation seemed caught up in that sound. 'In London, after their encounter in Tibet, Master Mahasamatman sought to increase his power a hundredfold by extracting the mental energy of a most... unique alien mind,' he said. 'There is no other like it on your world.'

Lethbridge-Stewart nodded. 'I know the fellow you speak of,' he said, smiling tightly. 'I wish he were here.' He frowned. 'The rats. The infection. The coma patients... I think I understand. With that original avenue closed, that *unique alien mind* lost to it, the Intelligence now thinks several thousand ordinary *human* minds should suffice in its place, is that it?'

Jemba-Wa looked startled. Considered. Let it turn to a bitter smile. 'You grossly underestimate your ageless ally, rambling the corridors of space and time in his idiot box. Or perhaps you *overestimate* the average human mind, as so many tend to do. Several thousand dull human minds to replace that magnificent alien consciousness? They wouldn't come close. But a *million* might do.'

Staring at the man, Lethbridge-Stewart was struck dumb with horror. He could think of nothing to say in response.

The little man's eyes flashed mystically, brightening into that plague-like yellow.

It hadn't been so very far away at all, Lethbridge-Stewart realised.

'Now do you understand?' the Great Intelligence asked him through Jemba-Wa's mouth, making its hostage take an involuntary step back.

Behind him, over the sound of gushing water, Lethbridge-Stewart could hear the familiar *clud! clud! clud!* of approaching Yeti, and his heart sank.

'I want your minds,' the Intelligence said with triumphant satisfaction. 'All of them.'

Sally blanched, thinking of what Alistair had told her of Owain's destiny. Then she remembered Jemba-Wa breaking off during his interrogation of her, whispering, *'Immense power!'* What Owain had long feared seemed to be happening here. Now.

She patted Owain's arm. 'Tell them,' she said. 'It's okay.'

He lowered his head, ashamed, then raised it. With Sally's reassuring hand on his arm, he quickly told the others about Cornwall. About his brother Lewis. About Remington Manor, haunted by a future remnant of the Great Intelligence. About its hunger to connect with him, even as it sought to destroy Lethbridge-Stewart.

He did not mention destiny. He did not mention the name Mahasamatman. These things he kept to himself.

Sally decided it was enough. She squeezed his arm encouragingly, smiling at him. Owain's head hung low, his cheeks burning. But when he looked up, his eyes were bright. 'I don't know how fully aware it is that I'm here, that I've been tapping into its energy, but I think it might be able to...' He faltered, then groaned. 'I'm such a fool! I tried to sense it. In the tunnels when I knew Uncle Alistair was in danger.'

Travers grunted. 'That's a door that swings both ways, yes?'

Owain nodded.

'You're saying it sensed Owain the way Owain sensed it,' Sally said.

Travers shook his head. 'That was unfocused malice. Unharnessed negative energy enhanced by the infected sleepers. Completely beyond Owain's control.'

'Can it take him over if it *does* zero in on him?' Adrienne asked.

As Sally patted Owain's shoulder reassuringly again, Travers pondered. 'That may be its goal, yes. To enter him. Use him as a weapon. Or... Or...'

He trailed off, as if something else, something even more troubling, had occurred to him. Sally gestured for him to go on, but he shook his head. 'No, I'm just postulating here.' He smiled at Owain. 'As I said before, if you were truly a guided instrument of the Intelligence, my boy, I would almost surely be dead. And as we can see, that is not currently the case.'

Owain nodded gratefully.

Sally looked at Travers, then turned to regard Adrienne. 'At any rate, it's worse than just knowing Owain's here. I think it knows now that we're *all* here. The Intelligence sees us as a threat. And perhaps Owain as an opportunity. Are you still armed?'

'Check,' Adrienne, patting her sidearm. 'We about to have company, you think?'

Sally nodded. 'We should set up defences, find a way to keep them out.'

Travers waved a hand at the other sleepers. 'We have to protect these poor souls,' he said fiercely. 'And particularly that of this boy!'

I'm not a boy, Owain thought dizzily. He closed his eyes once more, and tried to close his mind as well. Even now, though, he could feel the Intelligence out there in the ether, restless, like phantom hands riffling through the card catalogue of living minds across this sector of the city. He knew it was searching for him, but sensed it still hadn't quite put it all together. It was still somehow blind, despite the presence of the coma patients.

Jemba-Wa wavered, gasping. All at once he had become completely unsteady on his feet. Gun or no, Lethbridge-Stewart rushed forward to catch him before he could spill over backwards, cracking his skull on the track or the wall.

The little man was light as a feather. There was a brief, stuttering flash of yellow light in Jemba-Wa's eyes, like a signal gone erratic, blocked at the source. Then the light was gone altogether. Only the old man's ordinary, ice-chip eyes stared back at Lethbridge-Stewart.

Jemba-Wa looked down at the gun as if truly seeing it for the first time, looked back up excitedly at Lethbridge-Stewart. 'He's gone,' he whispered.

'What?'

'*He's gone!*' Jemba-Wa steadied himself, pushed the handgun into Lethbridge-Stewart's palm, and turned to push him down the tunnel the way they'd come. 'The Master's power is gone. Something else has commanded his full attention.'

Lethbridge-Stewart gawped in confusion, looking down at the gun. Beyond Jemba-Wa, he could see two Yeti tromping up the corridor towards them. Perhaps his captor had been planning to hand him off; perhaps Jemba-Wa had merely wanted to oversee the work at the next station. Either way, the Yeti stopped, puzzled. They were less than sixty feet away.

'Go!' Jemba-Wa thundered. 'Now, while there's time! *Go now!*'

Clutching the gun, Lethbridge-Stewart turned and ran. Behind him, he heard the Yeti roar, and the two of them gave thunderous chase. There was a weak shout from Jemba-Wa, trying to stop them, trying to gain control.

A harsh *whump* of impact. Jemba-Wa screamed in pain as the Yeti slammed him aside, coldly indifferent to whatever damage their speed and bulk had done to him.

So much for favoured-servant status, Lethbridge-Stewart thought grimly.

He only had moments before the Yeti were upon him.

He ran.

Owain gasped as the hands in his mind almost immediately changed, became fists wielding a piercing, sun-bright torch. The light seemed to illuminate all of Owain's being, filling him with terrifying brilliance from his mind outward.

Hello, James-that-was, it whispered. *Hello, Owain.*

'It's found me!' he gasped. 'Professor! Sedate me! Sedate me right now!'

Travers had been standing by the door to the hall, keeping an eye out for Kramer, who'd gone to check on the status of the military convoy. Now he turned back, brows furrowing in dismay. He hurried to the gurney where Owain remained firmly tied, his body now tensing and writhing in terror.

Standing on the other side of the narrow bed, Sally's eyes flicked to the tray of needles on the bedside table. She started towards them, trying to stick to the plan they'd formulated in the wake of Owain's revelations, but Travers shook his head. 'It may already be too late,' he intoned ominously. 'And if he is indeed as powerful as we suppose, we might need his abilities.'

Owain barely heard this. He lay back, eyes closed in horror. 'You don't understand!' he cried out. 'I'm not strong enough! I can't hold it off!'

CHAPTER FOURTEEN
Peril in the Streets

LETHBRIDGE-STEWART fell less than two minutes after wading into the deepest point of the swirling water.

He'd continued to run at full speed up to that point, lifting each dripping foot higher and higher to clear the sucking, pulling floodwaters. He had come to a curve in the track, where the water suddenly deepened from knee-high to well over halfway up his thighs. Running had simply become impossible. He toppled forward, legs buckling, and fell full-length, going completely under for a moment and drawing in a surprised, nasty mouthful of stinking brine.

He emerged spitting and retching, unable to see, certain the two Yeti would land on him any second. Then he heard them roaring again; not in triumph this time, but in agony. He spun around, spraying water every which way, and cleared his eyes in time to watch the Yeti die.

They had been running on all fours, and to his eye, it looked like the moment they had hit the water, their control spheres had burst in their chests. They were small explosions, but, for the Yeti, decidedly lethal ones.

As Lethbridge-Stewart watched, the massive, dripping shapes writhed, limbs flailing in their death throes, great yellow eyes flashing like emergency strobes. Smoke poured from their shattered chest plates. They roared, bodies bursting with green and blue energy. First one, then the other collapsed into the water and fell still. The black surface foamed and crackled but did not spread the robots' electrical malady. Standing there, dripping, Lethbridge-Stewart received no shock.

'What in heaven's name,' he wondered, pushing his wet

fringe off his forehead, looking around in disbelief. There was still the distant sound of screeching rats, but if they were watching from some dim side corridor they showed no sign of picking up the chase on their late, larger compatriots' behalf.

The waters were rising, but he wasn't far now from the first pump station. And its emergency ladder.

He turned and slogged on through the floodwaters, leaving the dead Yeti to spit and spark behind him, their fur trailing limply in the rising pool.

Once there had been a Tibetan youth who had dreamed restless dreams under a brilliant blue sky.

Now there was a badly injured old man, his left arm almost surely shattered in two or three places. The hip on that side ached horribly as well when he moved it. He lay propped against a tunnel wall, watching the rats run past, a steady stream of squeaking pestilence. He stared at them with no emotions whatsoever, and wondered whether any of this might still be made right.

Jemba-Wa had been terrified of the underground once upon a time, when he'd first come to this strange, towering city of metal and glass and staring, uncaring strangers. No surprise there, for a child of the high steppes. He'd never even taken issue with his cosy cave in the windswept heights above the monastery. With its firelight and familiar machinery and stores of raw materials he could shape into creatures lifted from pure imagination, it was the palace and workplace he had dreamed of since childhood.

But here, the cloying darkness and close, curving walls of the endless subterranean maze had made him feel like running mad, especially because it was *full* of squeaking pests and choked with the creeping stench of overheated electrics and old human filth. His cave, in comparison, had been clean and warm and smelled of fresh wood smoke, and no rodents or other pests encroached on his sanctuary so high up in the frigid, nearly sterile Himalayas. Here though, he had discovered true claustrophobia, true terror of the unknown and bottomless dark.

Jemba-Wa remembered Master Mahasamatman directing him down here, knowing the object he – it – sought was nestled somewhere in the creeping black. Jemba-Wa had nearly panicked and ran babbling, all worries about that deadly third rail temporarily forgotten in the shadow of the Master's latest order, his cruel directive to descend into the grim, filthy blackness, without even Kabadom along to comfort him. The Yeti was simply too big to fit where he had to go.

He'd wept tears of exhaustion and fear and shame, and Master Mahasamatman ignored them all. And in the end, down he went.Into the very bowels of hell itself.

It's like being blind, and he moves at a snail's pace. His weak torch offers no relief and eventually he discards it. In his shoulder bag are a compact shovel and a water bottle. The rumble of distant trains and the humming third rail are constant sources of terror.

After an eternity, the tunnel branches off into a disused passage. Jemba-Wa finds a shattered place in the tunnel wall, perhaps an old passage reopened by a minor quake. From it emanates the essence of something very old. Alien. A sound so low and rhythmic it takes on an almost mechanical hum. He doesn't want to climb in there, but the Master wills him forward. Jagged granite cuts his palms, knees, belly. He wonders how long until the blood draws the rats.

After another eternity, he begins to see faint yellow light. The gap widens and he tumbles into a dripping cavern full of glowing debris shards. At their centre, in a bowl-shaped crater, is a much larger glowing chunk. A smashed meteor. Oozing from it is a metallic liquid so cold and repugnant he is loath to touch it, but he empties his water bottle and scoops in half-a-litre's worth of the stuff. He wonders how long it has been here. And why it has never dried up.

Then, as he gathers the shards of the meteor itself, something even stranger happens. Jemba-Wa abruptly sees visions: early people, tall and sun-browned, their faces painted with clay and berries. They stand over a burned scar in the lush greenery: the smoking hole made by the strange sky rock. Some counsel flight; others speak protective incantations. One counts coup on the rock, demonstrating his bravery. Later, Jemba-Wa inexplicably knows, this man will run mad. Ride his horse off a cliff to escape the unseen voice, which speaks the tongue of the people though it hails from a world a thousand-thousand moons away.

The vision continues. Forbidding the people to go near it, the elders bury the sky rock and speak of it no more. Soon the first white men come across the great water, and ask the name of this idyllic place. The people call it Manahatouh, 'the island where there is wood for bows'. But it is not its only name, Jemba-Wa knows. Secretly, they call it Manahactanienk. 'The island of bad drunkenness.' It is as close as they can come to describing the mad whisper of the sky rock, the way it works on the mind. Soon they will sell the island to these foreigners for a pittance, glad to be rid of it.

Lost in the visions, Jemba-Wa does not feel his impatient Master take control of his body, greedily gathering up every piece of the broken meteor. When at last he comes back to himself, he is out of the tight cleft, staggering once more through pitch-black train tunnels, seeking a way up and out, dazed by the visions. He knows now why his master was so eager to find this ancient treasure; it had encountered the meteor and its semi-sentient metallic-liquid passenger before. Both had drifted in the cosmos, tumbling towards Earth. Their paths intersected, causing a titanic collision on the metaphysical plane. The Intelligence was strengthened by the alien energy. It fell to the planet below, the meteor hurled into its own decaying orbit. Bringing it to the island that would become Manhattan.

Jemba-Wa staggers out of the tunnel, weeping, the Master's trophy slung over his back.

The old man lay in the tunnel, haunted by his memories. He tried to will away the pain, realising what a fool he'd been all these long years. He forced himself to his feet, crying out at the pain in his hip and his broken arm.

He had to walk, so walk he did. Perhaps there was still time to save Lethbridge-Stewart, and stop the madness that had engulfed New York.

In the streets above, Army and National Guard units moved to join the pitched battle, but it wasn't a fight any of them were prepared for. The convoy from Fort Drum, five hours out under the best road and weather conditions, was caught behind a fifteen-vehicle pileup on Interstate 81 north of Scranton, Pennsylvania. They radioed in to warn it might be dawn before they arrived.

A half-dozen troop carriers loaded with armed National Guardsmen from Fort Hamilton came roaring triumphantly across the Brooklyn Bridge. The line of trucks zigzagged up side roads, cut across 14th Street and blasted their way north on 8th Avenue to Hell's Kitchen, only to catch a red light at the blind intersection of 8th and West 37th Street. Not chancing it, the lead driver braked to a halt, confident they were less than three minutes from the action.

Halfway down the city block to their right, the massive pane-glass front of the Garment District's tallest fabrics shop abruptly shattered outwards, disgorging what looked to the pimply young soldier riding shotgun in the lead truck like a solid wall of grey water. With the street lights blown out, he could perhaps be forgiven for mistaking a teeming horde of rats for an oncoming comber, and to his credit he *did* shout a warning. But it did no good. Nearly a hundred thousand rats sluiced down West 37th in a cresting wave. They swamped the convoy, surging through open windows, lunging over tailgates and leaping on the surprised, screaming men and women within.

Not one soldier from Fort Hamilton got off a single shot.

Hanging up the phone, Kramer ran a hand across her eyes.

'That bad?' Sally asked, standing nearby.

Kramer nodded her thanks to the night nurse and led Sally upstairs. She related what news she'd received from the UN, including the delayed arrival of the troops from Fort Drum and the debacle in the Garment District.

'It's bad enough we just lost six truckloads of fighting men,' she murmured, keeping her voice low so she wouldn't spook the occasional nurse or doctor that strode past. 'But according to an eyewitness, they're all lying in their vehicles or in the street, eyes wide open and bright yellow, chanting away for all they're worth. We're just giving the enemy more reinforcements of his own.'

A flurry of footsteps behind them, and they turned to see Professor Travers and Doctor Supravhal hurrying up the steps. They fell into step with the women, heading back to ICU.

'Security is barricading all the entrances, locking the hospital up tight,' the tired-faced doctor told them cautiously. 'I hope you know what you are doing, Lieutenant.'

Kramer nodded. 'So do I.'

'How long until they come, do you think?' Sally asked pensively.

None of them had to ask who she meant.

Filthy but unbowed, Lethbridge-Stewart shoved the manhole cover up as quietly as possible and peered out of the dark crescent.

Distantly, sirens beat at the night with a steady, panicked rhythm. Occasionally, far-off gunshots provided a staccato counterpoint. Across the intersection, Lethbridge-Stewart saw a horde of rats chasing a shouting homeless man, who was pedalling a rusty old bicycle for all he was worth. Cyclist and vermin disappeared into the downpour, heading southeast. Then the street was deserted once more.

He shoved the manhole cover aside and clambered out, staggering to his feet. He breathed deeply. No city had ever smelled so sweet. 'Nearly home and dry,' he murmured. There was a timely flash of lightning, and he realised to his surprise that it was still raining. 'Well, nearly home, anyway.' *Dry* would have to wait.

Lethbridge-Stewart turned slowly, noting the street signs. West 43rd Street and 7th Avenue. He was back in Hell's Kitchen, likely no more than a couple of streets down from Manhattan General. He hoped Owain and Sally would be there.

There was a phone booth at the far corner of 43rd, where it crossed 8th Avenue.

Too bright on this side, Lethbridge-Stewart thought. The shadows thrown by the buildings on the opposite side of the street would hide him more effectively. Looking both ways before he crossed – *safety first*, he mused, *even in these desperate times* – he dashed towards the glass booth and the paid telephone waiting inside.

Jemba-Wa had reached the hip-deep water leading to the lowest point in that section of the tunnel. The pooling

179

darkness was now covered with a floating layer of trash: egg cartons, old fast-food drink containers, sodden newspapers and other detritus picked up and carried along by the rising tide. The trash seemed to cluster around the lifeless, floating Yeti, perhaps tangling in their wet fur, perhaps just drawn to the larger shapes like tiny satellites in a watery orbit. The two Yeti had quit sparking and sizzling and were now just humped shapes laying face-down in the dark water. Jemba-Wa shivered.

He was steeling himself to wade in, continue following Lethbridge-Stewart in the direction Jemba-Wa had last seem him headed, when an unseen force clutched at his throat, shaking him like a rag-doll. It hurled him into the greasy, trash-littered water. Jemba-Wa cried out as his broken arm struck unyielding stone. He swallowed a mouthful of salty river water, lunged up gasping and vomited it back up. The vice-like grip was still at his throat, and the air filled with the fury of his unseen assailant.

Traitor! What have you done?

Coughing, flailing, Jemba-Wa hung in the psychic grip of the Great Intelligence. There were no eyes to stare defiantly into, no face to spit upon. He merely gasped and flailed, and finally drew enough air to shout back, 'Go on! Kill me! *Kill me!* My life clearly means no more to you than any other you have stolen over the long ages!'

Roaring in helpless fury, the Intelligence released him, and Jemba-Wa fell into the water once more, going under a second time and thrashing back to his feet, wiping water from his face, sucking in ragged lungfuls of air.

How? the Intelligence asked, almost piteously. *How could you betray me?*

'You promised to send me home,' Jemba-Wa whispered in return, rubbing at his damaged throat. 'But you only took me further and further from it. I didn't think anything could be worse than being pulled out of my own time and dropped into this city of crime and chaos...' He struggled to clear his throat, and when he spoke again his voice was stronger, vindictive. 'But you sent me into the darkness, forced me down into hell. All for your precious metal. Your *meteor.*'

He could tell the Intelligence was losing interest, was no

longer fully focused on him. Its restless, hungry mind had once more turned to its campaign for power. Jemba-Wa knew it was spreading itself thinner and thinner. Even with the rats providing new victims and thus new sources of mental power, the Intelligence itself was still driving most of the rats. And it was tiring.

Then its mind turned once more to Owain Vine, and Jemba-Wa understood that it believed it could still gain all the power it needed and more.

'No,' he whispered.

It is no matter, the Intelligence hissed at him. *Stay down here and die, or climb out and face the rats like all the others. I know where the boy is. The seed of my power, untapped and raw, lies within him.*

'No!' Jemba-Wa shouted.

But the Intelligence was gone, abandoning its good and faithful servant. Jemba-Wa slumped against a wall, groaning in despair. Then he hauled himself up again and began wading laboriously through the rising water, which was now at his waist.

I will not stay here and die, he thought stubbornly, staggering toward the pump station. *Nor will these vermin have me. I will... I—*

He stopped twenty feet from the ruined facility where he'd previous caught up with Lethbridge-Stewart. Stood there, swaying, face twisted in misery.

Another humped shape lolled in the water outside the pump house door. Even from here, Jemba-Wa could tell by the grey-white fur that it was Kabadom.

His old friend.

Jemba-Wa struggled forward, knowing it was too late. He knew too that the hulking Yeti might have been sent to punish or even kill him, and still didn't care. He reached the collapsed Yeti, saw the pall of smoke above it. It was still sparking, humming like an old generator winding down.

But it was too late. Kabadom, like the other Yeti which had encountered the salt water, had been destroyed.

Jemba-Wa supposed programming wasn't everything. Perhaps the oldest of his Yeti creations had been faithfully trying to follow its human creator, to protect him from their furious master. Perhaps, in the end, it had been more loyal to him than to the Great Intelligence.

Or perhaps it had come this way in pursuit of Lethbridge-Stewart, and died needlessly like its fellows.

'My fault,' Jemba-Wa whispered. And it was, of course. He had altered the chemistry of the new control spheres, had added a susceptibility to salt water as an Achilles heel, a safeguard against the possibility that he might one day need to defy his old master. It was the deep cavern that had done it, terrifying him to the point of rebellion, robbing him of any last hope of home. He had manipulated the new spheres, and by upgrading Kabadom he had unintentionally guaranteed that his guardian paid the same price as all the others.

Jemba-Wa touched the wet white fur. 'Goodbye, old friend,' he murmured.

It had taken Lethbridge-Stewart fifteen minutes to convince the operator to put his call through to Manhattan General, and another three minutes for the harried Nurse Joyner to accept the call. Then she slammed down the receiver, haring off in search of Sally or Kramer.

'Brigadier?' It was Kramer.

'Ah, Lieutenant,' he said briskly, turning slowly in the phone booth to look down 8th Avenue. 'I don't have much time, so I need you to listen very closely.'

Much of the city appeared dark below West 42nd Street, but to the north, there were still a few street lights. One of these illuminated the wrought-iron fencing and signage of a distant subway entrance. He couldn't read the sign, but recognised the pattern of words and symbols as common to most of New York's subway entrances.

Movement on the pavement around the entrance. Furtive shapes scurried back and forth. Rats, big enough to be visible through the rain. Maybe a dozen of them.

As he told Kramer about how the seawater appeared to destroy the Yeti outright, giving them a possible weapon to use against them, he let his gaze climb to the booth's small, bright light. It had automatically come on when he entered. He wondered if he could break the light somehow. He still had Jemba-Wa's pistol in his belt, but didn't think it worth risking a ricochet. Still, he didn't like that beacon. Not with a handful of potentially sick rats so close.

Kramer was asking him something.

'Say again?' he said.

'I asked where you are,' Kramer said. 'Sally's been going out of her mind, and Owain... Well, we're not sure what's to be done about Owain.'

The smile that had begun to wreathe his face at the mention of Sally's presence in the hospital disappeared again in a flash. He wanted to ask what had happened to Owain, but knew his time might be very short indeed.

'I want to speak to both of them,' he said abruptly, eyes closing in pain. 'But you must assure me first that you'll share this information with the authorities. Salt water may be a weapon against them. We might be able to get emergency repair teams back down there and get the flood control systems back online. You've got to—'

He broke off, gaping. His knuckles went white on the receiver.

A *dozen* rats, had he said?

A roiling pack of vermin now burst up from the subway station, following those first tentative vanguards of the pack. They spilled into the street in all directions. In a moment, there were thousands, a rippling, gestalt mass.

Even from here, Lethbridge-Stewart could see thousands of pairs of burning yellow eyes. More than half the pack was infected, he guessed. He muttered a curse.

'Brigadier?' Growing concern on the other end of the line.

'One minute!' he shouted. Clamping the receiver between his chin and shoulder, shielding his eyes as best he could, he drew the handgun from his belt and began to hammer at the metal mesh protecting the overhead bulb.

A flurry of chatter on the line. 'Alistair!' Sally now. 'Alistair, are you all right?'

'Hello, darling!' he called back, still pounding at the light. No luck. The mesh was too tough. 'A bit busy at the moment!' Hoping they were too far away to notice, he glanced over to see if the rats were paying him any mind.

'Alistair!'

It wasn't a matter of a few rats spotting him, he realised

183

with cold horror. They were *all* staring at him. All the ravening, yellow-eyed thousands of them.

And without warning they rushed his way, rolling at him like a solid grey avalanche of slick, wet flesh and piercing gold eyes.

'Alistair, where are you?' Sally nearly screamed.

'Phone booth!' he answered. 'I'm facing several thousand rats coming down 8th Avenue towards me. Tell Kramer to get the army mobilised. Salt water is the key!'

There was no time to run for it. They'd be on him in seconds. He looked around helplessly, cursed, slammed the door and put his body against it.

Lord help me now, he thought.

He grimaced as the throng reached him. The first wave leaped, hundreds of grey bodies slamming into the sides of the booth at a height of three or four feet. Their bodies made harsh thudding sounds, like birds inadvertently flying into closed windows. *Big* birds.

Yet the glass held.

Sally was in his ear again. It sounded like she was crying. He started to say something else, and then the main mob of rats slammed into the phone booth three deep, the sheer force of them rocking the big glass box nearly six inches off its base.

Both the overhead light and the phone receiver abruptly went dark and dead.

CHAPTER SIXTEEN
Showdown

SALLY RAN for the front entrance, with Adrienne close behind. They dodged through small clutches of hospital staff; nurses and orderlies wheeling patients out of first-floor rooms, preparing to safely tuck them away on upper floors where it was hoped they'd be safer in case the rats and their savage allies did attack the hospital. Adrienne looked around wildly.

'This isn't what I thought I'd be doing when I got up this morning,' she grumbled.

'What was he saying about salt water?' Sally shouted to her friend as she skated around an orderly pushing an old woman in a wheelchair, her saline drip rattling and bobbing on a pole attached to her chair.

'He said it might be a weapon we can use against the Yeti,' Adrienne explained. 'And something about using it to get the flood control systems back online, sending emergency teams into the subway to get the systems back. I don't—' She saw the barricaded front entrance below them and across the lobby, and groaned in frustration. 'It's blocked off, damn it! We'll have to get out another way.'

Sally ignored her. She'd hurl a chair through a front window if need be, but she would not spend another minute locked in this hospital while Alistair might be out there fighting for his life. 'We have to scramble whatever forces we can muster,' she said briskly as they hurried through the lobby. 'Get armed troops to the pump stations, take on the Yeti directly, see about finding ways to use salt water to—'

Adrienne was about to reply when there was a tremendous hammering at the locked and barricaded front doors. Everyone in the room stopped, heads turning, eyes widening in surprise. There was a single small cry, quickly stifled.

The two women looked at the door, saw the dust settling around its exterior edges beyond the piled desks and filing cabinets. A second powerful blow, and the left door seemed to jump inwards half an inch. More dust settled. Wood groaned.

'Everyone!' Adrienne shouted, drawing her pistol. 'Get out of here! Move!'

Cries of terror and surprise. People began to stumble away. Others merely stood watching in shock. A third mighty impact, and the left door snapped off its hinges, crashing inwards, wedged amid the jumble of shelving and other hardware. There was a tremendous, bestial roar, and Sally saw bright amber eyes glowing through the gap in the entryway. Adrienne snapped off two rounds, aiming for those piercing yellow eyes, and began to drag Sally away as the first Yeti smashed a fourth time at the front doors. This time it succeeded in shoving the entire barricade back half a foot. The remaining door would not survive another blow, and more Yeti shifted and pressed forwards behind the leader, ready to hurl aside the improvised blockade.

The rats swarmed in through two dozen gaps in the stacked furniture, and the first real screams of pain and horror pealed across the lobby. Adrienne continued dragging Sally away, cutting behind the eternally patient Nurse Joyner's information desk and pushing through a door marked 'Service'.

More triumphant roars behind them as the Yeti relentlessly pushed their way inside, punctuated by the high, chittering shriek of attacking rats.

They were in a grey corridor, empty except for a fire extinguisher on one wall and an abandoned mop and bucket beneath it. 'What about Travers and Owain?' Sally gasped as Adrienne pointed her at the far end of the hall towards the 'Exit' door.

'They'll have to take their chances,' Adrienne said reluctantly. 'We have to get out of here and stop the Yeti.'

They ran.

The sheer weight of the squirming, gnashing rodents was at first simply astonishing, but astonishment very quickly gave way to alarm as Lethbridge-Stewart, trapped inside the booth, the glass all around him teeming to a level of more than two feet with gnawing, snarling vermin, began to grasp the full implications of the situation at hand. He'd briefly put his back against the wall opposite the entry, pressing his right boot firmly into the hinged centre of the folding door to keep it wedged flat and shut against the pressure of the onslaught. Before long, however, he realised the powerful muscles of his thigh and calf weren't enough. He had to lunge forward and throw his whole weight against the door once more, holding it closed as the surging, squalling rats fought to push their way inside. To push their way to *him*.

They're rats, he thought, bewildered. *Bloody* rats.

The phone receiver dangled forgotten from its useless wall unit, all the cables sheared through when the unsuspected weight of the horde had smashed into the booth. The pay phone was about as useful as a paperweight now, though he fancied if worse came to worst he might be able to wrench the heavy thing off the wall and use it to bludgeon the first dozen or so rats that wormed their way in.

Amazingly, three cars passed him on the street. Two were civilian vehicles, rocketing down 8th Avenue like criminals on the lam; perhaps looters, perhaps New Yorkers finally fleeing the nightmare that had uncoiled from the depths below. The third had been a police cruiser, all its lights on and sirens blaring, screaming past in the other direction, angling toward the Meatpacking District and points south. The rats were drenched, and Lethbridge-Stewart noted with regret that none of them were fazed by this. The energy that drove them *had* to be cousin to the power of the Yeti.

More and more of them poured out of the distant subway entrance, some the size and weight of housecats. The newcomers roved up and down the street, looking for ways into the dark buildings that lined it, seeking out the human inhabitants within.

Sickened by the sight, Lethbridge-Stewart held on as the writhing, squealing mass continued to swell around him, the rats piled up three feet deep outside the phone booth, all glaring yellow eyes and teeth and claws splayed against the glass.

Just let us in, they seemed to implore him. *Let us in and this will all be over.*

Lethbridge-Stewart concentrated on keeping pressure on the door, holding it shut against them. If even one managed to slip through…

Owain looked up as Travers re-entered the coma ward, rubbing his hands nervously. 'That was definitely the crash of the barricade at the front door,' Travers reported, his eyes flicking nervously back and forth, glancing at the prone, chanting sleepers. Their voices had risen since the professor had stepped out. Owain found himself wondering how long it would be until they began to shout in their slippery, not-quite-Tibetan tongue.

'I can also hear the sound of fighting downstairs, and… and some screams,' Travers added. He looked down at the tied, bedridden youth sympathetically. 'No gunshots, though. I believe Lieutenant Kramer and Corporal Wright successfully, erm, made their getaway, as it were.'

Owain closed his eyes, trying to focus on what had happened on the train. His mind side-slipped briefly, and he wanted to give in to worry, thinking about Simon, lost since the ambush in the subway. Thinking about Uncle Alistair, lost there too. Maybe safe now, but more likely in the thick of it, according to what Aunt Sally had shared of their escape from the warehouse, and Uncle Alistair's stubborn insistence on following the Yeti back underground.

Thinking about screams downstairs. Screams, and no gunshots.

Owain resisted panic, fought to quell the unfocused, uncomprehending part of his mind that was still the boy Owain Vine, still Lewis's twin, still a naïve young man of Bledoe. He considered the teachings of the gurus, the lessons of the Buddha, and controlled his thoughts. Contained his fear. Soothed it into silence.

He reached deeper, and found what he needed.

If you do this, he told himself cautiously, *it could take hold of you again.*

'Owain?' Travers asked cautiously.

I was channelling blind, stupid power last time. If I can tap into

188

the energy, but hold the will of the Intelligence at bay...

'Are you all right, my boy?'

Owain opened his eyes, and saw Travers' face go slack with shock. It was no surprise to Owain, as he knew his eyes had changed colour once again, glowing fiercely in the darkened room. He could feel them, the focal point of the ancient mind and soul coursing through him.

His own soul, evolved and reincarnated through the endless centuries ahead, now reflected back on him.

'Untie me, Professor,' Owain said quietly. There was a deep, ringing echo in his voice, as if he were speaking from across a vast stone cathedral. Travers hesitated, shaking his head in what Owain supposed might be unwitting negation, his confusion and uncertainty so profound the man wasn't even aware he was trying to refute it. 'There is nothing to fear, Professor,' he said. 'Untie me, please.'

Still sceptical, Travers slowly moved to the gurney, fingers fumbling at the straps. 'Dear boy,' he murmured in an awed tone. 'Dear boy...'

Owain's voice never wavered. That echoing note reverberated as he spoke, a clear, hopeful counterpoint to the grim cadence of the sleepers' chant. 'I'm not a boy. I'm not sure what I am now. But hurry. Untie me. You'll need my help.'

Kramer and Sally bolted out of a side exit not far from the hospital's ER, and despite the close proximity of the tumultuous assault – cavernous roars from the Yeti, screams from the civilians, and everywhere the insistent, nerve-wracking *reek-and-squeak* of the rats – the young lieutenant let her British friend lead her around the side of the building, cautiously winding their way back to the main entrance. They were braced to find an enemy horde out there, but the street was empty once more.

The massive front doors of Manhattan General Hospital had been smashed in.

The enemy were already inside.

There was no time and no sense trying to dash back in to do what they could to help; they both knew the only thing they could do in there was succumb to the infection or die badly beneath great metal claws.

'There,' Sally hissed.

She pointed to a taxi, presumably the one she had commandeered earlier.

They ran to the yellow cab and leaped in, Kramer inspecting the compartment wildly, lunging up on her knees to check the back, gun up, making sure the vehicle was clear of lurking vermin. She kept imagining she could hear that dry-hands-rubbing sound that had preceded the horde bursting out of the subway.

Sally started the car, threw it into reverse and stomped on the gas. Shortly they were speeding up 8th Avenue, along mostly deserted streets. Kramer stared out of her window, shaking her head in disbelief.

Friday night in the Big Apple, just months after the Summer of Love, baby... Yet only the occasional flickering neon sign – and the random swarm of rats clustered outside a walk-up apartment – gave any sign there was still life here. She saw more bodies on sidewalks, others sprawled in doorways of various buildings, and shuddered, putting her forehead against the glass.

Some of them appeared to be chanting.

Next to her, the demurely pretty woman who intended to soon become Mrs Alistair Gordon Lethbridge-Stewart drove with confidence. She grilled Kramer as she pulled away from the old hospital, rapping questions in rapid-fire succession, and Kramer, who understood her idea immediately, explained how to get to the place Sally had in mind. Kramer grinned broadly as she did so. She liked the plan very much. She'd always wanted to ride in one of those.

It took them less than five minutes to draw within eyesight of their destination: 782 8th Avenue, home to the FDNY Engine 54 firehouse.

Kramer touched her friend's shoulder, pointing in triumph. There were closer New York City firehouses, she knew, but they were smaller, and might lack what Sally was after. Kramer was about to say something else when she happened to glance down at the road in front of them, just in time to see the dark pavement appear to... *writhe.*

'Hold on!' Sally abruptly screamed, seeing it at the same

time.

Water? Kramer wondered.

It was rats.

There weren't many of them, maybe a few hundred, but they were passing *en masse* across 8th Avenue just as the taxi came speeding out of the dark. The streetlights were out here, so perhaps the rodents were using the shadows to slip across the road unseen. Or perhaps it was just bad timing.

They rolled over the pack at speed, and both of them heard – or felt – small living things crunch and splatter under the taxi's tires. Sally maintained control of the car, resisting the impulse to brake or turn the wheel, and they passed over without issue.

Until a furless Yeti lurched into the road ahead of them, massive arms outstretched as if to catch the yellow cab in its remorseless claws.

Sally screamed again – in thwarted, frustrated anger this time, Kramer knew – and tried to jig past the enormous shape. Kramer felt her seatbelt lock as the taxi slewed and began to pitch left. She knew they were going over before the vehicle flipped, and braced herself for the crash.

In the hospital the power had gone out with an echoing snap of thrown breakers. Travers and Owain heard a metallic scream of protest from long-dormant emergency generators coming to life, winding up to full power somewhere below them. And that full power meant 'partial power' in comparison to normal. Emergency lights glowed a deep red at the end of each hall and above each doorway, throwing dark shadows everywhere. The formerly familiar shapes of ordinary objects – blood pressure machines and bedside tables and vases and rows of get-well-soon cards – took on unnatural angles and weird new depths.

Travers unbuckled the gurney's built-in wrist and leg cuffs and helped Owain slowly to his feet, patiently ignoring the youth's curses as the blood began to flow more vigorously again to his numbed limbs. Owain immediately limped through the door and out into the hallway, ignoring Travers' thin, panicked calls of protest. After a moment, Travers followed him grimly.

Now they stood at the top of the staircase leading down to the main floor. Owain was very pale, but the intense blue light in his eyes did not waver.

More of the same below them: human cries and Yeti roars and everywhere the rats, the rats, the rats. Something was thrown into the closed doors at the bottom of the staircase, striking hard enough to make the door jump visibly even in the gloom, and something slid to the ground with a groan. A moment later something else began clawing and scrabbling at the door. Owain put a hand on Travers' chest and began backing away.

Travers didn't need to be told twice. He turned and followed Owain, almost scuttling in his terror, clasping his hands and muttering, 'Oh dear, oh dear.'

Another hard blow, and the door behind and below them audibly splintered. Owain moved more rapidly, re-entering intensive care with Travers hustling in behind him. Travers turned and shoved the room's heavy double-doors shut, switching the lock below the handle on the right. Stared in consternation at it.

More crashing in the hall, still distant. It sounded as if the downstairs door had given way.

Travers looked around. The sleepers were chanting again, and Owain was, momentarily, nowhere to be seen. Then the boy came back from the antechamber, eyes blazing blue in the darkness. He caught sight of Travers' face.

'Don't worry,' he said.

He was carrying a mop that had been propped in a bucket in one corner of the back room. Unscrewing the mop head from the handle, he went back to the door. There he dropped the mop head, brought the handle up, and broke it over his knee in one swift move, snapping the thick wood pole almost exactly at its centre point. He laid the two pieces of wood side by side on his left palm, then ran them through the matching, squared-off door handles, wedging them in place so even if the lock gave they'd continue to slow down the enemy. For another few moments, anyway. They wouldn't last very long against the might of the Yeti.

Owain looked at Travers, who returned the look with mounting worry. Owain smiled.

'Don't worry, Professor,' he said again. 'We're not the ones in the real danger.'

Travers' eyebrows rose in surprised scepticism at that, and wondered whose situation could be more perilous than theirs.

Lethbridge-Stewart watched the metal frame of the phone booth begin to push out of true as the flimsy construct buckled under the relentless pressure of the rat pile. They were chest-high to him now, working themselves into some final, writhing frenzy as if they sensed the end coming.

'You've run out of time, old chap,' he said in a slightly bemused voice. 'Damned unpleasant way to finish up.' He wondered how painful the bites would be, how quickly the infection would take hold, sending him spinning down into unconsciousness. He watched the vermin grunt and surge and gnash. Would they bite him to death in their eagerness to infect him? Was it possible?

He drew Jemba-Wa's gun, checked the clip. Grunted in satisfaction. Good show. The first nine beggars that poured through, he'd give *them* what for, at any rate.

Glass cracked. He looked down. One of the big panes near the floor, above the blue metal footing of the booth, had a splintered, milky star running through its centre. A chunk of glass lay on the flooring, and a whiskered snout poked through the gap, jagged yellow teeth exposed.

Lethbridge-Stewart raised the pistol. 'Right,' he said. 'For Queen and Coun—'

He heard the ceaseless squeaking noise of the vermin change, that shared note of rage and insistence abruptly rising higher, becoming a keening squawk of surprise and a mixed chorus of outrage and confusion. He glanced around, craning his neck to look behind him at the horde piled against the phone booth door, and saw a remarkable thing.

The writhing mound of grey bodies had begun to shudder and shift, and now, incredibly, they were *parting*.

Like the Sea of Reeds before Moses, he thought, awestruck.

Rats tumbled away from the door, spreading out to the left and right of the booth, leaving a narrow path of bare wet street. Staggering up this temporary corridor towards

Lethbridge-Stewart, limping along in a weirdly empty circle that seemed to move with him, was Jemba-Wa. He looked close to collapse, but as he drew closer he remained shielded from the tempest of frenzied rodents all around him. The rats leaped and scampered but could not pass back into the protected space the old man occupied, neither could they swarm the front of the phone booth once more.

Deciding to chance it, Lethbridge-Stewart pushed open the door, wincing at the pervasive stink of the rat army, glancing back and forth at the walls of rodents snarling and leering at him, mere inches away yet unable, by dint of some new magic, to attack or even approach any closer.

'Hurry,' Jemba-Wa said raggedly, and now Lethbridge-Stewart could see how deathly pale he was, how his left arm dangled at a sickening angle. He sensed that Jemba-Wa was at the very point of collapse. Whatever power he'd called forth, the agents of the Great Intelligence were unable to overcome it. But Lethbridge-Stewart was certain their enemy could reassert its power any moment.

He walked carefully to Jemba-Wa, the pistol still gripped in his right hand, and put out a steadying hand, careful not to touch the badly broken left arm. 'Are you all right?' he asked warily.

'We haven't much time,' Jemba-Wa croaked, and he swayed on his feet.

Lethbridge-Stewart barely darted forward in time to keep him from falling, wondering when the roiling sea of rats would collapse inward and engulf them.

Sally shook her head, trying to clear the ringing in her ears, and slowly came to the realisation that she was hanging upside-down.

Gunshots. Four of them, fast and close, and light spilled across her. Someone had raked open the door of the yellow cab – she was still in the yellow cab – and was leaning in to fumble at her seat belt. Two more gunshots, and Sally clearly heard Adrienne say, 'Hurry. It's getting close.'

Sally looked at the man fooling with her seatbelt. He was young, no more than twenty-five. Pin-up calendar handsome, even upside-down. She was about to tell him this, matter-offactly, when she heard a click and dropped into his waiting arms.

'Good catch,' she heard herself say.

'Thanks,' he replied, his New York accent rich and nasal. He carefully lifted her out, helping her to her feet as she again shook her head, still vainly trying to clear it. 'Gave yourself a knock,' he said. 'Can you walk?'

'Of course,' she replied.

'Good. Can you run?'

'I—'

Another gunshot. Then, right behind her, Adrienne's voice, taut with tension: 'It's on top of us, go, *now!*'

Sally was hauled into motion. She gasped, almost laughed, and winced as her head lurched and throbbed. She was moving along between two people – Adrienne and the pin-up guy, she assumed – both of them lifting and half-carrying her between them. They were running away from the overturned taxi, headed toward a tall brick building with some sort of waving banner in the front, a billowing sail nearly as big as the front of the building itself.

Flag, she thought. *It's the American flag.*

Below the massive flag were two large, closed garage doors, the roll-up kind she associated, for some reason, with dockside warehouses and shipping containers. She suspected these, however, were designed to discharge fire trucks, given the big sign above them, intermittently visible below the blowing, flapping flag: 'FDNY Engine 54, Ladder 4, Battalion 9'.

Next to it, an open door. A squat, fat man was leaning out of it, waving one hairy reddish arm at them. 'Come on, come on, come on!' he shouted.

Behind them, something roared. The sound was prehistoric, enraged. Sally jerked in her rescuers' arms but did not scream. Her head ached miserably, yet she felt herself getting the giggles. 'Oh, wonderful,' she said with daffy good cheer.

'Deep breath,' Adrienne said in her ear, gasping a little.

The squat man jumped back inside, clearing the way for the three of them to enter. They turned as a unit as they did so, sliding sideways through the door – the pin-up guy, then Sally, then Adrienne – and the fellow slammed it behind them, throwing a heavy security bolt for good measure. It was a solid metal door, the chunky steel bar slotting snugly into brackets a good three inches thick. If anything could withstand the wrath of a Yeti, Sally supposed this door was it.

'Check her out,' someone said, and Sally glanced up to see her pin-up guy waving another man over. This one had carroty red hair and carried a medical kit, and as Pin-up and Adrienne eased her into a chair, he shone a small penlight into her eyes.

'She got a pretty good bop on the crown,' Pin-up said.

Sally looked him up and down, and finally made sense of his kit: heavy dark workman's trousers with big cuffs. Rubber boots. Suspenders over a strappy t-shirt.

'You're a *fireman!*' she said happily. And then leaned over and threw up.

As Sally groaned and wiped at her mouth, Kramer put a soothing hand to the back of her friend's neck, trying to comfort her. 'She might be concussed,' she told the tubby man, who seemed to be the boss. 'We rolled the car when that Yeti appeared. Clipped it pretty good. That probably kept us from rolling badly.'

'Yeah, we saw,' the squat man replied, his accent steeped in Brooklyn. 'Your rear fender caught it full in the chest, sent it flying. Prolly all that kept it offa youse while my ladder man, Chet here, got your friend outa the car. And I don't want to jinx us, but it sure looked like it was moving slow when it got up.'

Chet, the handsome young firefighter, smiled brightly at the mention of his name. Kramer returned it with a grin of her own, secretly irritated to find herself wishing for fresh makeup, and fighting an urge to smooth her hair, to un-muss it a bit.

Damned New York firefighters, she thought.

She looked back towards the man she thought of as the boss. 'You're in charge?'

He nodded. 'Chief Lester Morgan. Good to meetcha.'

She pointed at the far wall of the station house, which included a big secretarial desk. It was home to a bank of communications equipment far more sophisticated than she would have expected. *Only in New York*, she thought.

'Can you contact all the fire stations in the city from here?' she asked.

'All of 'em in all five boroughs, plus half the state and seaside Jersey,' Chief Morgan told her. 'Though if you're new round here you prolly assumed we leave New Jersey to burn.'

Chuckles from Chet and the medic. Kramer smiled, sure it was an old joke.

Morgan was still swelling with pride. 'Even with the power out like it is, we're backed up twenty-four-seven by the best generators in the city. We can roll in two minutes, every ladder and every pumper we got from Staten Island to the Bronx.'

'Good deal,' Kramer said. She glanced at Sally, saw her friend was still wrestling with her nausea, and went ahead. 'Chief, I'm Lieutenant Adrienne Kramer, United Nations Security Taskforce, authorisation Blue-Baker-Echo-Niner-Cobra-Helo. I want you to get on the horn right now, on my authority, and roll those trucks.'

Morgan raised a brow. 'You got a particular destination in mind?'

'I do. But first, tell me… What do your pumpers spray?'

He shrugged. 'We draw direct from the rivers. Straight outa the East River to starboard of 5th Avenue, straight outa the Hudson to port, if you catch my drift.'

Kramer closed her eyes in relief. 'Okay,' she said. 'We need the longest hoses and most powerful pumpers you've got. Send all of them to the MTA hydropump stations closest to their location. That's twelve primary stations to cover, right? Get them as close as possible and run the hoses the rest of the way. Some of them might have access hatches leading directly down from street level.'

Morgan looked dubious. 'You wanna flood the facilities that keep the subways from flooding?' he asked.

Kramer nodded. 'That I do.'

'And if anything… *big* gets in their way?'

His gloomy uncertainty was starting to damage her calm. Kramer folded her arms. 'Turn the water on them. See how long they stay in the way.'

He chuckled, snapped the fingers of his right hand and gave her a thumbs-up, and headed for the radio station. Behind them, outside the barred door through which they'd entered, something big roared as if accepting Kramer's challenge.

CHAPTER SEVENTEEN
Showdown

FOR LETHBRIDGE-STEWART and the unconscious Jemba-Wa, the end had come quickly... and it had been bloody.

So bloody.

Sirens had continued to wail throughout the city. The crack of gunfire suggested people were at last emerging from hiding to fight back. But even so, Lethbridge-Stewart could only watch helplessly as the Great Intelligence's rodent army crept into the collapsing circle. Whatever magic had created it – protecting the old man as he approached, protecting them both as they tried to flee – had nearly expired, leaving them to be engulfed by the writhing, biting mass.

Then, without warning, some kind of power surge had rolled over them. Lethbridge-Stewart felt it pass *through* him, and for a moment swore he could hear Owain's voice, tiny but triumphant: *I may be you one day, but not yet. Not now. This soul is mine, not yours.* All around them, the rats began to twitch and tremble as if caught up in some kind of grand mal seizure. For a good number of them the trembling ceased as quickly as it had begun, because they abruptly exploded in crimson gobbets of flesh and fur.

So many of them, and so close; he and Jemba-Wa were instantly splashed with gore. The rain smeared and spread it, thinning red to pink, but even so he promised himself that as soon as he could find a change of clothes, these would go into the nearest rubbish container. Or incinerator. He just hoped that this time he wouldn't end up with a spare jacket belonging to a lieutenant colonel, like he had in the London Underground – not that anybody seemed to notice. Still, best not to push his luck a second time.

Lifting the small, lightweight figure in his arms, Lethbridge-Stewart took stock of their surroundings. He was fairly certain the hospital was no more than four or five streets north of them, and he started in that direction. As he went, gingerly navigating through the noisome piles of dead rats, he saw a few still feebly twitching. Not all of them had burst and died instantly. Some had run in screaming circles and simply fallen over and expired. Others seemed to recover after these bouts of spasms and staggered away, creeping down subway steps and into sewer drains.

He suspected that the infected rats, the physical manifestations of the control force wielded by the Intelligence, had been the ones that had detonated like furry grenades. He felt no sympathy or distress over this. They were vermin, and the city was better off with them dead and gone.

'All things serve the universal good,' croaked a voice.

Lethbridge-Stewart looked down, and found Jemba-Wa's bright eyes fixed on his. 'Welcome back,' he said. 'I have to get you some help.'

'There is no need. Not anymore.'

Lethbridge-Stewart looked down sharply. Those brilliant ice-chip eyes... like the last embers of a tiny campfire trying in vain to light up an otherwise deserted island.

Except this island, he realised, was also sinking. Fast.

'The devil you say,' he shot back, ignoring the man's words and the evidence of his own eyes. Lethbridge-Stewart continued walking, carrying the old craftsman like an infant. Jemba-Wa was light as a feather now, almost completely used up. But Lethbridge-Stewart was stubbornly determined to get him some medical attention.

Saved my life after all, he thought brusquely. *It's the least I can do.*

In Gramercy Park, a pickup truck full of off-duty police officers skidded through the intersection of 3rd Avenue and East 19th Street. It braked hard, and the cops huddled in the back rose up, opening fire on three Yeti barring the 3rd Avenue subway entrance, the nearest access point to HydroPump Station 4M-East-East River. The Yeti bugled mocking fury at their attackers as rounds spanged futilely off their tough hide. Two of the hulking brutes dropped to all fours, preparing to charge the pickup... When a big red FDNY pumper truck careered around the corner of East 19th Street, someone laying on the klaxon usually used to scatter smaller vehicles out of its path on the way to a fire. Mounted on the rear of the truck was a massive water cannon, and this abruptly erupted as well, blasting a huge, arcing geyser of foaming spray at the station entrance.

The Yeti were blown off their feet. Two blew up immediately, their control spheres erupting, glowing eyes going dark as they crumpled to the streaming surface of the street. The third stumbled blindly for a moment as the water drenched its heavy black-and-tan fur, and it erupted in gouts of smoke and blue-green flame, collapsing backwards and cartwheeling down the twenty-nine steps which descended to the 3rd Avenue train platform. The men in the pickup truck cheered.

Sitting in the spacious cab of the red truck between Chet the fireman, who was driving, and her dear friend Adrienne, who was monitoring local reports over a massive set of headphones, Sally Wright winced a little at the others' boisterous cheers and hooting. She put a hand to the thick white bandage on her head.

'Can we dial down the noise a tad?' she asked woefully.

'Sorry, miss,' Chet whispered dutifully.

'Never mind her, Chet,' Adrienne said briskly, a wide smile creasing her face. 'She's just mad you wouldn't let her drive.' She reached forward, took the truck's communications handset from its hook, and toggled it. She had used it earlier to verify that all available FDNY crews and other first responders across the city were converging on their nearest pumping stations.

Now she keyed the squawk to announce she was breaking in, gave the chatter a second to clear, and spoke into the mic. 'All FDNY and first responders, this is Kramer. Salt water verified as a weapon, repeat, salt water is verified as a lethal weapon against cybernetic invaders. Open your hoses and give them salty hell!'

The storm had begun to pass by the time Lethbridge-Stewart, still carrying Jemba-Wa, saw the vaguely familiar street signs. They were close to Manhattan General now, he was sure of it.

The rain had tapered off, leaving the streets fairly clean, except for the endless dead rats everywhere: strewn across the wet expanse of the road, littering steps and pavements, lying in ominous heaps around the doorways and low-level windows they'd been trying to penetrate.

Some *were* still alive; these lay on their sides, panting in their final throes. They served no master anymore, nor paid him any mind, intent only on the act of dying.

He'd expected Jemba-Wa to rapidly grow heavy due to his own fatigue and exhaustion, but the little man seemed to weigh next to nothing. Even so, as they came to a long, low wooden bench demarking a city bus stop, the man groaned and begged Lethbridge-Stewart to put him down for a moment, just a brief moment.

He did so, knowing Jemba-Wa was well past making some hare-brained escape attempt. Well past everything, in fact, except perhaps his dying declaration. He went to the bench, made the man as comfortable as he could, and sat next to him.

Jemba-Wa sat looking around at the darkened, corpse-littered thoroughfare. He shook his head. 'So much waste.'

Lethbridge-Stewart cleared his throat. 'I wanted to thank you,' he said.

'Thank Owain,' the little man husked. 'He was able to reflect the Intelligence's power back on the Yeti, and the Intelligence itself.'

The street filled with the sound of oncoming engines. The wail of sirens rose in tandem, quickly drowning out even the engine roar as the vehicles sped into view. It was a convoy of crimson pumper trucks tailed by one massive, articulated hook-and-ladder rig. Lethbridge-Stewart had never seen such a welcome sight in his life.

The ladder truck driver braked as he neared the bench where the two men rested. He stopped and rolled down his window. He was a round-faced man with a tattoo of a bikini-clad woman on his exposed forearm, *Nancy Jean* inscribed underneath.

Lethbridge-Stewart blinked in surprise as the fellow addressed him. 'Hey there. You wouldn't happen to be

Letherbridge-Steward, would ya?'

'*Lethbridge*-Stew*art*,' he corrected the man gently. 'I am, sir.'

'Sorry, I'm lousy with names,' the fellow said. 'UN coordinator, lady name of Kramer? Asked us to look out for you. Would you fellas like a lift to Man-General? Kramer said Corporal Wright and a guy named Owain would meet you there.'

Permitting himself a small smile of relief and pride, Lethbridge-Stewart indicated Jemba-Wa. 'Can you assist me with this gentleman, please? I'm very much afraid he might be dying.'

Dawn broke over the city, bringing to a close a long, wet night that had begun to feel like it might never come to an end. But the last of the Yeti had been chased down and exterminated with the firehoses, and the infected rats had died in gruesome fashion. Their uninfected pack mates had slunk away unharmed, and in days to come, city officials would proudly point to research that suggested that Manhattan's rat population was down by more than thirty-five percent. The official cause? A new strain of pesticide, one that had no harmful side effects for human beings. Or wouldn't... once they tinkered a bit more with the formula.

Best of all, the coma victims began to rouse almost at once, with no memory of what had happened to them. They included several hundred individuals all over the city, and the original seventeen victims in ICU at Manhattan General. Two days from now, Pat Damiani would take his favourite bedside lamp and go home. Mrs Hagerstrom would collect Grendel from one of her neighbours and do the same.

Now, however, in the damp morning light on the last Saturday in October, the people of New York concentrated on doing what they had always done best: picking up, brushing off and getting back to the business of the day. Construction workers helped long-haired college types out of barricaded buildings, and free-spirited young people carefully guided dignified elderly strangers into the light. All of them stood together and took in the beauty of the dawn, their politics and their laundry list of differences forgotten – at least for the moment – in their shared joy at being alive to savour yet another magnificent morning in the City of Dreams.

Kramer had been kept busy for hours, guiding the fire teams against the remaining Yeti. She left them to mop up while she liaised with UN leadership, keeping her bosses abreast of developments. She was sure that at any minute she'd simply drop in her tracks if she didn't soon crawl into something remotely resembling a bed, preferably to sleep for eight or ten uninterrupted hours. She envied Sally, who had returned to Manhattan General and found a spare bed to rest for a bit.

There would be time for her own sleep later, Kramer knew. For the moment, working in a temporary office stacked with yellowing files that smelled ominously of mothballs, she concentrated on writing and issuing the official word on behalf of the United Nations. She was pleased to report the stellar work of the Metropolitan Transportation Authority and the US Army Corps of Engineers. Less than twelve hours after the loss of the first pump house, they were replacing the smashed machinery and taking back the tunnels under Hell's Kitchen from the floodwaters.

She was less pleased about how she'd been instructed to write up the rest: sewer rats, some exhibiting signs of rabies, driven into the city by flash flooding, and escaped bears from Central Park Zoo, which reportedly had menaced a few civilians before being tranquilised and returned to their enclosures. It was all soberly drafted, of course, and would be delivered with no trace of levity, but it amused and irked her in equal measure that John Q Public would swallow the whole thing without argument. *And why not?* she wondered bitterly. *Bodies get shipped home daily from southeast Asia, and these days anyone who stands up and tells the truth is likely to catch a bullet for his trouble. Just ask the Kennedys, God rest them. Just ask Doctor King.*

In the age of Vietnam and home-grown assassins, nobody wanted to hear about Yeti in the New York City Subway.

She thought about Detective Paul Dawson, her friend, and knew she'd have to sweep his death under the rug too. *Death by misadventure; subway train hit him during an investigation. It happens; I'm so sorry for your loss.*

'I *am* sorry, Paulie,' she said aloud. 'I wish I could do better by you.'

Someday she would, she swore it. Someday, she would apply what she'd seen here, taking advantage of all that she'd discovered to be lurking behind the flimsy curtain of normalcy. She would make weapons of that knowledge, and fight to prevent the sort of thing that had happened to Paul from happening to anyone else.

Lethbridge-Stewart wasn't the only soldier true to a cause, and this particular cause drew her and captivated her like no work she'd ever done before.

She'd be damned if they were going to keep her out of it.

New York had had one heck of a night, the newsmen on the TV said.

By breakfast time, most of America – and the world – had begun hearing about rabid rats and runaway bears and the superstorm that had drenched the Big Apple. Anyone suffering rat bites was encouraged to contact US Army medical staff working out of Manhattan General Hospital immediately. It was all perfunctory; Kramer, Travers and Lethbridge-Stewart knew that with the defeat of the Great Intelligence, the coma patients and any other bite victim would continue to make a full recovery, barring any other infectious diseases the rats might be carrying, and Kramer also quietly noted that the Yeti bodies – lifeless hulks now that the control spheres had been destroyed – were being whisked away by persons unknown for study. She had no doubt Lethbridge-Stewart was behind it, and had even heard the words *Argosy Isle* mentioned. She promised to open a dialogue with the Fifth Operational Corps; she and Lethbridge-Stewart had much to talk about.

Beyond that, it was over.

Or very nearly so.

Jemba-Wa lay on a narrow bed in one of Manhattan General's private rooms, various monitors and machines beeping quietly beside his bed, and handcuffs locking him to the metal railing. He lay silently, breathing in shallow gasps. A cheerful nurse had run an IV line into the crook of one withered arm to replenish his fluids, but to Lethbridge-

Stewart she looked like she was just going through the motions, waiting for the piercing bleat of the Code Blue alarm which meant all his monitors had flatlined. Despite all Jemba-Wa had done to instigate the chaos in the subways, despite the role he'd played in the London Event, Lethbridge-Stewart found himself saddened by the way the little Tibetan man was just slipping away. It didn't seem fair really, when you considered the way he'd been pressed into service, and kept there for more than two centuries.

Lethbridge-Stewart stood by the bed, one arm around Sally. As it turned out, she hadn't suffered a concussion in the wreck of the taxi, just a bad bruise and a knotted bump under her hairline. Doctor Supravhal had dosed her with a powerful injection of naproxen, before finally calling it a day himself and clocking out, almost ten hours later than he'd been scheduled to depart, and she soon reported feeling much better, with only a mild, lingering ache behind her eyes.

Primarily responsible for her upswing in health and good humour was seeing Lethbridge-Stewart arrive, battered and bedraggled but alive. She confided this to him as he held her tight, praising her for her bravery, both of them talking a mile a minute, and then they simply stopped each other's nattering with a kiss.

It had been a joyful reunion. For both of them.

Now the couple stood with Professor Travers and Owain, whose own reunion with Lethbridge-Stewart had been a warm and heartfelt relief, all of them wishing there were something to be done for the dying old man in the hospital bed.

'He beat the hold that the Intelligence had on him,' Owain murmured thickly. 'He was stronger than he believed.'

Lethbridge-Stewart nodded. 'I understand you were as well. Quite a lot stronger.'

Owain returned his gaze for a moment, then let his eyes drift. 'We'll talk, Uncle. We've... quite a lot to talk about. But not right now.'

Lethbridge-Stewart agreed. It could wait.

On the bed, Jemba-Wa opened his eyes. Blue ice-chips. No sign of the Intelligence. His life signs were feeble, according to the machinery, yet he smiled wanly as he regarded them.

He caught Lethbridge-Stewart's gaze, and one hand twitched in a weak 'come here' gesture.

Lethbridge-Stewart leaned close. 'Yes, Jemba-Wa?'

'Mahasamatman promised I would go home again one day. I believe that time is come.' Jemba-Wa blinked, and his blue, blue eyes shimmered wetly. 'Thank you for helping me to be free of him. Even if just for a little while.'

'No, don't surrender,' Lethbridge-Stewart said brusquely. 'Fight it, man.'

Jemba-Wa shook his head. 'Inevitable,' he said, every syllable an achievement.

'Is it getting brighter in here?' Sally asked.

It was. The light was emanating from Jemba-Wa's brutalised form. Bright, white light. And it was growing more radiant all the time.

'Brigadier!' Travers hissed, alarmed.

Lethbridge-Stewart held up a restraining hand. They had nothing to fear from Jemba-Wa anymore.

Jemba-Wa spoke again. 'In my passing, I may be able to help one of you.'

The light continued to grow brighter, making all of them step back. Lethbridge-Stewart shielded his eyes with one hand. Wincing, looking through his fingers, he saw Jemba-Wa raise a trembling hand of his own.

Towards Travers.

The professor stepped forward. 'Do you mean you can take me back?' he asked cautiously. He leaned over, and the two shared brief words. The rest could hear nothing of this exchange; the tumult of the vortex, somehow flowing from Jemba-Wa's body and cycling slowly within it at the same time, had begun to spin up to a windy roar. Then Travers turned to them, his face alight with excitement. Even before he spoke, Lethbridge-Stewart could tell his mind was made up.

'This is what I've waited five years for!' Travers shouted over the bellow of the vortex. 'I already know, as do you, that I'm destined to return to my own time, to live out my measure of years and take part in the London Event, to witness the birth of my children!'

Lethbridge-Stewart started to say something, but Travers threw up a hand. 'No, don't tell me anything! Best a man not know too much about his own destiny!' He fixed Owain with a sober look. 'And best a man never permit destiny to override his duty to those he loves, eh? Thank you for that useful reminder, young Mister Vine.'

Owain smiled, raising a hand in farewell.

Travers had to squint against the gale now. 'Whether I will remember *this* bizarre sojourn, I can't say!' he bellowed. 'But logic dictates I *will* have my family. A son... and a daughter! And she'll be the very image of her mother.' He looked at Jemba-Wa, took the man's thin fingers in both his beefy palms, still addressing Lethbridge-Stewart. '*Faith*, sir! More than anything, it's my deepest desire to see Anne grow into the woman I know will make me proud. So I surrender to logic... *and* to faith!'

Lethbridge-Stewart nodded. He started to extend a hand, but realised the powerful light was now so bright that he could see the bones of Travers' hands through the skin itself, and thought better of it. And *still* it grew brighter, pouring from Jemba-Wa's body. Lethbridge-Stewart guessed his death had been designed to signal the vortex to open, to return the little man's remains to the era from which he'd been drawn. He *would* go home again, as promised.

Though for no other purpose than to be buried... likely by bewildered, grieving friends and family. It was a cruel joke.

He hoped it would be the Intelligence's last.

'Goodbye to you all,' Travers called. 'We *will* meet again!'

'Thank you, Professor!' Owain shouted, shielding his eyes against the light.

Travers nodded, beaming. Then he looked around, seemingly in surprise, as if looking at something only he could see. Something beyond the visual range of the people in the hospital room. And very clearly alarmed, he said, 'Oh dear!'

Before he could say more, there was a grinding roar and a flash of the brightest light yet, forcing everyone to look away, the radiance searing, nearly unbearable. Sally burrowed her face into Lethbridge-Stewart's shoulder.

And abruptly, there was silence once more.

The bed was empty. So was the space beside it, where Travers had stood.

Lethbridge-Stewart, Sally and Owain looked at one

another, none quite able to find words. Lethbridge-Stewart blinked. The after-image of the two men, one prone, one standing over him, was still pulsing on the insides of his eyelids, only just beginning to fade.

Surrender to logic and *to faith*, Travers had said. Lethbridge-Stewart sensed a great truth there, one that would severely test his obdurate nature in the months and years to come.

For now he smiled wryly at his fiancée and nephew. 'Marvellous holiday, eh?'

EPILOGUE

BEHIND THE smoky glass of a phone booth halfway down the street from the hospital, hidden under a New York Mets cap and dark sunglasses, the man who had called himself Simon watched keenly as Lethbridge-Stewart, Owain and their friends left the hospital, hailed a cab and drove away, their business here finished. He nodded to himself and turned to the pay phone. He lifted the receiver, and dialled the plastic rotary wheel. Paused. Listened. There was a click, and a male voice said, 'Central.'

'Pinto. Blackstar. Coleridge,' he said. His drawl was gone, replaced by precise inflections more Western European than American. 'Caldera. Brightheart. Inferno.'

'Verified,' the voice said tonelessly. 'Hold, please.'

He waited, watching the street. A vendor was setting up his hot dog stand nearby, whistling as he put out condiments and a stack of napkins. Already, the meat-scented steam was wafting up from the boiler, and Simon's nostrils flared. What these people consented to put into their bodies!

Another click on the line. 'Report.' An older man's voice, English, clipped, military in tone.

'I found him, General. Just like you said. Owain Vine is the one.'

'You are certain?'

'Of course I am.'

A considered silence. Then, 'Good. Send your full report and keep track of him.'

'Yes, sir,' Simon said and put the phone down. He wasn't sure why General Gore wanted Owain, but that didn't matter. He had his orders.

He took off the baseball cap and spun it out into traffic, where it was quickly crushed under speeding taxi tyres. Simon coolly regarded the tidal flow of pedestrians. He watched the clean-up crews go about their filthy business, letting nobody rush them. He lit a cigarette, began to whistle, and fell in with the passers-by, heels clicking.

A moment later, he disappeared into the crowd.

PROFESSOR EDWARD TRAVERS opened his eyes, staring upwards, trying to remember where he was, and why. He was on his back, staring up at stars in a dark night sky.

I'm lying in a bloody field.

It was a start. His head pounded miserably. His body ached. Blood trickled from his right nostril.

He sat up quickly, wincing in anguish at the fresh bolt of pain in his head. His mind cleared, and he abruptly remembered how he'd come to be lying here. *The little Tibetan chappie, that toymaker. A final act of redemption.*

But… had it worked?

He looked around; he didn't recognise the area. A hillock was nearby, in the distance a copse of trees. And nearby, looking around in a confused manner, was a young man dressed in a Victorian looking suit. Travers clambered to his feet, the sound alerting the younger man.

'I say, who the dickens are you?' the man asked.

Travers regarded him. He seemed familiar, with his blue eyes and dark hair, but Travers couldn't for the life of him think where he'd seen the man before. 'I'm Edward Travers,' he said. 'Where the blazes am I?'

'Well, I can't be sure, but it seems to me we're somewhere near Pryford. We may be in the valley of the Wey.' The young man shook his head, and looked around the empty field. 'Although I've no idea how I came to be here. I was just leaving my house on Euston Road when…'

'Yes, yes, all very interesting I'm sure,' Travers snapped. 'Just tell me who you are.'

'Oh.' For a moment the man seemed puzzled, then stepped forward and offered a hand. 'I'm Herbert, although my friends call me HG.'

Travers blinked. Now he knew why the man looked familiar. He had seen a rare photograph of the young man in a book some years ago. The man had been a little older then, but now Travers had heard the name… 'HG,' he said, feeling more than a little puzzled himself. 'HG… *Wells?*'

'You've heard of me?' Herbert asked, now suspicious.

'Yes, you could say that. You could say that indeed.'

Continued in
Travers & Wells: Other Wars, Other Worlds

MAKER

THE BLADE is a blur in dextrous fingers, flashing and turning, coaxing the hidden shape out of the chunk of old pine almost of its own accord, creating something out of nothing—
Maker.

The knife stills. Bits of wood drift down, then stop. The tiny pile of shavings between the carver's booted feet has grown inappreciably but steadily as he works.

Then it comes again: *Maker.*

The slim youth's head snaps up, keen eyes glancing warily around. The word has come to him so quietly in the stillness of the cloud-shadowed day that he is almost sure it is a product of his mind, rather than a living voice.

He sits against a shelf of dirty shale and rock, an overhang that marks the first sharp rise of the Nyainqêntanglha mountains. Around him, there is no movement but the muddy backs and occasional raised heads of his herd, languorously chewing their cud and staring stupidly back at him. They are a motley, mixed-breed lot, their varying style of horns and their mismatched colouring indicating their regular interbreeding with the local wild *argali* and Himalayan bluehorn populations.

He hates the sheep. It has fallen to him to tend them since he was nine years old. That was a decade ago. The seventeenth century has given way to the eighteenth, and still he knows no world but his village, the mountains and these stupid bloody sheep.

Do you hear me, Maker?

He abruptly rises to his feet, his breath clouding in the

213

chilly air, his sudden movement causing the sheep to baa and bleat in surprise – but he just stands there, looking around in confusion. They return to their docile feeding, comforted by his presence, confident of his protection. There are lynxes about, and foxes, and on rare occasions a starving, desperate wolf pack or a lone snow leopard, searching for meat for her cubs. They do not lack for predators. Today, however, there is only the storm-scudded sky, the wind and the shepherd. The sheep are not bright enough to be alarmed by ghosts.

What is it you make? the voice enquires.

'Who speaks to me?' the youth calls out. Instinctively, he slips the half-carved wooden shape into a pocket of his flowing *pulu* robes, hiding it from view. The knife remains in his other hand, held up defensively.

A killing weapon, the voice observes. *Which you use instead for creation. You are a contradiction, boy. You are a wonder.*

'I am no boy.'

No. You are so much more. And none see it, do they? None truly know you. But I know you.

The youth's face goes dark with hot blood, and all the unhappiness in his heart, all the bitter things he swallows down every day as he tends the stupid sheep, boil up and choke him.

The townsfolk called him 'clever' since he was very small – Jemba-Wa, *the clever fox* – but over time it was his physical self, not his mind, that decided for them who he was, what he was capable of being. He had always been small for his age, born early to a mother who died while he was still a baby, and small he remained, even though he stuffed himself on bread and *tsampas*, clamouring for two breakfasts every morning until his father laughed and shook a finger at him. It didn't help anyway; small he remained.

Once, his people had thought him clever because of the exquisite wood cutlery and toys he taught himself to carve by the time he was eight. Before he was ten, he had even mastered ornate spiritual items: prayer wheels and wooden fish, Tibetan singing bowls and their elaborately designed mallets. He used spare kindling and the occasional discarded chunk of timber to carve his treasures, wielding one of his father's spare blades with his small, nimble fingers, ignoring the endless slashes and gashes he earned until his hands grew nimble.

And always, the things he carved he gave away as gifts. Before long, every home in the village contained a number of Jemba-Wa's treasures.

But all the while, his peers grew large and he did not. Friends drifted away; some became tormenters and bullies. The adolescent girls of the village who cooed over his craftsmanship – Amrita, comely and bright-eyed, and Bhasundara, broad of hip and cheekbone, beautiful as a highland storm – became young women who would not meet his gaze, who drifted from his orbit, pulled away by the attention of the bigger, stronger boys. In them, he knew, the maidens saw a promise of husbands. Of babies and security. He could not support them by carving wooden fish.

Before long, his smallness was all anyone could see in him. His cleverness, once appreciated for the skill it spawned, was forgotten. Never mind that many of the village elders who criticised his useless, dreamy nature – and chided his father for failing to make a man of him – were also those whose places of prayer were adorned with *muyu* and *rin gongs* of his making. Whose children played daily with his elegant wooden horses and yaks, his carved figurines of hunters and sorcerers and queens.

He possessed an eye for art and beauty, and a mind, if not the means, for designing complex machines, things almost beyond imagining. He had a way with gears and wheels, an innate understanding of steam and iron and engines... But there was no opportunity to pursue these endeavors, no need for them in a corner of the world that still rode beasts of burden, still made fire with flint, still painted white wards on the bellies of gravid cows.

What did the things of his dreams matter, when his muscles were undeveloped and his shoulders no broader than those of a child? He was hopeless as a farmer or shepherd, unable to plough or plant, too weak to haul a decent supply of water from the village well or help defend the women and children from Mongol raiders.

He couldn't even manage the community herd, two dozen

long-haired yaks, the village's chief resource for labour and trade. He had been knocked flying more than once by one or another of the bulls, and on one occasion had chased helplessly after the entire stampeding herd, spooked into flight by his clumsy ineptitude. They had crashed right through the centre of the village, smashing several hide-stretching racks and fouling a week's worth of drying goat meat and mutton.

His father, mortified, stood with him to receive the ruling of the elders. Jemba-Wa, then fourteen, was ordered back to his old job as sheepherder – a duty he'd already held for two or three years longer than was expected of a boy his age. Docile, easy to drive with a shout or a kick, so dumb they were liable to stand fast even as hungry wolves bore down upon them, the sheep were usually tended by a pair of unmarried village women with no prospects, or by unruly little boys whose behaviour had brought shame on their families.

The boy's own shame, as he received the elders' decree, was bigger than the world.

'Better a cold voice speaking true than the false warmth of a liar's smile,' his father had said, doing his best to hide his own humiliation. 'Leave the yaks to the big lads, Clever Fox.' They both knew 'the big lads' included boys two or three years younger than Jemba-Wa, some already a foot taller than he would ever grow to be. Those boys knew it too; cruel and handsome, all of them stupid as his sheep, they snickered behind their hands as they passed him with their herd, or when he trudged home alone from the hills, dirty and stinking from minding his own.

He hated those boys.

He hated the sheep.

He hates.

Jemba-Wa listens, spellbound, the forgotten, bleating sheep milling around him, as the voice whispers to him all the sharpest, darkest truths of his life. By the time it falls silent once more, he is red-faced with anger and sorrow, his chest rising and falling rapidly. *How* the voice knows all these things seems far less important to him now than does the fact

216

that it speaks with care. With concern.

Even with… compassion?

Finally, the voice repeats a thing it has said to him once before: *You are so much more.*

'I'm not,' he whispers back, slipping his carving knife into the pocket of his *pulu*, where it joins the piece he had been working on.

In his heart, his father's words echo: *Better a cold voice speaking true than the false warmth of a liar's smile.* But it is so cold here at the foot of the mountains. So cold. He yearns for a little warmth.

I am never mistaken about potential, the voice goes on. *You have the gifts of a master craftsman. People would come from miles away to buy your creations. You should be known from one edge of the horizon to the other.*

'No one ever comes here.'

Then you must come to me – for I will set you to work. For me, you shall make wondrous things of metal and glass. An army of machines, powered by science and engineering the likes of which your world has never known. Yours alone to wield – the craftsman of a new age.

Jemba-Wa gasps, blinking back tears. He realises the day has grown even darker, the tangle of storm clouds masking the sun's descent as evening comes on. He glances around at his sheep, retrieves his ironwood stick, and gives them the short series of whistles that signals 'Home'. They stir, begin turning toward the distant village.

Come to me, the voice insists.

'I have to bring in the sheep now,' he says uncertainly.

You require a demonstration of my power. I understand.

Above and behind him, there is a sudden noise like rending cloth, but deeper and more organic. A snarl, then a whole chorus of snarls. The sheep start and bleat in response.

Even before Jemba-Wa has whirled about, raising his staff, he knows what he will see there, on the ridge above him. He has wandered too far with his sheep this day, let his mind stray too long from his duty; he knows what that means, for himself and for his flock, but until this moment he has never fully grasped it.

He thinks fleetingly of the knife in his pocket. Knows it

can do him no good.

There are four of them, heads hunched low against massive shoulders, ears laid flat, muzzles pulled back to reveal sharp fangs. Dirty, yellowing claws curl over the lip of the rock above him, and their flat, black eyes never waver from those of the shepherd boy. As if on cue, those eyes go a preternatural reddish-yellow, glowing fiercely, and the quartet of highland wolves splits into two pairs, slinking down either side of the rock shelf, flanking him, meaning to cut off any hope of escape.

The oldest sheep bleat in terror, moments away from bolting into mad flight, but most of the herd just clusters in shock and confusion around the herdsman. Jemba-Wa shouts at them, shoves a couple aside, trying to crouch with his staff at the ready. Trying in this final, fatal moment to find his courage—

They are not here for you, Maker.

'What?' he gasps, eyes once more casting around hopelessly for the source of the voice. If the wolves hear it, they are not swayed from their path.

They are mine. Temporarily, of course. I have not yet gained enough control over the corporeal realm to do more than push weak minds, prod hungry souls. But I gain strength daily. Let me show you.

All the sheep are screaming now, most hunkered in place and shuddering as if gripped by fever. One of the old ones tries to bolt, and the wolf on the far left lunges into motion, jaws yawning wide to catch the animal by the throat. The triangular head snaps right, left, and blood flies. The sheep's wailing is cut short, its body flung into a heap. The wolf returns its attention to Jemba-Wa, muzzle dripping.

'Why don't they all run?' the boy cries miserably. 'Some will live if they run!'

The sheep are the tethers which tie you to a wasted life. I will cut those ties – and set you free.

Jemba-Wa looks more closely at the filthy animals in his keep – and he sees their eyes, too, have taken on that queer lambent cast. The force controlling the wolves now also controls the sheep, holding them in place.

He thinks of his long hatred for them, the way they

symbolise everything small and grimy and stupid about life in his village. Life among small men. The shame of his father. The self-interest and short-sighted arrogance of the elders.

Come, the voice whispers. *Leave them. Leave them all to the fate they deserve.*

The wolves have cornered them all, pinning them against the shelf of rock under the grey, funereal sky.

'Where must I go?' Jemba-Wa hears himself saying.

And he begins to push through the flock, muscling his way out of their woolly, stinking mass. The wolves regard him balefully with those piercing eyes – and let him pass.

The voice is thick with satisfaction now: *Walk north. I have much to tell you on your journey. There is so very much work to do.*

Staff in hand, Jemba-Wa walks north, streaming eyes fixed on the horizon. He tells himself he does not hear the agonized shrieking of the sheep as the wolves fall upon them. He tells himself he will not miss those he leaves behind.

He walks away from his village and his world, in the direction his new god commands.

One hand goes to the pocket of his *pulu*, but he does not take out the knife. Instead, his fingers curl around the half-carved thing he'd been crafting when the voice first spoke to him. It is *mi rgod*, the Furred Giant, the totem of his land.

The Yeti.

Screams and snarls behind him.

Jemba-Wa does not look back.

KKLAK! THE DOCTOR WHO ART OF CHRIS ACHILLÉOS

Kklak!: The Doctor Who Art of Chris Achilléos covers for the official Target novelisations, which began in the early '70s, defined a generation's image of the Doctor and his adventures – particularly after the show disappeared from British screens in the late '80s.

Lavishly detailed, with psychedelic overtones and an unapologetically pulpy sensibility, these covers perfectly captured the eccentric appeal of the classic series.

Kklak!: The Doctor Who Art of Chris Achilléos collects the entirety of Achilléos' *Doctor Who* artwork in chronological order, along with commentary from Achilléos himself (as well as some fans) – presenting the definitive guide to his seminal work. The book also includes a small contribution from twelfth Doctor Peter Capaldi and a foreword from Achilléos' long-time friend and collaborator, the late Terrance Dicks.